# Duck, Hunting
## The Diary of Mallory Rathbone
Carissa Hardcastle

Hardcastle Publishing House

Also by Carissa Hardcastle


**The *Leaves May Fall* series**
Leaves May Fall
Mountains Will Crumble
A Code of Conduct


To Hell You Ride

Content Information: *Duck, Hunting* is an unhinged little novel of horror that contains themes that may be disturbing to some readers. If you're reading this and thinking, "Great, bring it on, I'm ready!" then continue on, and enjoy the ride. If you'd rather be prepared for what you might find within the following pages, I've tried to include everything you might want to be aware of ahead of time.

This is a story of violence, gore, strong language, sex, domestic violence, child abuse, drug and alcohol use (including an instance of uninformed/nonconsensual drugging), mentions of off-page rape, murder, and—if you somehow missed it—cannibalism. Some minor characters act in ways that are misogynistic, racist, and/or homophobic. Protect your mental health first and foremost.

That said, I hope you have a great time with Mallory and her brothers.

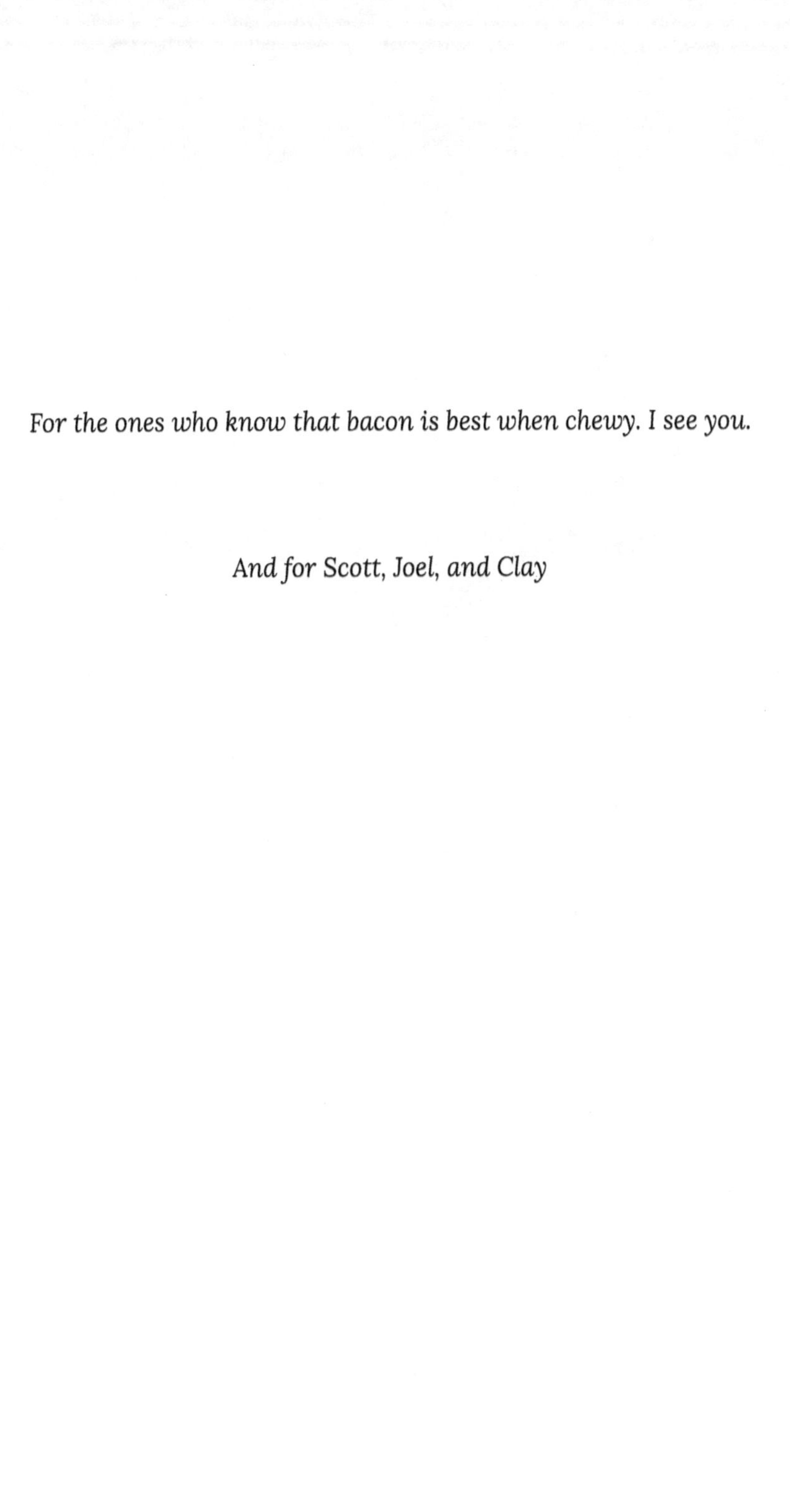

For the ones who know that bacon is best when chewy. I see you.


And for Scott, Joel, and Clay

"It's not as if she were a maniac, a raving thing. She just goes—a little mad sometimes. We all go a little mad sometimes. Haven't you?" – Norman Bates, *Psycho* (1960)

Birthdays:

Thomas Milton - May 21, 1938

Graham Conrad – February 19, 1940

Sidney David – May 26, 1944

Mallory Joy – June 3rd, 1945

Lyle James – August 3rd, 1951

Olive Nicoll Piermont – April 14th, 1945

Makoto Nomura – November 26th, 1943

# DELIGHTED

**Part One**

I've been thinking a lot lately about stuff from when I was younger, before it was just me and the boys. It's strange the days that stick out in your memory when there wasn't anything at the time to mark it as out of the ordinary, isn't it? For instance, I remember one day in either late June or early July of 1951, before Lyle was born.

My fingers curled over my knees, the knobby joints knocking together as I crouched in a chokecherry bush, wind whistling through the branches. Footsteps sounded behind me, and I forced myself to still, fighting the urge to look. Movement would draw attention.

"Where are you, little mallard?"

My teeth sank into my bottom lip, nails digging into my knees through the cotton of my dress.

"Come out, come out," sang a second voice.

I was only ... hot creepers, math ... six? And I couldn't stop the shiver that ran up my spine. Leaves rustled around me, and I pressed my palm over my mouth to muffle any sound that might escape.

"Hey, Graham, where do ducks like to roost?"

I dropped my hands to the ground on either side of me, all of my muscles tensing as two sets of footsteps grew closer.

"Ducks like to roost ... in the BUSHES!"

I sprang forward with a shriek, feeling fingertips graze my back as I pushed through the branches and into the open, sprinting as fast as my little legs would go.

"RUN, Ducky!"

I risked a glance behind me to see a small shape fall from a tree overhead, landing on the taller of my pursuers, who fell to the ground with a startled cry. But the other leaped over the bush I'd been hiding in and quickly began shortening the distance between us.

Facing forward, I flew across the meadow, another shrill scream tearing from my throat as I raced for the chicken coop that would be my salvation. I stretched my hands out, fingers reaching for the wooden panels still several yards away.

"Gotcha."

A palm pressed against my shoulder blade, and my steps slowed, a laugh bubbling up as I twirled around. "I almost made it," I huffed.

Graham smiled, sunlight pulling out the red in his auburn hair. "You're getting pretty fast. Give it a couple years, and I bet you'll be outrunning us all." He punched me in the arm, and I beamed at him.

"You almost had us this time!" Tommy called, walking up to us with Sid on his back.

I rubbed my arm when Graham looked away, watching my brothers congregate. Tommy released Sid's legs, allowing him to drop to the ground. "You're lucky you didn't put a hole in my pants pulling a move like that, punk," Tommy told him, ruffling his mop of bright red hair.

Sid ducked away, swatting at Tommy's hand and scampering to my side. He slung his arm over my shoulders, enveloping me in the familiar dirt and sweat smell of boy. "Would've been worth it if it had worked," he said.

"Too bad I'm wise to your tactics now." Tommy gave us a sideways grin. "You can try again tomorrow. Let's get cleaned up for dinner before Dad gets home."

The thought of going inside, scrubbing up, and being roped into helping out in the kitchen made me crinkle my nose. I'd just been handed more responsibility around the house that summer, Daddy telling me that I was old enough to start contributing more, especially with Momma being pregnant. I knew setting the table was inevitable, but that didn't mean I couldn't put it off a little longer. With wide eyes and lower lip protruding, I looked up at Tommy. "One more game?"

Tommy, our ring leader by order of birth, folded his arms across his chest with all the self-importance a thirteen-year-old could muster and pursed his lips as he considered. "Okay, one more."

Sid and I whooped, and Graham grabbed Tommy's arm, running toward the chicken coop and counting loudly, "One, two, three …"

Sid grabbed my hand, and we took off across the yard. "Let's go to the pond," I panted.

"Reeds or dock?"

"Reeds." And we sprinted, Graham's voice fading away. When we'd settled in the rushes and cattails at the edge of the pond, I began to second-guess the choice. The mud here was thick and sticky, and I worried that it wouldn't let go of my feet. But it was too late to change direction now. Graham was already calling out, "Ready or not, here we come!"

Sid squeezed my hand, our palms sweaty against each other as wind blew the reeds over our heads. There was confidence in that squeeze that said he knew we could beat our older brothers. His faith filled my whole little body. I knew I was smaller than the three of them—slower, clumsier, weaker. But Sid wasn't holding any of that against me that bright afternoon. We were a team, and he knew we could win.

I was determined not to let him down.

Wind tugged strands of red-blonde hair across my face as we watched Tommy and Graham plod across the yard, eyeing each other in silent communication before splitting up. Graham headed back toward the trees where we'd hidden last time, and Tommy stalked toward the pond.

I tensed, and Sid tightened his hold on me, his small hand gripping mine as though afraid I would bolt.

Then Tommy passed us, and I turned until my mouth was almost brushing his ear. "I'll lead him away from the coop," I breathed, quieter than a whisper. One of the first things we learned in our house was the art of actually talking quietly.

Sid nodded, releasing me, and I gathered my skirt, making sure it wouldn't get caught underfoot. Once I could no longer hear Tommy's footsteps, I ran.

"They're by the pond!" Tommy called, giving chase.

I didn't dare look behind me, angling toward the driveway instead of the chicken coop, no thoughts in my head aside from propelling myself forward and giving Sid the chance to reach safety. My feet left the sparse grass, hitting the hard-packed dirt of the drive, and a joyful giggle bubbled from my chest that I'd made it this far without Tommy catching me.

I rounded the back of my father's deep green truck, slamming my palms against the bed to halt my momentum, and peeked around to see if Sid had made it to the coop.

Tommy had been hot on my heels, and my eyes landed on him

first. I couldn't hold back a wide, wicked grin, knowing that my plan had worked. He was far faster than me, of course, but he was also a sucker. He'd gone easy on me, leaving Sid an opportunity to outpace Graham.

Tommy's eyes flicked behind me, the color draining from his face only moments before Daddy's hand clapped down over my shoulder. His fingers dug into my flesh, and I swallowed down the urge to squeak at the unexpected pressure. He whipped me around to face him, my feet sliding in the dirt.

No trace of that triumphant grin was left on my lips as I looked up at the man looming over me, taking in my state of filth. "What in God's good name do you think you're doing out here, ruining your clothes and covered in grime?" he growled, and I flinched. "Were you raised in a barn, huh? Who taught you to be wildin' out here like a ruffian, because I know your momma is trying to raise a lady. Look at you." He gave me a hard shake, and my throat closed up, clogged with tears that were more from fear than the biting grip that dwarfed my shoulder.

"I'm sorry, sir," Tommy interjected, stepping closer and taking the weight of that glare from me. "Momma asked me to keep an eye on her while she got supper ready. I made her go play down by the pond because I was tired of listening to her whining. I should've watched her better."

I looked over my shoulder at Tommy, my mouth dry. I wanted to shake my head, to say something, but Daddy's hand on me kept my tongue stuck to the roof of my mouth.

Tommy reached a hand out to me, but his eyes stayed on our father. "I'll get her washed off and back inside, sir."

I tried to take his hand, but Daddy looked down at me and gave me another firm shake that nearly wrenched me off my feet. "You go straight to the back porch. Don't go inside and don't touch anything. If you want to act like a boy, you can get treated like one. Wait for your brother."

I nodded frantically.

"Use your words when you answer me," he demanded, and I flinched again, unable to hold in a little yelp.

"Yes, sir." He released me, and I turned. Tommy didn't look at me as I passed him, and I lunged into a run, not wanting to hear what I knew would come next.

Skirting around the back porch, I met Graham and Sid, already hosing the mud off their feet. They'd seen Daddy's truck and had the foresight to stay scarce and clean up while I'd run right to it, too caught up in the thrill of the chase to register what it meant.

Graham held his hand out, and I walked over so he could help me rinse off. The water was cold on my toes, and I didn't look at either of them as we all tried to pretend we didn't hear the faint smack of leather against flesh.

My lip trembled as Graham took my hands, gently digging free the dirt caked beneath my nails while water ran over my fingers. I didn't want to speak, knowing my voice would come out high and whining. It wasn't because of what Tommy had said—I knew he'd only been trying to take the heat from me, to save me from the lashing that he was taking in my stead, but I didn't want to sound small and weak. I didn't want to cry when I wasn't the one being punished.

Graham was just finishing wiping dirt and sweat from my face, helping me dry off with a clean corner of a towel, when Tommy trudged around the corner. His hands were shoved into his pockets, his face set in a stoic, grim line.

I threw my arms around him as soon as he set foot on the porch, burying my face against his belly. "I'm sorry, Tommy."

His hand smoothed over my hair, his other arm going around my shoulders. "It's alright, Duck." I clung to him tighter, and he put his hands on my shoulders, pushing me away. I didn't miss the wince he tried to hide as he knelt to my level. "I'm fine. There's nothing he can do to hurt me."

"Because you're the biggest and strongest?" I searched his face for any tell of a lie, the wind pushing a strawberry blonde curl over his forehead.

He brushed it back, giving me a lopsided grin. "That's right, little mallard. I'm invincible. Now go help Momma finish getting dinner ready while I clean up. You, too, Sid." His gaze turned from me to our brother.

I was too young at the time to understand the deep shine of pain that lit Tommy's eyes, or the bitter hatred buried beneath it. He was our big brother, our leader and protector, and I trusted whatever he said without question. I didn't know the full breadth of what he was protecting us from. I was too young to realize he was still just a kid himself, growing up way too quickly to make sure that none of us had to.

Today started nice and slow, my favorite kind of summer morning. I slept until a stream of sunlight cut through the crack in my curtains, a bright streak burning red against the backs of my eyelids. I rolled over, taking a moment to settle into consciousness before stretching and finally opening my eyes.

On my way to the bathroom, I peeked into the boys' room. Lyle was still passed out in his bed, one foot hanging carelessly off the edge and auburn waves that were long overdue for a trim fanning over his forehead and cheeks. Benny, our border collie, raised his head, his muscles tensing as he prepared to hop down from the bed. I held my hand out, fingers splayed, and he sighed, resting his head on Lyle's calf. My two babies—though Lyle's reaction to the sentiment would be much more loathsome than Benny's.

If Benny was inside, that meant Tommy was already up.

As I neared the door that sealed off the newer addition from the rest of the house, I heard the faint notes of Booker T. and the M.G.s' *Green Onions* filtering through the wood, and when I opened it, my mouth immediately watered at the smell of bacon wafting down the hall.

I padded into the kitchen, still rubbing sleep from my eyes as I watched Tommy in front of the stove. His strawberry blonde hair, usually the twin color to mine, was dark with water, the curls at the top of his head resting in neat little clumps that wouldn't last the day.

He glanced over his shoulder, giving me his customary grin. "Good morning, sister."

"Morning," I replied, leaning against the counter as *Green Onions* turned over to *Rinky-Dink*. "You're up early for someone who was out so late." The words came out conversationally, but I looked up at him as I stole a strip of meat from the plate next to me, letting him see the accusatory question in my eyes.

Tommy reached out to muss my hair. "Thus the bacon, Duck. I have eggs and cinnamon toast on the menu as well."

I rolled my eyes. "Well, if you're making breakfast." I wanted to stay mad at him for missing dinner, for not making it home until after dark when I'd expected him earlier. But when I took a bite of bacon—the edges crisp and caramelized, but the meat retaining that firm bit of bounce as I chewed—I sagged against the counter. I just can't nail bacon the way Tommy does. The asshole knows it, too, and smirked as I took another bite of the rich, oily decadence.

Honestly, a pig could never offer up something this heavenly.

"I picked up a last-minute job down the mountain for today," Tommy said as I snagged another piece. "I don't know how long it'll take me, so would you mind going out to the cabin? He's about ready for collection."

I frowned, shaking my head. "I can't; we've got guests checking in this afternoon. I won't be able to make it out there and back on a bike in time."

Tommy's mouth pressed into a thin line as he pulled the last of the bacon from the pan. "I'll stop by Graham's on my way out, see if he can take care of it. Otherwise, I guess I can run out tonight ..."

"You know—" I swung one foot across the linoleum noncha-lantly. "If I got a motorcycle, I'd be able to help you two out a lot more."

No reply, just the crack of an egg, followed by a splat that was almost instantly devoured by the crackling of bacon grease bubbling against the whites. Tommy dropped a few more eggs in, raising one eyebrow as he stirred them together with a spatula.

"I knowww," I dragged out the word as he liberally sprinkled in salt and pepper. "'We've talked about this.' But, really, I think it's a great idea."

He didn't respond, just kept pushing the eggs around.

"It's my money. I can do with it what I want." I walked across the kitchen, grabbing a carton of milk from the fridge.

My brother still said nothing.

My brows pulled into a glare, but I knew the look was more pouty than what I was going for. "I can catch a ride into town with anyone, you know. Just because you won't take me doesn't mean that I can't hop in a car with Piney—or one of the ladies from church even—the next time they head into the valley. A salesman won't tell me no if I hand him cash."

Tommy grabbed a cup from the cupboard by his head, setting it on the counter in front of me. I snatched it away to pour my milk. He was irritating me on purpose, but that didn't stop my blood from running warm under my skin. Maddeningly, he still said nothing as he turned off the stove, leaving the eggs to sit for a moment longer as he dropped a couple slices of bread into the toaster.

But I was done with his charade. "I deserve to make my own choices." I spat the words, fists clenched at my sides. Then I walked out the back door, letting the screen slam behind me. Without stopping to even put on boots, I stormed over to the chicken coop, unlatching the door and letting them toddle free, clucking and bobbing their heads as they scratched at the ground, still damp with morning dew.

I tossed a scoop of feed in front of them, then ducked into their coop to collect eggs. I hadn't brought a basket with me, so I tucked what I found into the pockets of my robe.

Tommy was waiting on the porch by the time I was done, one foot crossed in front of the other and shoulder propped against a post. Danny (our bloodhound) sat at his feet, staring dolefully up at the two plates he balanced in one hand, the other holding my forgotten glass of milk.

I sighed, wanting to hold on to my anger a little longer, at least until I'd had time to expel it somewhere. But my stomach gurgled plaintively, and I trudged back up to the house.

I stopped before stepping onto the porch, tipping my chin up to meet Tommy's eyes. I let the depth of my disgruntlement shine through, glaring at him even as he held out a plate.

I took it, and he sat, patting the porch next to him on the opposite side of Danny, where he set my glass. When I didn't move, he sighed, tugging on the hem of my robe. "I'm sorry if you don't feel like you have any independence, Duck." He looked up at me, mossy blue eyes bright with sincerity. "I don't want you to feel trapped here. I'll talk to Graham about borrowing the wagon a few days out of the week so you can use the truck."

Now it was my turn to sigh, and I lowered myself next to him, careful of the eggs in my pockets. "It's not about having a car or even independence," I admitted, taking a bite of toast. Butter, cinnamon, and sugar coated the roof of my mouth, and that little monster in the back of my head bristled, mad that I was so easily placated. That Tommy knew me well enough to do it so seamlessly.

"People don't pay enough attention on these windy roads. If anything were to happen to you ..."

I shoveled a forkful of eggs into my mouth, feeling guilty for making him feel guilty and hating that I felt that way. We'd been having the same conversation for a year. Me wanting a motorcycle. Tommy and Graham refusing to take me to buy one with the argument that they were dangerous, that the risk of being thrown from it in the event of an accident was too high.

"It's not about controlling you or keeping you from leaving here. I don't want you to feel tied down."

I took another slow bite of eggs, trying to collect my emotions, which were now wild and all over the place. "I don't want to leave, Tommy," I eventually said, my voice quiet. I took a long drink of milk. "I just ... I don't know. I want the thrill of it, I guess. The power. It's freeing." A man had let me ride his bike, once, and it had set my blood to singing like almost nothing else.

"You weren't raised for a life of docile pleasures, I suppose." Tommy huffed a laugh, laying a strip of bacon across his cinnamon toast and taking a bite.

"Where were you last night?" I stabbed around at my eggs, finally admitting the real reason behind my erratic temper.

"A job ran late, and I stopped for a drink on the way home. I'm sorry, Duck. I should have called."

I looked at him, searching his face for a lie. "It's okay." I chewed on my bacon, looking out over the yard. It was quiet for a while before I finally said, "I can take care of him this afternoon after check-in, if you can pick me up from the cabin before dinner."

Tommy bumped his shoulder into mine, tossing an errant curl from his forehead. "I don't know that I'd do without you, you know that?"

"Yeah." A small smile played across my lips as I dropped my gaze back to my plate. "I know."

I don't know what I would do without him, either.

He left for the day after eating, and I made sure everything was ready for the guests' arrival. A couple hours later, I was lying on the dock, hair strewn across weather-worn wood and bare feet drifting in the water. One arm was draped across my face, blocking the sun, and the other was toying idly with the soft, velvety length of Danny's ear.

The bloodhound lifted his head with a soft huff, alerting me moments before the chug of an engine sounded up the drive.

I sat up, shielding my eyes from the glare as I watched a cloud of dirt get closer to the house. "Come on, Danny-dog, let's go greet them." Danny watched as I stood, then set his head back down between his paws, thick tail thumping against the dock. "Okay, fine, you old man, but don't be upset when Benny gets all the extra love."

Right on cue, the border collie came streaking around the other side of the pond, barking as he devoured the distance between him and the house. I let out a sharp whistle, and he curved in my direction.

Danny lifted his head, offering a half-hearted *awoowoo*, and I rolled my eyes at him. Bending down to give his haunches a parting pat, I walked off the dock to meet Benny, who leaped into the air, sailing past me only to turn and run circles around me as I made my way to the house. His sharp barks echoed across the yard, and I laughed, snapping my fingers and pointing beside me to bring him to heel. "I'm sure they'll love to say hello after they get settled in," I told him, scratching between his fluffy, black ears.

We walked through the back door into the mudroom off the kitchen, where I told him to sit. He did a tight little spin before obeying, pink tongue lolling.

Grabbing my leather-bound planner from the counter where I'd left it this morning, I hurried into the entry.

"... was out back just a second ago. Lemme go get her."

I walked in on the tail end of Lyle's commentary, my attention focused on flipping to the current week and his words directed over his shoulder as he moved toward the kitchen. We collided, and I caught him around the shoulder to steady him as I greeted the guests. "Hello." Due to the presence of strangers, I resisted the urge to ruff Lyle's hair before he scampered off. Taking a quick peek at my planner, I offered the couple standing in my house a friendly smile and held out my hand. "You must be the Brewers. I'm Mallory Rathbone, welcome to Delight."

"Thank you, Miss Rathbone. Donald Brewer, and my wife, Charlene." The man, balding but sporting a thick mustache and eyebrows to match, shook my hand before his wife stepped up to do the same.

Charlene was the polished kind of beautiful that almost never touches back-mountain towns like Delight. Her dark hair was smooth, short, and stylish, with a pink satin headband covering the part between her bangs and the teased bump at her crown. She had on a shade of lipstick that matched her headband, both complimenting her flowy yellow sundress and pumps.

I was instantly aware of my dirty, bare feet, curling my toes against the hardwood floor in a futile attempt to hide them. Tucking a lock of strawberry blonde hair behind my ear in an effort to keep her attention on my face, I consulted my planner again. "I have you staying with us through Saturday—that's two nights, three days. If you'll follow me to the office, I'll go ahead and get you all checked in and show you around."

The office is through the living room, its door glass-paneled to make up for the lack of windows. The space had been partitioned off from part of the den once we started the bed and breakfast.

We made small talk while I checked them in.

"It's our anniversary," Charlene told me when I asked what brought them to town. She peeked up at Donald with a mischievous smile. "Left the baby with my mother and decided to get out and have a few days to ourselves."

He grinned back at her in a lascivious way that made me dread what he'd say next. But he only signed his name on the indicated line with a simple, "Five years married tomorrow."

"Congratulations," I told them with my best hostess smile. "That's very exciting."

"Wood for five years," Charlene said, twining her fingers with Donald's. "We figured what better way to celebrate than a getaway to the forest? Plus, one of my friends at the salon told me she bought the most charming woodcraft sign from a local market—San Bernardino local, I mean, but the craftsman was from Delight."

"You must be talking about Piney." I selected a key from the tray in the desk drawer, closing the planner and leading them from the office. "I can give you directions to his store if you'd like."

"Oh, we'd love that, thank you!" she gushed.

"You're very welcome." I swept my hand to encompass the den and living room, giving a brief rundown of the communal areas and dining schedule (we provide breakfast and dinner) before directing them up the stairs. I showed them their room, the upstairs washroom, and handed over the key. "Holler if you need anything, and make yourselves at home," I finished, then left them to get settled.

"What's for dinner tonight?" Lyle asked when I walked into

the kitchen. He was sitting on the counter and chewing on a piece of jerky, Benny doing tricks at his feet for bits of it.

"Nothing if you keep putting your butt where we prepare our food," I answered pointedly.

He rolled his eyes, but slid down to the floor, holding out a piece of dried meat.

I took it, ripping off a bite and chewing thoughtfully as the taste of sweet hickory paired with a hint of cinnamon and rosemary filled my mouth. "Is this batch yours or Tommy's?" I asked, popping in the last bite and opening the fridge to peruse ingredients.

"Mine," he answered, casually leaning against the counter with his ankles crossed, but the gleam in his bright hazel eyes was all pride.

"It's really good. Rosemary was a nice touch." I closed the fridge and moved to the pantry. "Run out to the garage and grab me a couple pounds of ground chuck from the deep freezer. How does meatloaf sound?"

He eyed me suspiciously. "With mash?"

"Have I ever made meatloaf without mashed potatoes?"

"Need I remind you about the peas?"

I hefted a sack of potatoes from the pantry. "Listen here, you little shit. That was <u>one</u> time, and you were four. How do you even remember that?"

Lyle took a dramatic bite of jerky. "It was a traumatic experience. And we've got guests; watch your language."

"Go get me my meat and then get out of here before I show you a traumatic experience," I threatened, setting the potatoes on the counter and shooing him away. He flashed me a cheeky grin—one he got straight from Tommy—and ran off. I watched him disappear outside, a balloon expanding in my chest now that

I was alone.

Lyle is thirteen, getting ready to start high school, and his idea of a traumatic experience is eating (admittedly horrible) mushy peas when he was four.

We aren't a perfect family; I know that, but no one has ever laid a hand on him in anger, and no one ever will.

The fact that this is what gets to mark the first few pages of this new diary ... well, it feels good. Because this really is such a typical morning. I know I don't have anyone to impress, but I still wanted to record it all.

Anyway, enough of that. I've got work to do and shouldn't ~~doddle dawdle~~ delay any longer. I'm off to the cabin!

With the Brewers checked in and dinner prepped, I hopped on my bicycle—wearing sneakers, because I'm not a <u>complete</u> heathen—and headed out on the long trek around the lake.

We live in the densely wooded mountains, but just on the other side of the lake, things start to move back into the desert landscape that makes up most of Los Angeles County and the areas around it. Maybe it's because that side of the lake is closer to the desert, maybe it's just the steep inclines and cliffs that make it unideal for any sort of tourism, but the roads back there have never been as well developed. Which makes it perfect for the little cabin the boys have out there.

It really only belongs to Tommy and Graham—which is a story I'll explain later—but it's the ideal place for processing meat after a hunt, so we're all familiar with the space (outside of Lyle, who has only been to the cabin a couple of times, which I'll also get around to later).

Though most of the road is shaded by Ponderosa pines, a light sheen of sweat still coated my skin by the time I pulled up to the small, weather-worn cabin. I leaned my bike against the side, pulling my dress away from my body as I lunged up the steps to the front door. I dug the key from my pocket, and the slight resistance and subsequent click of the deadbolt turning were specifically familiar in a way that made my blood hum.

I bit my lip, trying to fight back an anticipatory smile. It'd been a while since I'd been to the cabin. I flexed my fingers, eager to let out a little pent up aggression.

The air inside was a little stagnant, so I opened a window at either end to let a breeze through and peeled my dress over my head, draping it neatly over the back of the couch so it didn't wrinkle. Stains are a pain I have neither the time nor the desire to deal with.

The closet in the bedroom is stocked with some of Tommy's and Graham's old clothes, and I snagged a t-shirt to cover my torso. It just hit the tops of my thighs, but did the job it needed to. My hair was already combed into a neat ponytail, and I tied a kerchief—old and stained, but clean nonetheless—around my head to protect it. Then I grabbed the tool bag from under the sink and pushed the coffee table off the rug in the living room.

One thing about California: it's rather prone to earthquakes. A fault line cuts through most of the state, which means modern homes are built on a solid concrete foundation—no crawl spaces or basements.

The cabin, though, has a basement. A basement that no one would ever think to look for because of the pre-mentioned fault line.

Underneath the living room rug is a trap-door style entrance to the basement. Instead of a handle, we just wedge a screwdriver between a couple of the floorboards. An entire section, roughly three feet by three feet, is connected on the underside and all comes up in a single piece. Once that's set aside, it's just a short trip down a steep wooden staircase that's almost more of a ladder to the hard-packed dirt floor below the cabin. I'm not positive how deep it is, exactly, but Graham is the tallest and he can stand without whacking his head, as long as he's mindful of the light fixture.

One other thing that might be worth mentioning: all processing takes place here, but sometimes that also includes a captive period to help with taste. We all know "you are what you eat," and oftentimes my brothers' choices in prey need a bit of a diet change before they're fit for consumption.

So I expected the clanking of chains that greeted me as I turned on the bright bulb hanging from the ceiling. The sound grew more frantic with the light, followed by muffled groans.

I dropped the bag to the floor and jumped back with a squeak, slapping both hands over my mouth when I saw the man chained to the wall, hands held above his head and a gag around his mouth. His face was swollen with bruising, blood crusted in his hair and beard. His clothes were in tatters. And one of his legs was gone from the knee down.

"Oh my God!" I gasped, hands shaking as they fluttered uselessly from my stomach back to my face. I took a faltering step forward, then stopped, taking in a shuddering breath to still myself before continuing. Crouching in front of the man, I reached out to peel the gag from his mouth.

"Help—you have to help me!" he gasped, his voice raw and gritty.

I shook my head, eyes wide. "What happened? What do I do?" Helplessness bled into my voice.

He swallowed once, twice. The effort looked painful. "Keys, find keys! We need to hurry before they come back!"

I sat back on my heels, brow furrowed. "Who?"

"The men who ..." he trailed off, his eyes darting around my face, then over my odd attire. "H-how did you ... w-what are you doing here?"

A grin split my face, and I spread my hands out in submission. "Ya got me."

He shook his head, slowly at first, and then speeding up. "Nononono."

"I _am_ here to help, just ... not you. Though I suppose that all really depends on what you count as helping," I talked over his protests, giving his body a more thorough once over. "See, I am going to help you contribute something good to the world—yippee!"

"You're crazy," he said, voice thick with tears and working up to a wail. "You're fucking crazy."

I rolled my eyes. "Rude. I mean it. Unfortunately, you won't be able to see the fruits of your sacrifice, but know that they will be very, very much enjoyed." I held his gaze with the last part, smiling with my teeth. There was plenty of femininity in the expression, just not the kind they teach you about in Sunday School. It was all predatory, nothing soft or sweet.

I leaned forward to pat his cheek, and he renewed his thrashing with a vigor. I hopped back, out of the way of his swinging leg, and went to collect my tools.

"You can't do this. You won't get away with this. AHHHH! Let me go, you worthless cunt!"

I snorted so hard I almost choked, turning back to him with eyebrows raised. "Well, Jesus, Bill. Are we really stooping to genitalia-based insults?"

"My name is David," he sniveled, though I think it was supposed to come out as a snarl.

"My most sincere apologies, David," I deadpanned, lugging the tool bag closer to him.

"Please, please, I have children. Lissy and James, they're just kids; show some humanity!"

I set the bag down well out of reach of his flailing leg, ignoring his pleading as I lined up the things I needed. He was rude, and I was still grumpy from this morning, so I wasn't inclined to save the man any undue pain.

Was that cruel of me? ~~Maybe.~~ Okay, fully. But I didn't feel bad about it then, and I don't now.

My brothers and I never hurt anyone who doesn't deserve it. Too many people get away with being rotten. We're ... karma's delivery folk, I suppose. This man was Tommy's pick, but if I know my brother, then the guy was more than likely guilty of abuse.

David was still thrashing about wildly, so I decided to start on an arm, since they had the least range of movement. I clasped his bicep just above the elbow, pressing into the wall with my weight to hold the arm still, then touched the tip of a four-inch hunting knife to the larger of the muscles in his forearm.

"When you're ready, David," I said calmly, giving him a grim, close-lipped smile.

(Before you get the wrong impression: I don't necessarily enjoy inflicting pain, that isn't my ... flavor preference... but sometimes it's the ~~principle principal~~ principle of the matter. I couldn't just let him insult me and then expect a quick death, now could I?)

"Fucking filthy cunt! You get away from me! I'll—" His words cut off into a scream that set my ears ringing as I sliced neatly through skin, drawing the blade up toward his wrist to release that pesky, chewy organ from the meat. Once that was done, I severed the tendon connecting that muscle to his upper arm, following the shape of it underneath until it was entirely cut free.

I released his arm to grab the cutlet, holding it in front of him so he could get a good look at it. "This'll feed someone's child," I told him.

He didn't seem to appreciate it. Shrugging, I laid the muscle neatly on the plastic sheeting next to me. Blood made his arm a little harder to grip, but I am a professional, so I held him down and removed the rest of the usable meat from his forearm.

He'd puked three times by the time I finished. Sour-smelling bile and half-digested chunks of his last meal coated his shirt. My stomach turned uncomfortably at the sight, and it was one of the rare times where I was unable to maintain control of my facial expression. My lips tugged down in a grimace.

He was much quieter, though, weeping softly, weakly. It was so pitiful that I was almost inclined to slit his throat and put him out of his misery.

I didn't, though. He only had a couple of minutes left in him at most, and would have even less once I started in on the rest of his arm. I decided to let him bleed out naturally. Men like him don't deserve the humane deaths we give to animals.

He was dead before I finished that first arm, and I unchained him, laying him out to make the rest of my job easier. Wiping my hands on a towel, I grabbed a cleaver, manipulating his arms at the joints to make them easier to chop through, allowing me smaller sections to work with. As disgruntled as I can sometimes be about the mess and physical effort involved, there's something about hard work that is quite satisfying, especially when the fruits of the labor are so enjoyable.

I was only halfway done when I heard the front door open. I sat back on my heels, rubbing my forehead against the sleeve of my shirt to wipe away the sweat beading there.

A familiar cadence of bootsteps walked across the floor, and Tommy poked his head over the entry. "How're we looking in here?"

"We should be able to finish up in a couple hours," I replied after a brief assessment.

"You're amazing, Duck. Let me change, and I'll be right down."

The work did go faster with Tommy there. I left the butchering to him, and started refining what I'd already harvested, slicing the best cuts into smaller steaks and cutlets, then separating the rest out into chunks for stew and grinding, and portioning out bundles of bone, muscle, and organ meat for the dogs. Everything got wrapped up in butcher paper and marked with a charcoal pencil as I went.

Once all the meat was packaged up and moved to the fridge upstairs, I helped Tommy disassemble what was left of David—the clothes, skin, leftover bones, and offal. That was placed in a porcelain tub and sprinkled with lye and water. This would stay here to decompose for a couple days before being disposed of in the depths of the national forest. (Please note that the boys have jerry-rigged a plastic shower curtain around the tub to help direct the fumes out of a vent bored specially for the purpose. The vent is obviously closed off when not in use.)

The job done, I placed my hands on my hips, blowing out a breath of exhaustion and hard work. Tommy lifted his hand for a high five, his customary lopsided grin in complete disagreement with the blood staining his fingers. I couldn't help but smile back as I slapped my palm to his.

"Go ahead and wash up. I'll get everything put away and set back to rights."

I didn't need to be told twice, bounding up the stairs and barely waiting to kick the bathroom door closed behind me before discarding my gore-splattered shirt. My hands were absolutely coated in congealed blood, but there was something satisfying about watching the water run from dark red to clear as I scrubbed them clean, then grabbed a rag to wipe off my legs.

Tommy knocked on the door before cracking it open, slipping a hand through to offer my dress.

"Oh, thanks!" I slipped it over my head.

"I've got to head back out after I drop you off," he said through the door. "I forgot I promised Mrs. Brown I would check something out at the church, but I'll be home before dinner is ready."

I knocked the bathroom door the rest of the way open, stepping out to pin him with a look. "You will be if you know what's good for you, Tommy Rathbone." I didn't have to tell him how much trouble he'd be in if he skipped out on dinner two nights in a row. Guests or not—that was family time.

Okay, quick pause. I understand that last bit might have been a lot, and I really don't want you to get the wrong idea. Let me clear some things up before I move on with the night, and have you reading about me feeding man-loaf to the Brewers thinking I'm an outright monster.

There are rules. We aren't barbarians or miscreants. What we do is resourceful and, really, no less ethical than hunting or fishing.

Rule One: no killing the innocent.

Taking this into account, eating people is even <u>more</u> ethical than eating beef or venison. A cow raised on a farm has hardly done anything wrong. People, though? They cheat. They lie. Men? They beat their wives and children. And so seldom is anyone ever held accountable for their actions. We only kill people if we've witnessed their misbehavior firsthand.

Rule Two: no killing the townsfolk.

The people of Delight are our biggest allies and our most steadfast alibi, which runs right into ...

Rule Three: be active members of the community.

No one wants to suspect their friends and neighbors are capable of hurting them or doing heinous things right under their noses, maybe doubly so when those friends and neighbors are nice kids who grew up to be contributing members of society despite their abusive father and absentee mother. So, regardless of what any true feelings about our neighbors might be, we act the part of perfect citizens. We go to church on Sunday. We donate to the bake drive, take meals to sick neighbors, and say hello in the market. The Rathbones are a friendly, good group of kids and staples in Delight. That reputation would be difficult to maintain if townsfolk went missing.

Rule Four: siblings only.

No mentioning what we do around other people. No involving or confiding in other people. No exceptions.

Rule Five: Don't be stupid.

This covers pretty much everything else, including choice of victim, timing, location—it is all calculated. There will always be risks, but we take the time to make sure they're recognized, reduced where possible, and planned for when not.

The waste not, want not portion isn't a rule so much as common sense. That's where the hunting started, of course, out of necessity. After that, it was just ... budget friendly? An acquired taste? Undeniably, though, hunting is _really_ fun.

Okay, actually, since I'm already on a tangent, let me take the time to introduce my family. You must think me such a discombobulated storyteller. "You" being the reader who will never be, because these thoughts are for no one but myself. But I did just hop right into the middle of things, and that feels wrong.

So, hello. I'm Mallory, or Duck to my brothers. I usually put this information ramble at the beginning of a new journal, but alas, we're now a few pages in, and I'm not starting over. Anyway, there are two reasons I journal as much as I do. First and perhaps most obvious, as a girl raised in a home overrun with boys, I've always needed a place to sort through my most raw thoughts and feelings without providing my brothers with more for teasing. And in case you haven't noticed (though, as <u>my</u> imaginary audience, of course you aren't that daft), there are a lot of things I can't vent to anyone else, either. Christ, imagine me walking down the street with Olive (my dearest and best friend) while rambling on about the cutlets I made of old David—and we'll just cut that off there before I get carried away. Second reason: I love telling stories. One day maybe I'll be among the ranks of Shirley Jackson and Richard Matheson, but even then I won't be able to tell <u>this</u> story, <u>my</u> story. I would never risk my family that way. But I don't mind taking the time each day to tell it here, where it's safe.

On with the introductions!

Tommy is the oldest, only by two years, but I think he always took pride in that label. Even when it was just Graham toddling after him, he liked being looked up to, and he took his self-appointed role as leader and protector seriously from the start.

For Graham, there was always Tommy, and to be honest, I'm not sure Tommy remembers much before Graham, either. By the time Sid came around four years later, the two were thick as thieves, and Graham was more than ready to emulate everything he'd been shown about being an older brother.

I came along when Sid was barely a year old, and we've been attached at the hip since. I mean, not physically now that he's gone, but we're still close. There's never been any secrets between us because we can read each other too well. I can't remember a time when we weren't in sync—we have simply always understood one another.

And then there's Lyle. Sometimes I feel bad because he's never had a set person the way the rest of us do, but we all band together to make sure he never feels like he's missing anything.

Lyle is the only one of us who has no memory of any other life. No memory of the fear that always followed our father's footsteps, the harsh words spat out of anger almost every night, or the sound of a wooden paddle connecting with bare skin. No memory of our mother, quiet and timid and unable or unwilling to protect us. He has no memory of parents at all, nor of the time directly after, when Tommy found himself head of the family at only fourteen, and he and Graham had to figure out how to take care of the lot of us. No memory of how we struggled.

But even in the hardest times, if there was one thing none of us ever wanted for, it was love. I know how that sounds, but it's true.

That's not to say that we never got into spats. We are siblings, after all. Tommy and Graham have roughed each other up once or twice—the Rathbone temper runs as hot as they come—but no one has raised a hand in anger against Sid, me, or Lyle since the day our father died.

It's a miracle, really, that Tommy was able to raise us to be so … emotionally healthy after the childhood he'd had.

I digress, but we're a close-knit family, and after those few first days on our own, we figured things out. In a way, relying on each other was already our normal.

Of course, things changed as we grew up. Graham is married now, living down on the lake with his wife, Priscilla, and working as an auto mechanic. Sid has been gone for three years—a fact that leaves an aching hole in my heart. He ran off to the navy at nineteen, and letters and the occasional phone call are all the contact we've had since. It's not been easy, but I meant it when I said we're still close. We both have to be careful with what's in our letters, but we've always been able to communicate well. And it won't be forever. He'll be back one day.

Tommy is still at home. He works as a sort of free-lance construction worker. Roads, houses, dams, pipelines—whenever something is being built, he ends up on a crew. In the slower months, he does general handyman work around town. And there's the bed and breakfast. I took over the summer after finishing high school, but all the legal stuff is in Tommy's name. As far as he's concerned, it's mine, but Uncle Sam says otherwise, thanks to the missing bits between my legs. I don't mind, though.

Sid left. Graham, though still close, left. Lyle is growing up and has the whole world at his fingertips. But Tommy is tied here, which means I'll always have someone.

Now that that's taken care of, let's move on to dinner. It was definitely an interesting one.

Danny's exuberant howls alerted me to Tommy's arrival home as I was chopping green beans. Soon after, the back door opened, the clatter of dog nails on the linoleum and excited panting almost covering the thud of boots.

"I know you're not about to track dirt through this kitchen," I called, punctuated by a distinctive *shnick* as the knife sliced through a group of pods and hit the cutting board.

"I wouldn't dream of it," Tommy replied. "Not as long as you're armed." I heard the thunk of discarded shoes as he toed them off, and he and the dogs entered the kitchen. "Of course, <u>they</u> get to track in whatever they please."

I bent down, letting Benny swipe his tongue over my cheek. "Of course they do," I agreed, tossing him and Danny each a segment of green bean. "Angel babies get to help clean up scraps in exchange for watching the chickens at night."

Tommy leaned against the fridge, folding his arms over his chest as he watched me work, a few strawberry curls falling over his forehead. "And what scraps can they expect tonight, dear sister?"

I eyed him suspiciously. "Meatloaf. Why?"

He ran a hand over the scruff on his face, going for nonchalant, but I knew he was just hiding a smile. His blue-green eyes sparkled with mischief, though his smile cleared by the time he dropped his hand, tucking his fingers into the pockets of his stained jeans with a casual shrug. "Just curious."

I returned my attention to the task at hand, not believing him, but not wanting to play into his game, either. "Whatever you're up to, I'll find out, eventually." I set the knife down, grabbing handfuls of quartered beans to toss into a pot. "Go shower. Don't forget we've got guests, so be presentable for dinner."

He rolled his eyes, reaching down to scratch Benny between the ears. "You see how I'm treated in my own house, Benny-boy? Like I don't know how to mind my manners?"

I added a measure of water and bone broth to the green beans and set them on the stove to cook.

"'Be presentable,' she tells me, as though I'm ever been anything but," he continued addressing the dogs as he left. Danny followed him, but Benny settled in the middle of the kitchen floor, watching intently for anything that might drop from the counter.

Not long after, the Brewers entered the dining room as I set the final dish on the table.

"Wow, Mallory, this looks delicious," Charlene complimented, taking a seat next to her husband, whose name had temporarily fled my mind.

I smoothed a hand over my hair, now down and carefully styled so that the ends swung softly over my shoulders, nonchalant. "Oh, it's nothing special."

Tommy walked in, showered and dressed in a collared shirt. He spread his hands out, eyebrow arched as though to ask "acceptable?"

I refrained from sticking my tongue out at him. "Tommy,

meet the Brewers. They'll be staying until Saturday. Mr. and Mrs. Brewer, this my brother, Tommy," I introduced as he took his seat.

Mr. Brewer leaned over to shake his hand. "Donald, please, and my wife, Charlene."

I cut into the meatloaf, offering the first servings to our guests, and Lyle began slopping potatoes onto his plate, topping them with a pat of butter. He'd fully mixed it together by the time I'd doled out meatloaf for me and Tommy, but before I could place his serving on its fluffy bed of starch, a knock sounded at the door.

Danny's baleful howl sounded from the back only a second later.

I looked at Tommy just in time to catch him swallowing back a grin. "I'll go see who it is."

I narrowed my eyes, watching him go. Lyle shared none of my suspicions, taking the spatula from my hand to serve himself.

"Pardon my interruption, I hadn't realized the time," a voice I vaguely recognized floated from the entryway.

"Nonsense, I insist you join us," Tommy replied, and soon led our visitor into the dining room. His dumb pond-water eyes sparkled as they met mine, a shit-eating grin pulling his mouth. He was up to something. "What do you think, Duck? Is there enough to go around?"

Standing next to my brother was Mitchell Price, a man with clean-cut, dark hair combed perfectly to the side and a face that was all straight, lean lines from his nose to his cheekbones to his chin. A tall drink of water if there ever was one, but not one I thirsted for on principle of occupation. "Why, of course. Lyle, would you please grab the preacher a place setting?"

Lyle paused, a bite halfway to his mouth. A glob of deep red ketchup fell from the utensil back to his plate before he shoved the forkful into his mouth and scooted his chair back to comply.

"Please, Mr. Price, have a seat," I turned my attention back to the new addition, registering Tommy's smugness as both men took their seats. I'd only exchanged a few words with Mr. Price since he'd arrived in Delight and had no real reason to feel wary of his presence outside of my brother's weird behavior. I felt like I was missing the punchline to a joke he thought was immensely clever. "Donald, Charlene, this is Mr. Price, who just joined as a junior pastor at our church. Mr. Price, the Brewers, our guests for the next few days."

"It's Mitch, please. A pleasure to meet you, and my sincere apologies for cutting in on your meal. I appreciate the generosity."

Lyle finally made it back with dinnerware, and I served Mitch while ignoring the abject humor rolling from Tommy.

The conversation turned to small talk from there, and I mostly tuned it out as I ate. The meatloaf was one of my better moments. I don't claim to be an excellent cook—almost everything I know is from trial and error—but I do know my way around a kitchen, and the spices I'd picked were doing what they needed to.

"I must say, Mallory, this is just divine," Charlene complimented.

I fought the urge to preen, but Donald cut in before I could thank her.

"It's such an interesting flavor. What kind of meat do you use, if you don't mind my asking?"

"It's a homemade blend," I answered, dabbing at my mouth with a napkin. "Beef, of course, and wild game—a secret family recipe. If I told you, I'd have to kill you." I winked at Charlene, who let out a dainty laugh.

"I've got a couple of the same caliber, so I understand how that goes," she assured me. I wouldn't bet on it.

"Wild game?" Donald helped himself to another serving of potatoes. "You fellas get some good hunting up here? I'm more of a fisherman myself, but I've bagged a turkey or two in my day. Do you hunt a lot of deer? Antelope?" he asked Tommy, then glanced at me when Charlene placed a hand over his. "Sorry, I don't mean to bring up delicate topics around the dinner table."

Tommy took a careful bite of meatloaf, examining his fork with an air of nonchalance before looking up at Donald with a wolfish gleam in his eyes. "Nonsense, Mallory is arguably the best hunter of us Rathbones."

I did preen this time, straightening my shoulders and tilting my chin up.

"Is that so?" Mitch asked.

I shrugged a shoulder, taking a sip of water. "I can hold my own, I suppose."

"Since when are you so modest?" Lyle spoke up, wiping ketchup from the corner of his mouth with the heel of his hand.

I pinned him with a look, but his eyes flicked to Tommy with an unapologetic smirk.

"It's an admirable quality," Mitch said. "A woman with the means to help support her family."

There was undoubtedly an interested light in his eyes that I pretended not to see. "Thank you, Mr. Price. I do what I can for these ill-bred buffoons." I glanced from Tommy to Lyle with mock disdain.

The conversation moved on after a chorus of light laughter, and my attention drifted back to the food, dissecting the textures and flavors to better make mental notes on where to improve.

I'd been a little hesitant about whether or not the butteriness of Ritz crackers would make the loaf too rich. Ground beef has a tendency to go a little dry, yes, but I don't actually use any, and human is almost dense in its oiliness. But the acidity of the garlic and onion minced in cut through that, and the added salt from the crackers helped bind the buttery taste to create a pleasantly silky flavor profile when all was said and done.

I really had outdone myself.

It made me eager to see how our guests would react to the sausage I'd cook with breakfast tomorrow—also homemade.

I glanced at Lyle, who was finishing up his second helping of meatloaf, devouring it with the endlessly hungry abandon of a teenage boy. He knows the secret recipe, of course. He's grown up on our admittedly non-standard diet.

That's just another one of those things Lyle has no memory of: a time when we didn't eat people.

When dinner was finished, I left Lyle to the dishes and slipped outside to put the chickens in for the night. Benny happily helped me round them up into their coop, much to the chagrin of the hens, who complained with indignant, fluttering clucks when his nose or paws got too close to them.

Danny stood at my feet, a low howl building in his chest. I turned to see Mitch walking down from the porch and rested my hand on the bloodhound's head, quieting him. "I see him, Danny-dog." He let out a bark that was more of a huff than anything, but sat down beside me, thick tail thumping the dirt. Benny darted toward Mitch, circling his heels as he made his way across the yard.

"I hope I'm not intruding," he called.

He was. "Not at all, Mr. Price." I whistled two sharp notes. "Benny, heel." The border collie ran over, tongue lolling.

"Mitch, please." He stopped in front of me, leaning down to

pat the dogs. This allowed me to see Tommy leaning against the porch behind him, that infernal smirk plastered onto his face, and I suddenly realized what this was. "Thank you again for dinner. I really didn't mean to impose."

"It's no problem at all." I smiled politely, avoiding prolonged eye contact as I waited for my suspicion to be confirmed.

"I ran into your brother earlier today—" there it was. "Divine intervention, truly, because I'd been looking for a chance to speak with him. You know that traveling carnival that rolled in yesterday is starting up this weekend, and I wanted to get his blessing to ask if you'd like to go with me."

"Oh?" My eyebrows lifted, and I refused to glance past him to where Tommy still watched us.

Mitch chuckled, running a hand through his thick, dark hair in a way that was arguably attractive. "He told me you were a woman in charge of yourself and that I should bring my intentions directly to you."

Jesus H. Christ. Of course he did. "Mr. Price—"

"Can you at least drop the 'mister'? I'm younger than two of your brothers." He caught my gaze, eyes bright and earnest as he squinted in the light of the setting sun. (Which, by the way, highlighted every chiseled line of his face. God truly does have his favorites.)

"Mitch," I conceded, tucking my hair behind my ear. "I'm flattered, truly—"

"Lyle can come, too, of course. Tommy, even. It doesn't have to be anything formal or official."

The thread of a different possibility started to weave its way through my mind. "No expectations?" I clarified, holding his eyes.

"No expectations," he agreed, tucking his hands into his pockets and rocking back on his heels.

"Okay then. I'll meet you Saturday morning."

"Eleven o'clock?"

"I'll be there, brothers in tow."

"It's not a date," he confirmed with a wink that really did work for him. He turned to leave, saying goodbye to Tommy before he walked around the house to where his car was parked out front.

I waited until I heard the engine sputter to life before approaching my brother, moving with measured, purposeful steps before shoving my palms against his chest. "You're so dumb." He laughed, and I shoved him again. "You meddling son of a bitch."

He swatted my hands away. "Don't talk about our poor mother that way."

"Why would you put it in his head to come here? That's the worst prank ever and not even clever."

He grinned, unperturbed, pulling a pack of cigarettes and a lighter from the porch railing. "I don't know, Duck, you seem pretty flustered."

"I'm not," I insisted, taking a step back and smoothing my hair. "And I'll have you know your little joke backfired."

"Oh, really?" He quirked a brow, lighting up and then passing it to me.

I folded an arm across my middle, smugly leaning against one of the porch's worn wooden posts as I took a long drag. "I can see your logic."

"What logic is that?" he pressed when I didn't continue, lighting a second cigarette for himself.

"Mitchel Price is a good man. Well-known in the community. Easy on the eyes." I trailed the toe of my sneaker across the rough grain of the porch beneath me. "A girl could do a lot worse for a husband." I bit my lip, looking at my feet with a shy smile. "Of course, I'd have to invite him to live here, too, but that could be fun. Just imagine, a man of the cloth, preparing a sermon about God's righteousness while chowing down on someone who may have shaken his hand the Sunday prior."

I peeked at Tommy while I talked, his expression morphing from skeptical to vaguely horrified to proudly amused. "You're sick in the mind, Mallory Joy."

"I was raised by the best." I blew smoke up into the air, then beamed at him. "I did tell him I would go to the carnival with him, though. You and Lyle, too."

"Me and Tommy what?" Lyle asked, the screen door slamming behind him as he joined us with a fistful of Red Vines.

Shaking his head with a laugh, Tommy plucked a licorice from Lyle's grip and took a bite. "Our sister pulled a fast one on us, bud."

"You invited the preacher over to get under her skin, didn't you?" His eyes moved from Tommy to me, wary of what might come next.

I lifted one shoulder, smug gaze trained on our older brother as I took another warm lungful of nicotine.

"I'm afraid she's enlisted us to spend a day at the carnival with Mr. Price."

Lyle rolled his eyes, taking a bite of licorice. "I didn't ask to be a part of this, and I'm not spending a day with the Bible-thumper."

I pouted. "But don't you think he'd make a great broth-er-in-law?"

"You can't be serious," he muttered around a shockingly bright red mouthful.

"I'm twenty now, LJ, I've got to hurry and hitch up before I become an old spinster."

"It's 'get hitched,' and you're not serious."

"Marriage is a sacred covenant of the Lord, not a joking matter." I sniffed primly.

Tommy nodded sagely. "It's my duty as patriarch of this family to make sure Duck finds a good match, someone reliable who can take care of her and lead her down a path of righteousness."

Despite myself, I gagged.

"Too much?" he asked with a grin.

"Wait," Lyle interjected. "Do we have to go to the carnival with him or not?"

"You don't have to," I laughed, reaching out to muss his hair, brown waves shining with streaks of red in the dying sunlight. "But I think it would be really fun if you did. And I'd owe you one. You could tease him and pull little tricks all day."

He wrinkled his nose. "But what if my friends see?"

I sighed. "Well, there's a valid argument. I wouldn't want to tarnish your reputation."

Lyle searched my face, unsure if he was being teased. "Right," he agreed slowly, taking another bite of licorice. "I'm gonna go meet up with Jake and Tanner. Briner got a new shipment today and promised he'd have inventory done before close."

"Home by nine, got it?" Tommy told him. "There's a few dimes in the truck you can snag on your way out."

Lyle's smile stretched wide. "Thanks, Tommy." He waved as he leapt from the porch, Benny getting up to follow, anticipating the fast chase of the bike down the lane.

I leaned back against the railing, closing my eyes and letting the last dregs of the sun's warmth soak into my skin while I finished the cigarette. "Did you ever think we'd make it to this point?"

"What do you mean?" Tommy asked, sitting on the steps to scratch Danny's long, velvety ears.

"Just ... the life we have. The point where you can put it in the preacher's head that he should come courting because you know it'll catch me off guard and watching that amuses you. The point where you're tossing Lyle spare change for a new *X-Men* comic without a second thought."

He looked up from Danny's head nestled in his lap. "Of course. That's the whole reason behind every decision I've ever made. Because I knew we'd get here."

I was filled with such a sense of contentment that I almost feel guilty now. Because how can I be content when Sid is on a boat halfway across the world? Where Graham's absence from my daily routine is just an unfortunate part of reality, the hole Sid left is like a gaping wound. No matter how much I remind myself that he had to do what was best for him, I can't help feeling abandoned. I may understand his reasons, but that never makes it any easier to adapt to the loss of my confidant, my conscience.

Being happy doesn't mean I don't miss him. I have to remind myself of that.

# DESIRED

## Part Two

I don't know if Daddy got worse after Lyle was born or if I was just getting old enough to see more than I used to. He was always mad, always on the brink of losing his temper. If we were too loud, or didn't listen, or whined too much, we were disciplined. If Momma did something to set him off, his temper would grow even shorter with us. Not that she ever did anything on purpose, but she was so wrapped up in the baby that she forgot to prioritize him sometimes, I think.

The only time we really got a reprieve was at church, where Daddy would talk with the other men after service, smoking cigarettes and chatting about whatever things men had to discuss amongst each other when they weren't at the bar after work.

Everything changed in early December of '51, just as fall was giving over into the chill of winter. So many little details about that night are seared into my memory, replayed often in my dreams.

"Mallory, go wash up and set the table."

"Yes, Momma," I mumbled, sprawled on my belly on the floor with *The Lion, the Witch, and the Wardrobe* spread open in front of me. Tommy and Graham were reading it to me and Sid, and I tried to include Lyle sometimes, but he mostly just slept and cried. I was impatient with the chapter-a-day pace the older boys had set and was determined to work my way ahead, slowly and clumsily sounding out the words as my finger moved along the page.

"<u>Mallory</u>." My name grew sharper on her lips. "Wash up and table."

Lyle started fussing in his bassinet, and I shoved up from the carpet. As much as I loved my baby brother, I'd much rather set the table than try to settle him. I heard my mother sigh tiredly as I scampered to the bathroom, book tucked under my arm.

Before the addition was built, there used to be a small bathroom next to an additional back door with a large window between them. I paused in front of the window, the dark expanse of the yard consuming my attention. Even though it was hardly past five o'clock, the sun had already set, and a sense of wonder built in my chest with the thought that maybe the shadowy forest out there belonged to an entirely different world.

I stepped up to the door, my little hand gripping the knob and my imagination telling me it was a portal out of this life. A portal to a place where men were nice and gave you tea next to a crackling fire and had hooves instead of feet. A place I could discover and then bring my brothers, and we could have an adventure together.

With a glance over my shoulder, I opened the door, slipping out into the cold with the book clutched to my chest.

The bite of the night air stole my breath, and I tugged the sleeves of my sweater—an old hand-me-down from sibling to sibling—over my fingers and tucked my hands beneath my arms. My socks didn't do much to protect my feet from the ground, but I was young enough and so deeply lost in my imagination that I hardly noticed.

My eyes were on the stars as I walked across the yard, and

I smiled, spotting different shapes than the ones Tommy had taught me. My gaze dropped to the trees, searching through the clouds of my breath for any movement that might lead me to a tea-brewing faun.

I crouched, wrapping my arms around myself to conserve warmth, but still too lost in my fantasy to turn around and go inside.

An owl swooped low through the forest, and my lips parted in awe that I'd seen it. I remembered Graham telling me they were entirely silent when they flew, which made them excellent predators. I shivered when its harsh cry cut through the night and hunkered down lower.

"MALLORY."

I wasn't sure how long I'd been huddled in my own thoughts when Daddy's voice jarred me back to reality, echoing across the still night. I stood hastily, whirling to face the house as he marched across the distance between us. I wanted to meet him halfway as much as I wanted to run the opposite direction, and the warring instincts left my feet rooted to the ground as he stormed up to me.

"What in God's name do you think you're doing out here?" he asked, his voice low. Dangerous.

"I was just—"

"I don't want to hear excuses, girl." He cut me off, grabbing me roughly by the shoulder and dragging me across the yard.

He seemed to tower over me, and my numb toes scrabbled for purchase on the ground as I tried to keep up with him. "Daddy, I'm sorry—"

"Your mother told you to wash up. She told you to set the table so she could look after your baby brother." He was taking me away from the house, and fear made my heart beat wildly in my chest. Against what I knew better, I thrashed against his hold.

"I'm sorry, I didn't mean to—"

"SHUT UP," he bellowed, and I cringed away from him, hot tears spilling down my cheeks. "You were told to wash up, but since you'd rather dally in the dirt like a ruffian, you can wash up like one, too."

With that, he threw me forward, my feet barely able to stay underneath me as I splashed into the pond.

The frigid water bit angrily at my toes, and I stumbled back toward the shore. "I'm sorry, Daddy. I'm sorry," I cried, tears blurring my vision as I reached for him, the muscles in my legs cramping from the shock of cold.

"Wash. Up," he ordered, gripping my grasping hands only to push me back out of reach.

My numbed feet tripped over a rock, and I fell backward, icy water surging over my chest. My entire body seemed to seize, and I gasped, choking on sobs as I struggled to right myself.

"Dad, she's just a kid!" Tommy's voice made me snap my head up, and I managed to get to my feet, my entire body racked with violent shivers.

"Stay out of this, son. She's old enough to know how to listen," Daddy snapped, turning his attention back to me. "Wash your hands, Mallory. Keep dallying, and there's a whooping in it for you, too."

I fell into the water again, my legs unable to listen to me anymore. "Daddy, please," I wailed, coughing as I fought to catch my breath in the cold. I couldn't stop crying, and I could feel my stomach convulse with each sob, with each violent tremor through my body. My sweater was soaked through, obscuring my outstretched hand as I reached for Tommy, completely past the point of words.

I couldn't push myself back up. Couldn't fight my way out of the water. Couldn't even hear the words I knew Daddy was shouting at me. I was soaked to the bone, hands and knees sinking into muck that I could barely even feel.

The world had reduced to an all-consuming, biting cold. I couldn't tell if I was choking on my breath or on water. But through the blur of tears, I saw Tommy.

I saw as he looked at me, his eyes wide with horror. I saw as his entire posture shifted, hardening with resolve as he looked at Daddy. And I saw when he bent down to pick up a rock.

Tommy stood, kicking his foot into the back of Daddy's knee so that he toppled forward, then swung the rock into his temple with enough force to make his head snap to the side. Tommy pulled his arm back and hit him again, and again, until Daddy slumped.

Then Tommy ran into the water, not even watching as Daddy fell face-first into the pond. He picked me up, clutching me to his chest as he splashed back to the shore. "It's okay, Duck. It's okay." He set me down, stripping the sodden clothes from my body and pulling his own shirt off.

"I d-d-dropped the b-b-book," I stuttered, from cold or from my hitching sobs.

"We'll get it. Don't worry about that," he soothed, yanking his shirt over my head. The front had patches of wet where he'd held me, but the back was dry and warm. He picked me back up, cradling me close, and walked back to the house. If he was scared, if he was at all unsettled by what had happened, I couldn't tell. His confidence bled into me the same as his body heat, and my crying had leveled off into quiet, hiccuping breaths by the time we reached the porch. "I need you to listen close and follow my lead," he whispered, moving his hand from my hair to open the back door. "Be Mallory-mallard, got it?" He set me down, meeting my eyes.

I nodded, sniffling.

Graham's head popped into the mudroom. I don't know if that had been planned or if it was just part of the way that the two of them were aligned, but Tommy didn't skip a beat. "Her clothes are down by the pond. Can you run and grab them?"

"And the b-book," I added, blinking tearfully up at Graham. "I b-brought N-Narnia outside."

He placed a comforting hand on my head. "I'll find it, Duck." His eyes met Tommy's, and something silent passed between them before Graham nodded and slipped outside.

Tommy looked me over while I stood in his shirt, residual shivers running through me. "Fuck, your lips are blue," he whispered, and it was the first time I can ever remember hearing him curse. He pulled me back into a hug, his arms tight around my shoulders. "Nobody is ever gonna hurt you again, okay? I promise I'll never let anyone ever hurt any of you again."

"Tommy? Is that you, honey?" Momma's footsteps tapped across the kitchen, and Tommy pulled back, meeting my eyes with a look that said it was showtime.

"Yeah, I found Duck out by the pond. I think she fell in."

"What? Oh my Lord, Mallory!" Momma came around the corner and scooped me up.

"Her clothes were wet, and it was cold, so I gave her my shirt."

Momma nodded, rocking me back and forth. "That was quick thinking. Did you see your father out there?"

"No, ma'am. Graham went to get her clothes, though. He'll let him know we found her."

She sighed, pressing my face to her neck. "What were you thinking? It's freezing out there! You could have gotten hurt."

She tsked, her voice dropping to a resigned mutter. "Let's go get you some fresh clothes before your daddy gets back in. Christ, Mallory, you're lucky he wasn't the one who found you."

"I'm sorry, Momma."

She took me upstairs and began to lecture me as she got me into clean, dry clothes, but I was still rattled, and she stopped when my eyes pooled with tears and my shoulders started shaking with hitched breaths. Kneeling in front of me, she took my face in her hands, brushing tears from my cheeks. "Just try to be more mindful, baby, okay?"

I nodded, sniffling.

"Good," she smiled stiffly, stood, and took my hand. "Now let's get downstairs and get everything all set before your daddy gets in, okay?"

Graham was inside by the time we came down.

"Is your dad on his way in?" Momma asked him, moving from behind me to fuss with the table settings. I knew she was worried about how he'd react to the interruption to dinner time.

"No, ma'am, I didn't see him," Graham answered.

Sid came up to me, his eyes questioning. I gnawed on my lip and shrugged, and he grabbed my hand in a show of solidarity before we took our seats at the table.

"Should we go look for him?" Tommy asked from across the kitchen. He'd replaced his shirt and was walking in slow circles with a sleeping Lyle in his arms.

Momma's hands flitted from the place setting in front of her to her hips, and she nodded, moving over to take the baby and place him back in the bassinet. "Would you please, honey? That would be so helpful."

Tommy and Graham headed back out.

Sid's gaze burned into the side of my face, and I realized I was staring toward the mudroom. My belly knotted in on itself as I waited for them to return, as I wondered what would happen. Would Daddy remember that Tommy had hit him? I became suddenly terrified that Daddy would throw Tommy into the water in my place. Would Graham be able to save him the way Tommy had saved me?

Sid squeezed my fingers, grounding me. I tried to prepare myself for whatever came next.

The door opened, Tommy stumbling in with Graham right on his heels. My heart leapt into my throat with the anticipation of Daddy following them.

But he didn't.

"He won't wake up," Graham gasped, tears lining his eyes as he ran up to Momma. "What do we do? He was lying in the pond, and he won't wake up!"

Momma wrapped her arms around him, her hands trembling as she looked at Tommy in question.

Tommy swallowed thickly. Once. Twice. A tear tracked down his cheek. "He must've tripped in the dark. He's not ... He's not ..."

She stood, shaking her head.

"He hit his head," Tommy continued softly, sniffling. "He was face down in the water."

Momma stumbled, her face going white as she hurried outside. Fear pushed me to my feet as I watched her disappear into the dark before looking up at Tommy.

He gave me a reassuring, if unsteady, smile. "Don't worry."

"What's happening?" Sid finally spoke up, rising to stand beside me.

"I've got them," Graham said, and Tommy nodded, running off after Momma. Graham took his glasses off, scrubbed his face, then slid them back on and took me and Sid both by the hands. A long, keening wail from outside raised goosebumps on my arms as he led us to the couch and knelt in front of us.

"Dad's dead," he said, and Sid curled closer to me.

"Was that Momma?" I asked, that sharp wail still echoing in my ears. "What's wrong?"

Graham's eyebrows pulled together. "You need to understand what happened."

I angrily swiped tears from my cheeks, not remembering when they even reappeared. "I know what happened."

"I know, but you need to <u>understand</u> it, okay?" He put both of his hands over mine. "Dad's ... He's dead, like when we kill chickens to cook for dinner."

"I <u>know</u>." I grew more upset that he thought I was too stupid to get what dead meant. "Tommy killed him."

Sid stiffened, looking from me to Graham. "What?"

Graham swallowed, wetting his lips and clutching my hands a little tighter. "That's not—You need to understand."

"I do!" I yanked free, scowling as I crossed my arms over my chest. "Daddy was in a fit. He was mad, and he was hurting me, but Tommy stopped him. Tommy protected me, but he saved all of us, too. Daddy can't hurt us anymore, so why is Momma screaming?"

Graham blinked, surprise flashing across his face before a sad softness replaced it. "She's upset because she loved him, Duck. Even though he was mean, she loved him."

"Well, I didn't," I insisted, arms still crossed. "I love you and Siddy and Tommy and baby Lyle and Momma, but he was mean and nasty, and she should be happy now."

Graham made a sound like he was hurt, and that softly sad emotion that I can now name as pity took over his entire expression. "The things he did ... none of it was okay. Nobody should treat another person the way he treated us." His eyes moved to Sid, watching as he processed everything. "But it's still okay to be sad, or to be confused."

Sid's little hand touched my cheek, a gentle pressure urging me to look at him. I did, dropping my petulant scowl because none of what was clustered in my chest was aimed at him. "He hurt you?" He dropped his hand to his lap, and it's hard for me to explain what passed between us, because it was both something so wholly simplistic in the way that most things are with youth, but also the sort of complicated understanding that's only possible between two people who know every part of each other. He nodded. "Then I'm glad, too."

Graham pulled us both into a hug, his breath hitching in his chest. I slid my arms around his neck, understanding that this comfort was more for him than for us.

When he finally pulled away, his cheeks were stained with tears. "Momma never had someone like Tommy to look out for her when she was growing up," he started. "She doesn't know who she is without Dad, and that's why she's so sad. But she'll figure it out. We'll help her, right?"

I nodded.

"You know how Dad was always nice to the neighbors? How everyone at church loved him so much? They won't understand why Tommy had to do what he did, so if anyone talks to you about what happened, you need to say that he had an accident, otherwise Tommy could get in trouble—a <u>lot</u> of trouble."

My chest tightened as the scene replayed behind my eyes, tears choking my throat, and my chin quivered as I met Graham's gaze. "I'll protect you guys always. I promise."

"Oh, Duck." He sighed again, smoothing my hair behind my ear.

Sid's hand wrapped around mine. "We stick together, right?" He looked from me to Graham, green eyes serious. "It's the five of us. Always and no matter what."

The corner of Graham's mouth lifted, and his gaze drifted to where Lyle lay in his bassinet, still sleeping. "The five of us. Always and no matter what."

That sentiment became something of a motto among us.

Before we get any further into things, I should mention that there is one single person in this world that I love as fiercely as I love my brothers: Olive Piermont.

In many ways, Olive is my exact opposite. Where I'm brash and loud, she's thoughtful and quiet. I'm always brushing crumbs or dirt from my clothes; she's pristine. My fair skin burns an angry red after time in the sun, while the brown of hers only deepens from tawny to bronze. We may not be what you could call two peas in a pod, but we've been best friends since we met almost a decade ago. Hot creepers, has it really been ten years?

Let me just get on with the day before I get to rambling.

After breakfast this morning, I set about making sure the house was ready for the next guests' arrival, then Tommy dropped me off in town to run a few errands.

My first stop was the library, where I grabbed a couple Westerns for the boys and perused the shelves for suspense, mystery, or horror for myself. I brought my selections up to the counter, only to find that the librarian had set something aside for me while entering new titles into their catalogue this week. God bless Mrs. Drear, honestly. A genuine smile split my face when I saw Shirley Jackson's name on the cover of *We Have Always Lived in the Castle*. She remembered how much I'd loved *The Haunting of Hill House* and wanted to make sure I had first dibs. I thanked her for thinking of me, and she waved me off, clearly pleased by my reaction, and told me it was no trouble for her favorite horror enthusiast.

The pleasure of that interaction put a little bounce in my step as I made my way to the grocery store down the street. I only needed a few things, but grabbed a cart for the convenience of not having to carry my tote full of books.

I was picking out a carton of strawberries to use for dessert tonight (for shortcake) when Olive sneaked up next to me. "I'd go for the peaches. They're in season."

I smiled, a burst of warmth spreading through my chest, and placed the strawberries in the cart. "If that's your way of asking for cobbler this evening, you're gonna have to be sweeter about it," I replied without looking at her.

"Oh, but what sort of guest would I be if I made last-minute demands?"

"The needy kind, who has a sweet tooth with cravings that change with the wind," I answered, walking over to the selection of peaches.

"The endearingly needy, with an endearingly changing sweet tooth?" she implored, hooking her arm through mine.

I steered us toward the display of peaches, humming an affirmative. Obviously, I was going to make her the cobbler. I'd been letting her dictate most of my sweets choices since we met. Which was fine, since I preferred savory treats anyway, but the thought did pull me back into a flood of memories of picking out candies with her and Sid, the two of them somehow always in agreement about which chocolate bar or flavor of taffy best fit the mood of the day.

"You're lost again, Mally," Olive prodded my side with her

elbow, jerking me from my thoughts.

I dropped my head to hers for a moment. "You're never allowed to leave me, okay?"

She squeezed my arm in assurance. "Have you heard from Sid lately?"

Of course, she cut to the heart of the matter without me even fully realizing it was there. "Not since his letter earlier this month." I grabbed a can of whipped cream.

"I'm sure his next update will come soon," Olive said, her voice laced with enough conviction for both of us. "And in the meantime, you've got me. Though I'm nowhere near stoic enough to make a proper substitute."

I laughed at that, heading toward the checkout. "You're much too malleable to be my conscience for me."

"I never could say no to you," she agreed, tapping my nose. "I've got to run. I've been gone from the shop too long as it is. Six o'clock tonight?"

"Six o'clock," I confirmed, watching her wiggle her fingers in a wave before spinning around to leave. My eyes tracked her despite myself, watching her long, dark curls bounce just above the flare of her hips as she moved down the steps to the sidewalk.

I forced my attention to the checkout lane before anyone could notice my staring, though I was well versed enough not to worry about my mask slipping. I know how to keep appearances. My emotions never make it to my face unless I want them to—I'm confident in that.

And where Olive is concerned, they will always stay hidden.

She's my best friend. Practically everyone in Delight knows we're an inseparable pair.

But no one in Delight knows that I am hopelessly in love with her.

I was trying not to get too into this earlier, but dammit, I feel like a ramble, so you're gonna get a ramble.

Love is … strange. I've always loved Olive, and I'm not sure when that love grew from friendship into something deeper and more yearning. But I can pinpoint the first time I realized it.

We were fifteen and sitting in church, of all places. A storm had rolled in, rain beating against the roof of the building hard enough to make Pastor Forsythe need to raise his voice to be heard. A clap of thunder sounded right overhead, and Olive jumped, her hand gripping my thigh reflexively as she brought the other to her mouth, stifling first a shriek and then a giggle at her overreaction.

All my focus was where her hand lay over the fabric of my dress, the heat from her skin searing into me, racing through my body and coming to rest low in my core. She looked at me, dark eyes full of warmth and laughter, and I knew with all-consuming certainty that I would do anything she ever asked of me. That I was powerless to deny her anything. When she pulled her hand away from her mouth, all I could think about was how her lips might feel pressed to mine. What she might taste like. And the thought sent a pulse of heat between my thighs.

I laughed along with her, clasping her hand to remove it from my leg and make it easier to banish the thought of her fingers sliding higher.

I've been harboring those feelings since, but have never acted on them nor let myself truly consider the possibility of doing so.

For one thing, homosexuality is illegal. I know that must seem like a weird line for me to draw, but this isn't about me. It's about Olive, and for as much as she follows along with my general mischief, she's a moral person. Which leads to a second point: homosexuality is a sin. Again, I couldn't care any less, but ... Olive.

The third point, though, has equal weight for both of us. I've seen what can happen if it comes out that someone has ... "inverted" desires. I know how quickly people can turn. Judge. Hate. Condemn. I don't precisely care for most of the people of Delight, but I know that my family's standing within the community is a large part of what makes our lifestyle possible, and more so, I would never turn that sort of negative attention to Olive.

So, with the knowledge that my feelings can never see the light of day, much less be voiced or exchanged, I bury them, content to have a best friend who wants to be such a prominent fixture in my life. I happily accept her platonic affection and covet any kind of love she has to give me.

It's better this way.

Especially because, like I said, Olive is a moral, God-fearing woman. Forget genitalia altogether, and we are still left with the fact that moral, God-fearing people don't have romantic relationships with cannibals.

Is that melodramatic? I don't know.

I'd like to say there are exceptions, like Priscilla, but that's a different situation. Priscilla is beautiful and sweet. She's not just in love with my brother, she's obsessed with him. She <u>lives</u> for his happiness and his praise (which he gives her in droves). Graham loves how much she loves him. Don't get me wrong, he's a good husband—loving, attentive, keeps his temper in check—but he isn't <u>in love</u> with her and feels no guilt keeping secrets from her. Rule four, remember? What we do is something the five of us will never tell a single other soul or admit to outside the safety of our own home.

So you can see how romantic relationships can be complicated. Graham made it work by finding someone who loves him deeply and basks in his attention without needing that same level of devotion in return. Tommy has only gotten into relationships with girls determined to leave our little town for the big city. They've all broken up with him when they realized he isn't willing to move.

As far as I know, Sid is both the only person on this earth who knows how I love Olive and the only one aside from me who's ever actually fallen in love. And now he's gone.

It really is better for everyone—my brothers, Olive, me—that I continue to pretend my love for her is no different from my love for my family.

~~Besides, just because I pretend my lust for her doesn't exist doesn't mean I have to ignore all my physical desires. And I've dated a bit, just never seriously.~~ That's not the point, and I'm getting off track. Back to the pertinent things.

After making my purchases, I walked down to the auto shop at the southern edge of Main Street. The large bay door was open, and I stood at the threshold cradling a paper bag of groceries.

Graham kneeled on the floor, a backwards California Angels baseball cap holding his thick auburn hair away from his face as he replaced the brake pads on the car in front of him. He glanced up, a crooked smile splitting his face. "Eh, what's up, Duck?"

I rolled my eyes at his Bugs Bunny impression, propping the bag on my hip. "Just wanted to check if you and Priscilla were still coming over tonight. We'll have a full house."

"Depends," he answered, turning back to the car. He lifted the tire into place with a slight grunt. "Is your boyfriend gonna be there?"

My face fell into an unamused expression. "That slick-nosed little weasel. Did Tommy come by here today?"

Graham laughed, tightening the lug nuts. "Nah, yesterday, before he went home. It's an attest to my own skills in reading people that I knew Mitch wouldn't wait before stopping by to speak with you."

"That's not how you use 'attest,'" I huffed.

Graham waved me off, not even bothering to look at me. "I'm skilled with people, not grammar."

"You're about to be skilled at not having a seat at the dinner table," I said primly.

He snorted, lowering the jack. "We'll be there, don't worry. Priscilla was going to make cinnamon-roasted carrots, I think. There should be enough for everyone."

"Don't let her stress about it if there's not. But since you'll be driving there anyway, can I steal your bike? Tommy's on a job across the lake, and I've got cold things."

"Wow, you want me to walk home *and* still have time to shower before dinner?"

"I do ask the world of you."

"It's a good thing you're my favorite sister."

"Lucky for me, for sure," I agreed.

"Dinner at six?"

"Dinner at six."

"You got it." He stood, moving closer as though to muss my hair with his greasy fingers.

I hopped back, warding him off with one hand. "Get back to work, Mr. Rathbone. I'll see you tonight."

"Later, Ducky-gator."

I rolled my eyes again, but blew him a parting kiss before turning away. His bike was propped against the side of the shop where he always left it, barring inclement weather when he drove to work instead. Setting my groceries and tote in the basket, I swung my leg over the side and pushed off.

The rest of the afternoon was uneventful. I checked in the Masons, an older couple with two teenage girls, and spent some time reading before starting dinner.

With so many people, I set the guests up inside with their own spread of pork Alfredo (which was, of course, a homemade imitation pork) and Priscilla's famous cinnamon-roasted pecan carrots, with a peach cobbler for dessert.

My family sat at the table on the back porch with the same spread (with the addition of a separate pan of pecan-free carrots, ~~obviously~~. Wait, have I mentioned my nut allergy yet? It's unfortunately severe. I've had two near-death experiences, one due to walnuts and the other due to almonds. I can't even tell you how alarming it is to be eating a slice of banana bread one moment and being entirely unable to breathe the next.)

There I go, rambling again. I told you I was in a mood today. Where was I? Dinner, right.

We were at the outside table, Danny and Benny lounging beneath our feet. Lyle peeked surreptitiously at Olive, his cheeks flushed in evidence of his boyhood crush whenever she joked with him. Priscilla and Olive dished out town gossip while Tommy and Graham talked about the last Angels game and the different vehicles they'd seen in the field north of town where the carnival had set up. I hopped back and forth between the two conversations, watching as Benny took off after a pair of Canada geese that landed in the yard. Tommy hollered at him to leave them be, a beer bottle paused halfway to his mouth.

It really was a perfect evening, almost. Unlike yesterday, I felt Sid's absence too strongly to be content. I took a sip of my own beer, shaking off the glum thoughts before they had a chance to take root, and rejoined the conversation with renewed eagerness.

After Graham and Priscilla left, Olive helped me collect all the dishes and bring them into the kitchen for washing. She was suspiciously quiet as she helped dry the cutlery, and I waited, curious where her mind was but knowing she would spill before long.

"Are you really courting Mitchell Price?"

I snorted, almost dropping the plate in my hands. "No, of course not. He expressed interest to Tommy," I explained, "who told him he was more than welcome to come ask me himself."

"But you're going to the carnival with him tomorrow?"

"Well, yes, but—"

"But you aren't meaning to date?" she interrupted. I looked at her, but she was intently studying the circular movements of the dish towel in her hands. Eventually, she peeked up at me, brown eyes framed by dark lashes. "Why not?"

I could tell by the way she looked at me that she was trying to puzzle something out, and my heart rate kicked into a higher gear. I shrugged, handing her a new plate. "He's a preacher. I don't ... I mean, honestly, can you imagine me as a preacher's wife?" I raised my eyebrows.

It was her turn to snort, though it was much more light and feminine than mine. "He's handsome, though, and kind. Even if your plan is to run the bed and breakfast until you're old and crotchety, there's no reason you should have to do it alone."

"Are you volunteering your companionship?" I asked coyly, batting my lashes.

Olive laughed, shoving me with her shoulder. "If we're destined to be old maids, then of course we'll be old maids together." She took another plate from me. "But I'd like to think there's love in the cards for us."

"Me, too," I quietly agreed.

"So why turn down Mitch's advances?" she pressed, unrelenting.

"Because I'm not interested in him in that way. I know what life with him would look like, and I don't think it's one where I would be happy." I looked at her again. "Why does it matter?"

Her teeth sunk into the swell of her bottom lip, and she

tucked a dark curl behind her ear, her cheeks flushing mauve. "I just ... well, I'd quite been hoping we could go on double dates."

My mouth dropped open. "Olive Piermont, have you been keeping secrets?"

"It just happened yesterday. I was going to tell you at the market, but I didn't know if we'd have time to talk, so ..." she shrugged, a worried smile pulling at her lips.

I shook off the cold bite of jealousy that pierced my heart. "Well, spill the beans. Who's the lucky guy who gets to woo you?"

"Jonah Forsythe."

That name was like a bucket of ice water to the face, and probably the only thing that could have made my control over my emotions slip.

I can live with Olive dating. I can live with Olive marrying. I'm fully prepared to love and support her through every one of life's milestones. But Olive can't be dating <u>Jonah</u>.

My stomach twisted into a knot, and I'd never had to struggle so hard to keep my despair—my disgust--from pulling the muscles in my face. I concentrated on the crockery in my hands, scrubbing too intently at a bit of baked-on sauce because I couldn't say anything, and all of my thoughts felt trapped in my chest, rolling up to the back of my tongue to spew from my throat.

But how could I tell Olive that she deserved more than what the pastor's son will ever be able to give her? How could I tell her that he is a coward and a liar and that I hate him so much it makes me ill when I have to stare at the back of his greased-back hair on Sunday mornings?

How could I tell her that he broke Sid's heart? That Jonah had been my brother's first love, his first kiss, had made him feel like there wasn't anything wrong with him and it was okay to feel the way he did, only to shatter his trust and run him out of town? Sid is gone because of <u>him</u>, but how could I tell her any of that when those aren't my secrets to share?

"Say something, Mally." Olive wrung the dish towel between her hands, peeking up at me.

I should have slit his throat and fed him to his parents—fucking rules be damned.

I forced a smile, though I can't say how believable it was, and touched a dollop of suds to her nose. "I'll give him a chance for you. But if he does you wrong, I'll wring his neck and bury him out in the woods."

Her shoulders drooped, something I couldn't quite catch flashing across her face before her smile returned as she wiped the bubbles from her nose and swatted me with the towel. "You and your violent mouth, Miss Rathbone. One would think you were raised by feral boys," she teased.

That elicited a genuine grin. "Imagine the terror I would be if Tommy and Graham hadn't wrangled me into a being fit for society."

"A terror, indeed," she agreed, taking the dish from me to dry. "I know he hasn't been your favorite after he and Sid had their falling out, but Jonah is … nice." She leaned into me. "But you know I could never be serious about someone who had any problems with you. If he can't be civil, then I'd rather know sooner than later … so … tomorrow?" she asked, looping the dampened towel around the back of my neck. "Jonah and me, Mitch and you … it could be fun."

I tipped my head forward until my nose touched hers, then pulled away. "Tomorrow," I agreed. Chuckling, I added, "Lyle will be relieved that he doesn't have to be the third wheel all day."

Olive laughed, setting the towel on the counter next to the

stack of clean dishes. "That's why I asked, of course, to keep my number one man happy."

So, there you have it. A normal day ~~filled with normal pining~~. Well, I don't know, but it's not as miserable as that implies. All in all, I'm looking forward to tomorrow because it means time with Olive, but there's an awful knot in my stomach at the prospect of her growing closer with Jonah. I hate him <u>I hate him</u> I hate him.

This morning was bright and sunny and promised to be a scorcher by mid-afternoon, but I held out hope that at least the wind might pick up to keep the heat from being overbearing. (Alas, it did not.) It was a much better lake day than carnival day, but I was excited about the prospect of an entirely new group of people in a new environment. The possibility of a new hunting ground had been on my mind since the carnival was first announced.

I made a quick batch of muffins for the guests, then dressed. This was much more of an ordeal than it should have been because have _you_ ever tried balancing looking nice enough to draw the attention you want without looking nice enough that your date-not-date thinks you put in the effort for him?

I slipped a prefilled syringe of epinephrine from my Ana-kit into my pocket (it's an annoying accessory, but a requirement when eating out) along with a few bills and was out the door. Tommy sipped coffee on the porch with the dogs, reclined back in a chair with his feet kicked up on the railing. He barely had time to open his mouth before I said a quick goodbye and hurried off to Olive's. No way in hell was I going to give him a chance to tease me about my double date. I'd released him and Lyle from chaperone duty the night before, and I would be damned if I let them turn my kind deed into an arsenal for their jokes.

A short ten-minute walk later, I saw Olive standing at the end of her driveway by a large wooden sculpture of a bear. The Piermonts' yard is full of woodland creatures in varying sizes that Piney (nobody calls him Mr. Piermont) sells to tourists at his shop on Main Street. (He's the one who made our bed and breakfast sign, too, as a gift. Refused to take payment for it when Tommy tried to offer. I think it was his way of thanking us for accepting Olive and her mother so immediately. Not everyone in Delight had been as kind when Piney first showed up in town with a Dominican wife and half-Dominican child. Luckily, most of the folk here are pretty devout Christians, and Pastor Forsythe wouldn't accept a lick of racism in his church. His son may be a worthless prick, but the man himself does have redeeming qualities. Sorry, babbling on again.)

Olive was a dream of tumbling curls in a sleeveless lilac blouse and a pair of matching shorts. The faintest sliver of bronze skin showed above her waistline when she lifted her hand to wave to me, her mauve-painted lips parting in a smile.

This moment of perfection was ruined by the bout of revulsion that turned my stomach when my vision widened to include the man standing next to her.

Jonah Forsythe: blond hair combed back, black aviators resting over his eyes, light blue, short-sleeve button down, open at the collar, and blue jeans starched so straight I'm surprised they could stand to touch his legs. (That's a gay joke. As a reminder, he ran my brother—the whole other half of me—out of town, so I'm entitled to a little internal nastiness.)

The corner of my lip wanted to twitch into a snarl, but I smiled, ignoring Jonah to pull Olive into a hug. Her curls brushed my cheek, lifting from her neck just enough to offer me a hint of her trademark scent of hyacinth and bergamot. Which is also sort of my trademark scent, on account of the fact that she loans it to me often. She's obsessed with it and claims she can smell it better on me than on herself.

Far be it for me to deny her pleasure.

"Hello, Jonah," I said after releasing Olive.

"Hello, Mallory. How's ... how are your brothers?" He slipped his thumbs through his belt loops.

"They're well, thank you for asking," I replied sweetly, refusing to give him any of what he refused to ask for and didn't deserve to hear—word on Sid. Looping my arm through Olive's, I led us down the road. "What are you most excited for, Miss Piermont?"

"Definitely the food. I haven't had a corn dog since the state fair in San Bernardino last fall," she sighed dreamily, then her arm tightened around mine, and she skipped forward a couple steps, dragging me along. "Ooo, and cotton candy!"

"I'm partial to caramel apples myself," Jonah said, keeping step on Olive's other side.

Nobody asked, but Olive looked over at him with an inviting smile, so I bit the side of my tongue to hold off a retort. I hated how easily he got under my skin. I was better than that, and I knew it was just Olive's involvement that was making me want to dig his throat out with my fingernails more than usual.

But then she giggled at something he said, and her fingertips dimpled the skin on my arm where she squeezed me. Her touch just made me feel even more conflicted. I can't let him hurt her like he hurt Sid, but I can't hurt her in the process of protecting her, either. It's still all so muddled and confusing, but was even more so in the moment. A slow ache built at the base of my skull, and everything inside me tensed, tight with energy.

More people from town joined us on the road as we neared

the carnival grounds—some on foot, kids on bikes, and families in cars—and I calmed myself down by imagining how I might kill them.

I could tackle a walker to the ground and smash their face into the road until they choked on blood and asphalt. Then push a cyclist in front of a car, and when the driver got out to check, pull the seatbelt free and wrap it around their neck until their eyes bulged from their head.

"Jesus, Mallory," you might say. "I thought you claimed not to enjoy inflicting pain." And you would be right. I don't. But there's comfort in knowing that I <u>could</u> overtake anyone if the need arose. ~~And there's an innate release in violence that~~ The point is I'm not actually doing any of this to random people, okay.

By the time we reached the entrance, I was a lot more settled in my skin and pulled fully back into the moment as the jumbled murmurs of the crowd and ticket sellers were joined by lively calliope music.

"Forsythe! Mallory!"

I turned, spotting Mitch waving to get our attention as he pushed his way through the crowd. My eyes caught on his light green polo, not for the way it fit across his broad shoulders, narrowing at his waist and tucked into khaki pants, but for the thick, deep green stripes that ran vertically down his chest, perfectly matching the green of the button down I wore, sleeves rolled and hem tied into a knot at of the waist of—yup—khaki shorts.

I blamed my already unsteady emotional state for the warmth that bloomed across my cheeks when I met his eyes. We <u>matched.</u>

I briefly entertained the idea of lying in the middle of the road to wait for someone to run me over.

"Price!" Jonah called back, lifting an arm enthusiastically, one hand resting against the small of Olive's back to keep her from being knocked away by the commotion of the crowd.

Mitch finally reached us, and he smiled down at me, guileless and friendly. "I dig the outfit."

"You must have read my mind this morning," I joked, gesturing at his shirt.

"Don't worry, it's a gift that only extends as far as fashion." He played along, winking. Why couldn't Olive be into <u>him</u>?

Jonah looked between us, one eyebrow cocked. "Shall we, then?"

"Where are your brothers?" Mitch asked, looking around.

"I gave them the day off, on account of Olive and Jonah being available to chaperone." I looped my arm back through hers, and she rolled her eyes.

"Don't worry, preacher, I'm not here to report back to the women's Bible study," she assured him.

"Mitch, please," he insisted. "And I expect they'll have their tongues wagging enough just seeing us in passing."

"Well, let's go give them something to gossip about." Olive grinned, leading us toward the ticket booth.

As soon as we stepped from the outer lot into the carnival, I felt like we'd been transported to another world. The air was thick with the cloying sweetness of spun sugar and kettle corn, and the calliope music flowed exuberantly over shrieks and laughter and the rattle of thrill rides. Even in the daylight, naked bulbs flashed along the tops of booths, advertising games, prizes, treats, and various acts; and the brightly painted structures matched the vibrant, clashing colors worn by the carnies themselves, easy to spot among the more mutely dressed guests.

"Step right up! Step right up and prove yer strength!"

"Ladies! Gentlemen! Boys and Girls! Who among you is brave enough to enter Digger's Haunted Graveyard?"

"Cotton candy! Ten cents!"

It was impossible to take it all in, but I would have stopped in my tracks to try had I still not been hooked to Olive, who tugged me along as I looked around.

Chaos. Complete and utter chaos. But each carny I spotted was clearly in their element, thriving in the environment as they pulled in patrons from the crowd. A genuine smile stretched my cheeks. A carnival is a place of magic. A place where people are so easily distracted. Anything can happen with just a little bit of know-how and intention.

The <u>perfect</u> hunting ground.

I gave Olive's arm an excited squeeze and then let her go, pointing ahead to the Ferris wheel. "There it is!"

"Isn't that more of a nighttime ride?" Jonah asked.

Olive shook her head, patting his arm as she followed me through the crowd. "It's tradition! Every fair and carnival, the Ferris wheel comes first. We get a bird's eye view of the entire grounds and see where all the best rides and booths are," she explained, then gave him a speculative glance. "I'm surprised you don't already know that."

"Smart," Mitch complimented, nodding slowly as he took in the looming wooden circle ahead of us.

"Sid started it," Olive said, and Jonah stiffened.

Mitch tilted his head, and I buried the sudden pierce of pain at his absence, exacerbated by Jonah's presence, under an easy smile. "My brother."

"Ah, the one who joined the army, right?"

The discomfort in Jonah's posture gave me a smug satisfaction. "Navy."

"Such a commendable act of bravery," Mitch said solemnly.

I fought the urge to slide my gaze to Jonah. "He's the best man

I know."

When we got to the front of the line for the Ferris wheel, I climbed in next to Mitch. His legs bounced a little as the ride shifted, brushing against mine briefly before he pulled them back in, leaving a respectable distance between us as we slowly worked our way up. That was a pleasantly surprising turn of events, and a bit of the tension eased in my shoulders as I relaxed back into the smooth wooden seat.

"So you're into thrill rides then?" he asked.

"Oh, absolutely. Most forms of thrill, really." I saw his knuckles go white as he gripped the seat bar. "And you?" I prompted coyly.

He caught me watching him and laughed, still the same friendly tenor, but with a note of unease. "Well, no. And, coincidentally, also feel the same about most thrills."

I raised a brow at that. "Not one for the unexpected, huh?"

"As a general rule, that would be correct."

I shook my head with a laugh. "And yet you work with teenagers."

He blinked for a moment, then joined me. "You have a point there. But I won't always work in the youth ministry. It's where I fit best now as a junior pastor, but there's a point where I'll age out, right?"

"You have ambition for a congregation of your own?"

He shrugged, gasping a bit as we lurched to a stop to let more passengers board, our cart gently swinging. I resisted the urge to throw my weight into the pendulum motion and push our swing harder. Was that actually a bead of sweat forming at his hairline? "I wouldn't call it an ambition, more of an open desire to serve wherever God needs me."

I made a humming sound in reply, unable to relate and also distracted by a crowd gathering in front of a booth below. I leaned forward to get a better look and then was further distracted by movement directly beneath us. Jonah stretched an arm out behind Olive along the back of their seat, and I envisioned myself leaping from my cart and grabbing hold of the appendage on my way down. I swung from it, ripping it free from his body as I landed on the framework of the Ferris wheel to watch as blood dripped from the arm and sprayed from the gaping wound in his shoulder. The rounded white bone poked—

"What about you?"

I snapped back to reality and twisted to look at Mitch, sitting back in my seat. "Pardon?"

"Do you have ambition?"

I meant to tell him that I was content running the bed and breakfast, but changed my mind when I spoke. "I want to write stories."

"What kind of stories?" he asked, regarding me like he really did care about the answer.

So I told him about my love of horror and thrillers, and he confessed to having a soft spot for science fiction and fantasy. We compared notes on our favorites, the conversation light and easy as the Ferris wheel looped us up and around a few continuous passes.

After we unloaded, the men let Olive and I dictate our path through the crowd. The morning went by in a whirlwind of games, snacks, and rides, and I was continually surprised by the way Mitch treated me. I had expected to spend the day avoiding the brush of his hand or side-stepping away from the warmth of his shoulder too close to mine. The last thing I needed was for his stunted man-brain to misread things and think I was trying to lead him on. But I'm pleased to report that Mitchel Price is a gentleman. The most he did was lightly grasp my elbow to guide me away from a pair of children speeding by from behind me, releasing me as soon as the threat of collision had passed.

And so, as the day went on, I found myself relaxing, at least where he was concerned. With him just a few years older than me, it was easy to interact with him the same way I would with Graham, and I let myself enjoy the loosely controlled chaos as well as the company—outside of Jonah, of course.

Later in the afternoon, I clasped a cup of frozen lemonade in one hand, worrying the plastic straw between my molars. Jonah was attempting to impress Olive with his knowledge of hair products, of all things, while they split a puff of cotton candy larger than both of their heads put together. I did my best to tune him out, watching the endless commotion as we stood in a patch of shade underneath a cottonwood, waiting while Mitch stood in line for food.

I was watching a clown, tall and skinny and wearing orange-and-red striped overalls, at least five sizes too big, stretched out around his waist by some sort of hoop. His face was painted the classic clown white, with broad, bright red lips, a red circle on his nose, and a black triangle beneath each eye.

He pulled long, thin balloons from a pocket inside of those outrageously oversized pants, made a show of taking huge, heaving breaths, then blew them up, deftly twisting them into swords and flowers and dogs.

His act was amusing enough, but I caught one side of his mouth lift under that garish red paint, and he subtly jerked his chin to the side, then shrugged, his attention returning to the crowd of children surrounding him.

Taking everything in with a practiced precision, my gaze moved the direction he'd been looking and landed on a raised ride operator's platform. A young man leaned on the railing, his arms crossed and still smirking from whatever that non-verbal conversation had been about.

He pulled a faded blue bandana from his back pocket, snapping it out and lifting his newsboy cap to wipe sweat from his forehead. Returning the bandana to its place, he pushed off from the railing and turned back to his controls. Golden hair peaked from underneath the back of his hat, and his arms were the deep tan of someone who worked outside all day. Swatches of grease decorated his hands and forearms, and I would bet that his dark-colored clothing was also stained.

I rolled the straw over in my mouth, teasing it open before squishing it flat again. I flicked my eyes in a cursory glance over my surroundings, but no one was watching me watch the ride jockey, so I continued. He just had that look to him, something in the way he carried himself, and I felt a telltale lurch of anticipation in my gut ...

I was already confident in my appraisal, but then I caught him.

As he helped a girl about my age down the rickety steel steps, he copped a feel, palming too much of an ass cheek for it to be an innocent brush. Her head whipped around to him, her cheeks flushed. And he winked.

<u>Bad boy</u>.

The hunt is special to me.

I have never been the kind of person who finds joy in killing a complete stranger. Where is the grit? Where is the connection? How are we any better than animals if we don't allow for that bit of personal touch?

Not that I judge my brothers for being more concise with these things than I am. Add it up to just another difference between our two sexes, perhaps, but there's something in the hunt that has always thrilled me more than the kill. A successful hunt is what truly warms me all the way to my core.

I find a guy who's never learned to value and respect other people, then get him to fully lower his guard, to trust me, to appreciate and even crave my attention and company. And just when he thinks he has me under his thumb—that's when the claws come out. God bless, I get goosebumps just thinking about it.

I haven't been able to indulge since just after the new year.

A young family had come to stay at the bed and breakfast: a husband, wife, and one darling little toddler. The husband was around Tommy's age and reminded me so much of my father that I almost froze up the first time I heard him lash out at his wife. He didn't yell at her in our direct presence, but I heard enough through the walls to know he was the kind of man who thought having a penis meant he had absolute authority and ownership of his family, that he was due respect and ultimate consideration in every part of life.

Disgusting pig. He was so stupidly easy to seduce.

It took only a few admiring glances, always avoiding direct eye contact in favor of a respectfully downcast gaze when initiating conversation. Some flustered, accidental touches. Some fanciful sighs when his wife was out of earshot about how hard he must work and how she must appreciate him so greatly.

He had only stayed for a weekend, but by the time Sunday rolled around, he was whispering nonsense to me about what a good wife I'd make one day. He even clasped my fingers and kissed them, though that wasn't half as bad as when he left—his wife and child in the car all ready to go, he'd stepped back inside to "make sure that everything was settled" and kissed my cheek, his hand planted firmly on my hip like he owned me, too.

God, he was such a satisfying slaughter.

After only two nights of winning him over, he was gone. I waited a week before I borrowed the truck and made the two and a half hour trek to Temecula and parked at his office, which he'd proudly told me all about. I arrived just after lunch, waiting in the back of the parking lot where I knew he took a walking smoke break most days. Sure enough, he'd come down the sidewalk, tossing a filter into the road as he made his way around the manicured bushes.

"I made it out of the mountains," I called, making a show of tightening my coat against the cold once I got his attention.

His eyes widened in surprise for a moment before he regained his composure, looking around and stepping closer. "Mallory? What are you doing here?"

I blinked, biting my lip and taking a step back in uncertainty. "I'm sorry. I shouldn't—I shouldn't have come. I just haven't been able to stop thinking about ... well, I remembered you talking about your lunchtime walks, and I thought maybe—no, I'm sorry, I'll go. This is so forward and entirely inappropriate." I held my hands out in front of me, shaking my head and retreating further back to the truck, and, consequently, out of view of the building's main doors.

He blinked, regaining his composure, and followed my retreat. "No, no, I was just surprised is all, I hadn't expected ..." he trailed off, shaking his head.

My lashes fluttered, and I leaned back against the truck, scuffing a boot across the pavement. "I don't mean to cause trouble. I'm honestly not even sure why I'm here."

With a final glance toward the office building, adjusting the front of his pants as he verified that we were out of view of doors and windows, he stepped closer, caging me in. My heart rate doubled, my stomach flipping with adrenaline. "I think I know why you're here, darling." He cupped my cheek, this thumb brushing my lips.

I gasped, mouth parting as I met his dark, hungry gaze with wide-eyed innocence, then looked over his shoulder. "I don't think we should—is there somewhere nearby we could ... talk?"

And just like that, he was getting into the truck. No one had seen me, and no one had seen him leave. He was all too happy to stop down a secluded road and follow me out of the cab. All too happy when I reached out to him, fingers trembling, heart thumping such a heavy rhythm I was sure he could see it in my throat. All too happy when his weight pressed against me, his face angling down to mine. He wasted no time in deepening the kiss, his tongue strangely cold and tasting of tobacco, one hand grabbing at a breast through the layer of my jacket.

He was already locked in, so I loosened the reins on my self control, a little anticipatory whimper working up my throat as I rushed to unbutton my coat. His hands were on my body, and while I kept one of mine on the back of his neck, he was unaware of the other, which pulled a four-inch hunting knife from an interior coat pocket.

He <u>was</u> aware when I stabbed into the delicate skin where his leg joined his pelvis, and he was not at all happy when I ripped the blade sideways, feeling the pull and snap of tendons and sinew as I opened the artery located there.

Adrenaline sang in my blood as he grabbed at his crotch, trying to staunch the blood flow as he sank to the ground and screamed.

"No, no, no, no," I cautioned, hauling him back up by the shoulders. The idiot actually helped me, too, staggering back upright on his good leg and leaning heavily against the truck.

"My leg, my leg," he whined, choking on tears.

"I know. Come on, let's get you some help," I said calmly despite the elation buzzing through my body, and helped him into the passenger seat, which was already lined with an old towel over a sheet of plastic. (Predictably, he'd been too single-minded to notice during the short drive.) When he was mostly sitting, I balanced just inside the truck, pulling his head toward me and driving the blade through the top of his shoulder, then pushing his head the other way and repeating. Small grunts of exertion forced past my teeth as I severed the nerves of his arms, and his legs started kicking as he tried to buck me off. But pain and surprise were on my side, and I tipped him forward to shove the knife tip between two knobs of his lower spine. He slumped against me, resuming his screaming.

"Please, stop that," I said, pushing free and slamming the door closed before making my way to the driver's side. I flexed my fingers in the cold air, shifting the knife from one hand to the other and focusing on taking slow, even breaths.

My teeth were still buzzing when I climbed back into the truck, my blood rushing with an electric levity. His screams had dropped into a warbling sort of moan that sounded vaguely erotic, and I knelt on the bench seat next to him, leaning over to spread his knees apart. Sluggish spurts of blood seeped from his leg, filling the cab with the warm smell of copper.

"You ... crazy bitch," he gasped, limbs paralyzed and quickly bleeding out. "I have a wife! A baby!"

I climbed onto his lap, my shins resting across his thighs, clear of his blood, and dragged my gaze from his wound up to his face. "That sure seemed to matter when you had your tongue down my throat," I commiserated, resting my hands on his cheeks.

His eyes clouded with fear, his pupils blown wide, and butterflies tumbled through my belly, exhilaration threatening to steal the breath from my lungs as I watched him realize his own dire helplessness at my hands.

I sat back, pressing one hand against his heart while I used the knife to give me a better vantage of that single, simple gash in his thigh. Every thump against my palm was matched by a surge of blood in the canyon I'd ripped into his skin. So much blood, and he wasn't even fighting me—<u>couldn't</u> fight me. I peeked back up to find him staring at me, terror in his eyes. He swallowed thickly, his tongue working in his mouth as he prepared to talk. I shook my head, pressing the flat of the blade to his lips. His own blood painted his mouth as whatever he'd been about to say dissolved into a single, drawn-out whimper.

My teeth sank into my lower lip, his pulse weak and slowing while my own raced with giddy elation. "So tough," I whispered. "Such a big, strong man you were." His eyelids drooped, and I leaned forward, feeling his final breath against my cheek. "But I'm stronger."

Adrenaline still buzzed through me when I slid from his lap and started up the truck. For all the anticipation that had swam in my stomach on the drive down, the entire ride back I was filled with that giddy energy.

We had a wheelbarrow at the cabin that I unceremoniously dumped him into to aid my laborious journey to the basement. But I did it. And damn if that man wasn't all the more delicious for my efforts and the thrill of the chase and trickery.

I didn't feel bad for his wife. She was downright gorgeous and only a few years older than me. She would land another man easily, and hopefully one that was a little less prone to anger and groping strangers.

Over six long months it's been since, and the thrill of it—the near-orgasmic satisfaction of everything coming together for that final moment of sinking a blade too deep to reverse—is once again a distant memory.

I crave that release like nothing else.

So the timing of the carnival really is perfect. Tommy may have just had a kill, but summer is our busy season at the bed and breakfast, so it's important to stock up while we can and while plenty of good candidates are still out and about.

And, honestly, a carny is too good of a target to pass up. They're practically vagabonds, and no one will raise the alarm if one goes missing after the next stop. Plus, it's better to start the hunt sooner; that way if ol' golden-haired grabby-hands isn't a good fit, I still have time to pick another.

But, oh, how I hope he'll do. I can't explain it outside of gut instinct, but intuition tells me he's meant for me. As great as the rest of my night was, he was definitely the highlight.

Okay, okay, back to it.

"What did I miss?" Mitch came back with a spiral of skewered tri-tip, pulling my attention away from the ride jockey, and I felt my cheeks warm.

"Mallory is always getting lost in the clouds." Olive slid an arm around my waist. "Leave her be for more than a moment, and she leaves the planet for a world of her own."

I tossed my hair with an indignant tut. "I'm not that bad," I defended. "And, actually, I was watching the clown in the big pants."

"Hmm." Mitch looked over to the clown in question, offering me the skewer. "Do you think he wears pants underneath the overalls?"

I ripped off a chunk of the tender meat, contemplating. "Surely at least a pair of shorts. Otherwise someone tall enough might see his unmentionables."

"What kind of skivvies do you suppose a clown wears?" Olive asked with a giggle.

"Maybe they're made out of balloons," I suggested.

"Highly doubtful," Jonah replied with a snort, and I resisted the urge to stick my tongue out at him.

But I did catch Mitch rolling his eyes, and we shared a quick, conspiratorial smile.

"Is anyone up for that pendulum ride?" I asked, pointing to the death trap labeled THE INVERSION where my chosen carny was posted. I just couldn't help wanting to get a closer look.

"I'll go," Olive said, her eyes wide as she took in the almost vertical swing of the large metal arm.

"I'll happily watch from the sidelines," Mitch said, raising his skewer in a salute. "I don't have enough faith in the stability of those things."

Jonah looked a tad wan as the screams of riders washed over us, but he stepped into line with me and Olive regardless.

I watched the operator as we neared the front. He was friendly, joking with anyone who interacted with him, be it fellow carny or patron, and his entire being—from posture to voice—exuded confidence. I chewed on the side of my lip, wondering if he really was a good fit after all. If he was that big of a personality, he might be missed.

Then his sparkling blue eyes caught mine, and he cocked his head to the side, a sheaf of gold falling across his forehead with the movement. "You ain't scared, are ya?" he challenged in a thick drawl, and I froze for a second, thinking he'd somehow been able to read my thoughts. "'Cause you shouldn't be," he continued, and I tethered myself back to reality. Of course, he was talking about the ride. "I put this beauty together myself." He leaned forward to pat one of the stabilizer legs, then fumbled comically with a screwdriver that he pulled from his back pocket.

With a ham like that, was I really expected not to bite?

Before I could respond, he turned back to the ride, which was coming to the end of its timed cycle. Olive, though, raised an eyebrow and elbowed my side with more than a bit of suggestion. I'd lightly flirted with conquests in front of her before, and I wondered how she would react if she learned how many of them were now dead and whether or not she would see the commitment and, dare I say, the romance in the fact that I'd fed bits of each of them to her.

I shook off the macabre thought as we boarded and waited for the operator to check our harnesses.

"You ready, darlin'?" he asked, giving the strap over my lap a perfunctory tug.

"You inspire the utmost confidence," I replied drily, meeting those jovial baby blues.

He winked, brushing the back of his hand across his forehead in a way that dislodged his newsboy cap. "Glad to hear it."

I lost sight of him as he moved around the contraption, but then Olive was grabbing my hand with a squeal, her feet kicking in anticipation, and I stopped worrying about the hunt to enjoy the moment.

And what a moment it was. My cheeks hurt from smiling when we got off the ride, a joy that only deepened when Jonah stumbled right off into the bushes to lose his lunch.

Olive put her hands over her mouth, still high on the exhilaration of the ride and trying to fight back her own smile and breathless laughter. "Poor thing," she cooed sympathetically, but she stayed next to me.

To top off what had been an unexpectedly delightful day, Mitch sent Jonah ahead after we parted with Olive at the end of her driveway. That almost made me nervous, but his hands stayed in his pockets as he walked me home, and his eyes roamed the trees for a while before he finally looked down at me. "I hope I'm not wildly misjudging this, but am I right to assume that you don't see something happening between us any more than I do?"

I gave him my best apologetic smile. "You got me."

He sighed, returning my smile with a nod. "I had a fantastic time today, and I did greatly enjoy your company, but ...”

"I have no desire to date you, and you don't know how much of a relief it is to hear you feel the same," I said, saving him the trouble of tact. "But I did enjoy myself. Thank you for inviting me."

"The pleasure was mine, Miss Rathbone."

He left me at my driveway with a handshake and a friendly wave, then I turned toward the house, leaning down to pet the dogs when they ran up to me.

"You look happy," Tommy said, sitting on the front porch with a cigarette and a plate of what looked like the remnants of barbecued cutlets.

I grinned. "Fried foods and thrill rides will do that, I suppose."

"Is that all?" he needled, trying to tease me.

I couldn't keep the smugness from my voice as I passed him. "Oh, I've decided I'm hunting."

I deliberately stayed in the common areas of the house, where Tommy couldn't talk to me with so many guests around. I admit, watching curiosity burn behind his friendly host mask all night had been the best sort of payback for the way he'd meddled with Mitch. Once it was dark, I excused myself to shower, and it wasn't until after, as I sat at my vanity brushing through towel-dried hair, that my brother finally got me alone.

"Hunting, huh?"

I met his eyes in the mirror, gently working through a knotted section. "I'm mostly sure I found my mark today, but even if he doesn't work out, I have every confidence that another one of those carnies will fit the bill." I bit my lip, savoring the way my blood fizzled at the thought of him. It had been too long since I'd been inspired into such deliciously palpable action. "I have a good feeling, though."

Tommy leaned against the door, crossing his arms over his

chest with an amused smirk. "Well, that didn't take long. Eager one, aren't you?"

I set my brush down and turned to face him. "They'll be in town for over a week. Maybe some of us can appreciate a bit of delayed gratification in our art."

He snorted a laugh. "Are you judging my craft?"

"You're the one who just called me eager."

He raised his hands in deference, and then I finally caved and told him about the encounter with probably too much excited detail. When I finished, Tommy nodded appreciatively. "I know you know what you're doing, but I'm around if you want a sounding board."

"Or any help?" I added for him.

"Of course, that's what big brothers are for. But only if you want it."

I smiled. "I'll let you know if I"—I stifled a yawn—"run into any snags."

"It's a plan." He walked across the space between us to pull me into a hug. "Night, Duck," he said, releasing me. "I love you."

"I love you, too," I replied. And then I was alone, left to document the day and soon to dream about carnivals with Olive and chasing a blue-eyed boy.

Hunker down, because this day was a _ride._

I'm delighted to report that seeing Mitch at church wasn't awkward in the least. I can't say the same for my brief interaction with Jonah, who invited Olive to sit with him and his mother. She and her parents always share a pew with us, and it was all I could do to keep from smugly grabbing her hand when she politely declined his invitation.

After church, I spent the day catching up on chores. Just the usual things, plus the Brewers had left yesterday, which meant a deep cleaning of their room. (You'll also be happy to hear that Donald is a nice man. I kept a pretty close eye on him around the house, and from what I could tell, he's head over heels for Charlene and treats her well. That would be a bit of a bummer if I didn't have the carnival to hunt.)

The Masons let me know that they would be out for dinner, which meant a break from cooking, too. Tonight would be a fend-for-yourself situation, and I was already looking forward to relaxing later with a bowl of cereal.

I was deciding between Cocoa Puffs and Frosted Flakes and dancing around with a broom to Lesley Gore when the front door opened.

"Special delivery," Olive sang as she stepped inside.

"My favorite kind." I beamed before stooping to sweep my pile of dirt and dog fur into the dustpan. "And right on time. I'm just about finished up here."

"Perfect, because it's too beautiful a day to waste inside playing housekeeper." She skipped into the living room to turn up the volume on the record player.

I moved into the kitchen, dumping the dustpan into the trash and propping the broom against the fridge. I barely had time to wipe my hands clean with a dish towel before Olive was in front of me, grabbing my hands and pulling me into a swing dance to *Sunshine, Lollipops, and Rainbows.*

We took turns leading, trying to outdo each other with swings and spins and so absorbed in dancing that we didn't notice we had company.

"Nobody told me there was a party."

I jumped, clutching Olive, who made a surprised sound somewhere between a shriek and a squeal, and then we collapsed against each other in breathless laughter.

"What are you doing here?" I asked my brother, moving to turn the volume down.

"Hello to you, too, Duck." Graham rolled his eyes, striding into the kitchen and straight to the fridge. "Is Tommy out back?"

"Is Priscilla with you?" I asked at the same time.

"Nah, she has an Avon party today. Or maybe it was Tupperware?" He shrugged, pulling a container of jerky from the fridge and digging in. "This is tasty. Lyle's?"

"He's been getting creative with spices."

"Kid's got a good palate. Anyway, Tommy and I were going to run down to San Bernardino today. Didn't he tell you?"

I frowned, crossing my arms and leaning back against the counter. "No. Why?"

He grabbed another strip of jerky and shrugged again, closing the container and replacing it in favor of the milk carton, which he opened and began to raise to his mouth.

I intercepted it with a huff. "We have guests." I glared, grabbing a glass and handing both to him.

He at least had the decency to look sheepish. "Sorry."

I crossed my arms again, watching as he took his time pouring the milk and finally closing the fridge. My foot began a staccato tap-tap-tap against the linoleum as he drank. "Why are you going to the city?" I repeated.

Hazel eyes flicked to Olive, who stood in the kitchen entrance to my left, then back to me. "Just the usual. Gonna pick up some stuff for around the house."

I bit into my cheek, taking a deep breath through my nose. "But you guys just replenished the staples last week."

Tommy came in, and the dogs rushed Graham, tails thumping loudly against the cabinets and fridge as they vied for attention. "Oh, good, you're here," our elder brother greeted, clapping Graham on the back. "Ducky, I think I forgot to mention we were going to the city today." He smiled at me, hand still resting on Graham's shoulder like all of this was normal.

I curled my hands into fists where they were pressed against my ribs, confusion and hurt tumbling into one another and quickly becoming anger. "For ... to restock?" I asked, holding his gaze.

He lifted one shoulder in a shrug—they were both so goddam casual about this—and moved across the kitchen to the sink for a cup of water, my eyes tracking him the entire way. "Yeah, nothing we really planned. We were just talking about it the other day and decided why not. Get out and stretch our legs a bit. You've got everything nailed down here."

Blood roared in my ears, and I chewed on my cheek to keep my eyes clear as an angry lump formed in my throat. We had just talked about my hunt last night. He knew it was my turn; they both knew. The only time they ever went into the city was when they were itching for action, and the selfish bastards couldn't even give me two goddam weeks to get my own.

And that's what hurt, what fueled my anger. Even though I knew Tommy could see the betrayal plastered across my face, he didn't so much as look ashamed, much less apologize. He just smiled that stupid, pleasant smile and walked over to me, slinging an arm around my shoulders and pulling me into a hug that I refused to participate in. "Hold down the fort, Mallory-mallard. We'll be back tonight," he said to the top of my head. "Lovely to see you, Olive. Keep her out of trouble, yeah?"

Then he grabbed his keys, and he and Graham were out the door.

I swallowed, reeling as heat rose in my chest and my fists clenched. It was my turn. The taste of copper flooded my mouth as I bit into the meat of my cheek.

I forced a deep breath, willing away the solid lump pushing at my throat. Tommy and Graham would never disregard me like that. If they hadn't looked apologetic, it's because they weren't doing anything they had to apologize for. Maybe they were just getting in some early scouting, maybe doing some legwork so that Lyle's first time in a couple months would go smoothly.

I breathed out through my mouth, emptying my lungs of oxygen.

Tommy and Graham would never do anything to hurt me. Everything they'd ever done had been with consideration of the rest of us. My entire life was built on the solidity of that fact. I couldn't start second-guessing it now. And they knew how much

I loved the hunt. They're the ones who raised me to crave it. Next week was Father's Day. I guess I couldn't really begrudge them wanting to go out and celebrate. They had by and far earned the right to call themselves fathers in every way that really mattered. But it was <u>my turn</u>, dammit, and it wasn't <u>fair</u>. They'd just had that guy I'd helped field dress out at the cabin. I hadn't had anyone in months. And Lyle would be fourteen in August, eager for his first. We couldn't take that many so close together—there were rules, and being greedy and uncontrolled like that was stupid. It would get us caught, and—my thoughts spiraled round and round.

"What's wrong, Mally?" Olive's soft voice broke through my cloud of anger, and I realized my vision had gone blurry with unshed tears.

"Nothing, I just ..." I shook out my hands, tipping my head back and blinking to coax the tears back into my body. "It would be nice to have that kind of freedom, is all," I finally said, settling for the barest relation to the truth. "They can just take off and go wherever they want, whenever they want."

Olive sighed, offering me a commiseratingly grim smile. "I know what you mean. It's like we're always beholden to some form of accountability as women. It's never just about us and what we need, is it? We've always got to be thinking of others—what comes next, what chores need to be completed, what foods are ready for the next meal and what still needs to be prepared, who is coming home at what time with what concerns, who might need something from us and at what point. Even when we're relaxing, it's not really relaxing because there's always something else that will need to be noted or taken care of. It's exhausting. No woman would be able to decide on a whim she needs to get out and stretch her legs without something falling apart later down the line." She shook her head, a line between her pinched brows as she glared down at her feet.

I don't know what I'd expected from her, but it hadn't been that. She so seldom got worked up about anything, which made it even easier for me to jump on the warpath when she did. And now I wanted to cup her face and tell her I would never hinder her from being able to do anything she wanted, that I would share life's burdens and make sure she felt free to think of her own happiness.

Good God, I love her so much, and moments like that make it so hard for me to remember all of the very real reasons why I can't tell her.

"We should go," I said, looking out the window to Graham's station wagon parked out front.

Olive laughed, crossing her arms over her chest. "If only."

"No, I mean it," I said, meeting those dark brown eyes. "Not, like, forever, but let's just go to the beach or something. We can forget the world for a while, come back tomorrow or … whenever."

"What about Lyle?" she asked, and my heart rate doubled with the thought that she might be considering it. I could easily forget the hunt, forget getting skipped over, if it meant time away from the world with her.

I waved a hand through the air, cool and casual. "He's almost fourteen. He can be by himself for a few hours until the boys get back."

"So, what, then we just take your brother's car and drive west until we hit water?"

"Sure," I shrugged. "Graham will figure out that I took it and will also figure out that I'll bring it back."

"And he's not gonna be royally … pissed?" She lowered her voice when she said it, rocking back on her heels to make sure we were alone.

"Oh, of course he is, but he'll get over it."

Olive shook her head at me. "You always have been trouble."

"Is that a yes?" I raised my eyebrows.

"You drive an incredibly hard bargain, Miss Rathbone." She placed her hands on my cheeks, my stomach flipping when she touched the tip of her nose to mine. "But I'll have to ask for a rain check on your offer of grand theft. Unfortunately, I promised my dad I'd open the shop for him tomorrow while he does deliveries."

I sighed as she took my hand and led me from the kitchen. "Well, let's not throw a wrench in Piney's plans."

We spent the afternoon wading in the pond and playing fetch with the dogs, and when Lyle turned up from whatever adventures he'd been on with his friends, we went inside for food and then played a few rounds of rummy—he whipped us both, the card sharp. As the sun was on its last legs, I walked with Olive back to her house, Danny padding along at my heels and Benny darting ahead of us, chasing a flock of quail from one tree to another.

I felt restless when I got home again. The temptation to walk down to the carnival was strong. I tried reading for a bit, but just couldn't sink into the pages, still a little wound up from the older boys leaving me behind. It <u>was</u> my turn. (Have I reiterated that enough?) And what was the harm in stopping by, being noticed? I thought of sparkling blue eyes, a mop of golden hair peeking out from the brim of a gray newsboy cap. The guy was nothing but trouble in a meat-suit, and I wanted to gobble him up—figuratively and literally.

"To hell with it," I muttered, swinging my feet over the side of my bed to lace up my sneakers. I could pull Lyle out with me, grab some fair food as a treat since I'd been rejected twice tonight.

"Hey, LJ, wanna go grab dessert from the fair?" I asked, poking my head into the boys' room.

He looked up from where he lay on his bed, comic book spread open in front of him. "Don't we still have cobbler?"

"Wouldn't you rather have a fresh churro?"

He brushed auburn waves from his eyes. (I really need to make time to trim his hair.) "Can I ride the tilt-a-whirl, too?"

I leaned a hip against the doorframe, crossing my arms in mock contemplation. "Oh, I don't know. Maybe ... if you can beat me down the drive." I ran off down the hall, stopping in the mudroom to pocket a couple of dollars from the old nail tin that Tommy keeps on the top shelf—his "secret stash for treats"—as Lyle's protests of not being ready followed. I barely remembered to turn back to grab a syringe from my Ana-kit in the kitchen, then slipped out the back door and jogged around to the front of the house.

Danny stood on the front porch, *awoo-wooing* at me as Benny followed me down the lane. Lyle came bursting through the front door, and Benny loped back to him. I picked up speed, laughing as Lyle chased after me, hollering that I was a cheater.

I slowed to a walk, letting him catch up near the end of the driveway. He swatted me away when I tried to muss his hair, but he couldn't quite hide his smile. "Benny, home," I commanded, pointing, and the border collie gave a little grumbling whine before turning back toward the house. The sun was down by now, though the sky to the west was still hued a soft indigo. I tilted my head back to watch the stars appear, and Lyle slid his hand into mine as we walked. He'd mostly grown out of the habit, and I peeked over at him to see him also staring up at the sky.

Times like this, he still seemed so young.

"Do Tommy and Graham always hunt together?" he asked,

softly enough that his voice wouldn't carry over the crunch of gravel beneath our shoes.

"Almost always, I think."

"But you and Sid never did?" He looked at me, curious, and I realized with a start that he was almost as tall as me now. I have no more than a few inches on him.

I considered his question for a while, thinking. "Not never," I finally said. "In the beginning, we did. He actually waited for me for his first, because he didn't want me to feel left out." I smiled at the memory, me dolefully looking on as Tommy and Graham prepared him for his first trip. He'd met my eyes and frowned, seeing how much I wanted to be a part of what the three of them would soon share, and told our brothers that he wouldn't hunt until I could.

Sweet, thoughtful Sid, whose heart was big and softer than a duckling's downy feathers. He never would've let Tommy and Graham leave like that without assuring that they weren't skipping over me or encroaching on Lyle's first.

"He never craved the hunt so much," I continued. "The last couple years before he left, he would let us go ahead of him more often than not." But he'd always helped out whenever we needed it.

"I miss him," Lyle said, dropping my hand to shove his into his pockets. His mouth curved up in a smile. "He's the only one who stands a chance against me at cards."

I laughed, shoving into his shoulder so that he stumbled a few steps away.

The carnival lights were bright and colorful, a welcoming glow over the crowds enjoying the warm summer night. I bought us each a churro, then wandered through the thrill rides, my gaze flitting over the carnies in search of my intended prey.

Lyle pulled me impatiently toward the tilt-a-whirl, and I posted up at a picnic table nearby while he stood in line. I was slowly working on my cinnamon sugar-coated pastry and content to people-watch rather than have my stomach whirled around while still plagued by the anxious knot of agitation in my gut. It was frankly annoying that I hadn't shaken it off by now, especially when I doubted Tommy or Graham had given me a second thought since leaving.

I huffed, frustrated with myself for still fixating on it, and took a deliberate bite of churro while watching a kid attempt to win a stuffed bear for a girl by slamming a hammer. It didn't look like too promising of a scene, so I moved on to a couple of parents trying to wrangle a hoard of kids that I sincerely hoped weren't all their own—

"Hello, strawberry."

I slowly turned to see who addressed me and found none other than my ride jockey, standing with one foot propped up on the bench beside me. Maybe it was because I hadn't expected him to approach me, or maybe I couldn't pack down my left over annoyance at my brothers, but I didn't respond to him the way I typically would with a mark.

Instead of smiling and fluttering my lashes, I held his gaze evenly, raising my eyebrows a little (I can't raise only one) and said, "Pardon?"

He grinned at me, undeterred, and hopped up to sit on the tabletop, both feet now planted on the bench next to me. "I thought that was you," he drawled.

He remembered me?

"Come on, miss thing, don't pretend like my bit with the screwdriver yesterday didn't leave an impression." His accent made "thing" come out "thang", so that it took me a second to decipher what exactly he'd said.

"Miss thing?" I questioned, eyebrows rising further.

"Well, I don't have a name, and I reckon calling you pretty little thing won't go over too well since you didn't seem to like the reference to your hair." He leaned forward on his elbows, blue eyes dark and sparkling in the carnival lights.

I blinked, touching my hair, then flipped the reddish blonde strands over my shoulder with an unladylike snort. "Does that sort of opening line typically work for you, blondie?"

"Oh, I'm hurt," he said, sounding entirely unhurt. "Do you really think I'm the kind of guy who'd run around trying to flirt with every pretty girl I see?"

I ate the final bite of my churro, crumpling the paper into a ball and wiping my hands off over the dirt to my side before finally meeting his eyes again. "Yep."

He removed his newsboy cap and placed it over his heart. "You wound me," he said with a radiant smile, shameless and apparently fond of a little pushback.

It's bad manners, I know, but I do love to play with my food.

I shifted to face him, and he rested his elbows on his knees, leaning forward as I spoke. "I apologize for any internal pain I caused, but can I suggest an exercise in introspection?"

He tilted his head to the side, red and purple light splashing across the gold of his hair as he twisted his hat around where it dangled between his knees. "You're welcome to suggest anything you like, miss thing."

I rolled my eyes to mask the way my insides swooped with the intensity of his stare and saw Lyle walking up in my periphery. "Noted," I answered, standing.

"You're leaving?" He sat up, a look of confusion flashing across his face.

Not used to rejection, also noted. "Time for me to call it a night," I offered in apology, giving a little wave of my fingers as I backed toward Lyle.

"Wait, what's your name?" he called after me.

I shrugged, smiling as I turned and looped my arm through Lyle's. "Not miss thang," I threw over my shoulder.

He shook his head, fitting his hat back over his hair as he watched me leave.

"Who's that?" Lyle asked.

"I'm not sure yet," I replied, weaving us through the dwindling crowd.

The truck was in the driveway when we got back home, and Graham's wagon was gone. The other car in the drive belonged to the Masons, and the lights off upstairs suggested they might have already retired to their rooms for the night after a long day out and about.

Which was great, because my good mood from the encounter with my carny boy had withered at the sight of Tommy's truck—this is not a common reaction for me, and that added confusion only made me feel less sociable.

"Tonight was fun," Lyle said as we started up the drive. "If you want to talk about what's happening with that guy, I'm around. So you can give Tommy an icy shoulder for a bit if you want and still brainstorm or whatever."

My chest expanded with so much love it hurt. Of course, it was always the five of us, that was law, but this show of solidarity earned him all the brownie points. I slung my arm around his shoulders and rested my head against his. "Thanks, LJ. You're pretty okay, you know that?"

I could just about hear his eyes roll, but he leaned into me and said, "I know. I had the four of you to watch, so I know exactly what <u>not</u> to do to make sure I end up groovier than all of you."

I barked out a laugh as he shrugged off my arm, scampering up to the door and ducking inside. I came barreling in after him, Benny running up with delight at the commotion and getting right under my feet so that I tripped over him. "Benny-boy, no, you're supposed to be on my side!" I chastised, pointing to try to sic him on Lyle.

Lyle did the job for me, patting his chest so that Benny hopped up, then dramatically falling to the floor to wrestle.

"Don't rile him up, guests are sleeping," Tommy reminded us, and I righted myself, taking a moment to compose my features before I looked at him.

He stood in the hallway, hands tucked casually in his pockets and a smirk playing at one corner of his mouth.

We looked at each other in silence, and I waited for him to mention his trip to the city or ask about what Lyle and I had been up to. But he said nothing. So I tilted my chin up, portraying that I couldn't care less what he did or what he thought of what I did, then breezed past him into the kitchen—

And stopped dead in my tracks, hands clapping over my mouth and eyes filling with tears, blurring the image of the man with fiery orange hair clipped into a high and tight leaning against the counter, a smile stretching his freckled cheeks.

"Hey, Ducky," Sid said.

<u>Sidney.</u>

A strangled noise escaped me, and next thing I knew I was across the room, throwing my arms around him. Sid caught me, spinning us in a half circle to keep my momentum from knocking us over as I cried into his shoulder.

"Sid!" Lyle called, rushing to join our embrace.

"I missed you," I choked out.

One of his hands left my back to clasp Lyle. "I missed you, too. I missed all of you so much."

I stood on my tiptoes, arms tight around Sid's neck, afraid that if I let him go, he'd be gone again. When the tears blurring my vision cleared, I met Tommy's gaze over his shoulder.

He leaned against the wall, one foot propped in front of the other, golden strawberry curls tumbling over his forehead and his mouth tipped up in that classic smirk, dimpling his cheek. He didn't say anything, but he gave me the slightest nod, and I understood he knew I'd doubted him, and he had let me, even though I should know better. He'd always come through before, and he always would.

I tightened my hold on Sid and nodded back.

Sid is home. And, more importantly, he's home to stay.

His term of enlistment is finally up, and he'd sneakily coordinated with Graham and Tommy to surprise me and Lyle.

<u>Sid is home.</u> I'm still reeling.

The two of us stayed up talking well into the night. Well, Sid talked. I mostly asked questions, needing to hear his voice to further cement the reality that he was here, that this was real. I was afraid to fall asleep and find out that it had all been a dream.

He was exhausted, I could tell. But he humored me, avoiding the darker parts of war in favor of regaling me with stories of jokes passed in the mess hall, the incomparable feeling of watching aircraft launch from the flight deck, and—my favorite of all—Mak. I knew of him from Sid's letters, of course, but do I even need to tell you how much detail men tend to leave out when unprompted? But face-to-face, I finally got the unabridged telling.

"We'd seen each other around, of course, but had never really talked until the first night we were both scheduled for fourth watch. It was considered the worst one, zero-two-hundred to zero-six. All it took was that first time on watch with him, and ..." he trailed off, and I knocked my shoulder into his.

"You liiiiiked him," I sang.

Sid shrugged, his mouth curving up in a half smile that was all boyish charm. "Finding ways to keep getting scheduled with him became almost like a second job." (He didn't reiterate, but I knew from his letters that Mak was practically always on fourth watch. Because his full name is Makoto Nomura, and despite how long it's been since V-E Day, the military—and the country—is still full of racist assholes.) "It would've looked suspicious if I asked to be scheduled for fourth watch all the time. I lost so many games of checkers and accepted so many candy bars and packs of smokes to keep up pretenses. We'd been underway for damn near eight months before I worked up the courage to hint that I was interested. I told him you'd mentioned a magazine article in one of your letters that said being around the ocean for long enough was supposed to make your lips over twice as soft as usual due to the salt air being exfoliating. But supposedly it happened so gradually that you couldn't tell on yourself, you could only feel it on someone else."

I laughed so loud that Sid shushed me, slapping the back of his hand against my thigh. "Subtle, Rathbone."

He ran a hand over the short length of his hair, biting back a grin and his eyes distant with fond memory. His whole countenance glowed. "Yeah, not my best moment, and I definitely shocked him. But we'd grown close enough by that point that he actually took the risk and flirted back." He sighed, a blush crawling up his neck. "He told me that sounded like a bunch of hogwash and asked if I could back up that claim with proof. I thought my knees were gonna give out, I was so nervous. I leaned back against the railing, all casual, but I don't think my heart has ever pounded so hard as it did when I grabbed the front of his uniform and pulled him right up against me. When he didn't push away from me, I kissed him."

I won't share the rest of those details here, because they're not mine, but Siddy has never been so ... so effervescent in his entire life. I'm tired out of my mind, sitting here in the early morning sun while recounting all of this, but I'm happier than I've been in a long time. Everything feels right. Life is good. And who needs sleep when there are brothers to catch up with?

Sid slept on a pallet of blankets on my floor, but despite the late night, he was up long before me. I faintly heard him and Tommy in the kitchen on my way to the bathroom and decided to let them be, heading back into my room to write about yesterday.

The whirlwind that was last night turned into an even bigger whirlwind of a day.

The Masons packed up and left early, which would have usually meant a low effort morning. Not today, of course. Breakfast was a whole event, with pancakes and hash browns and sausage and eggs. Graham and Priscilla even stopped by, so the whole family was together.

The five of us. Like it was always meant to be.

I almost cried when Sid and Lyle fought over the last helping of potatoes. This was the life I'd missed for three years. Tommy squeezed my shoulder when he walked behind me on his way to the kitchen for a fresh cup of coffee, and I was thankful he hadn't pointed out my emotions for the others to tease me.

Priscilla leaned into Graham, nudging him, and he patted her hand obligingly, waiting until Tommy came back in to sit up straighter in his chair. He cleared his throat. "We've got some news to share, and we've been waiting until we were all back together to do it."

I watched his posture, suddenly nervous because he looked nervous, flicking his gaze up to Tommy in the way he used to when they were younger and he'd wanted validation. Priscilla leaned into him, looking up at him with moony, adoring eyes.

My throat went dry, suddenly sure they were moving. We just got Sid back, and now Graham was going to move, probably up north to the San Joaquin Valley where her parents and sister had relocated last year. The food in my stomach churned, and there was nothing I could do to stop the blood draining from my face as my mind reeled. Was he really choosing her over us?

Priscilla caught my eye and gave me a nervous, hopeful smile.

If this bitch thought I was going to be okay with her stealing our brother—but then she spoke, and my thoughts weren't so much interrupted as completely derailed.

"We're going to have a baby." She beamed, dropping a hand to her belly. "I'm pregnant."

I blinked, dumbstruck. That sweet smile on her face started to waiver, and I remembered myself, jumping to my feet. "Oh! Oh my gosh, congratulations!" I darted around the table to hug her as the boys erupted into congratulations of their own. "A baby," I reiterated, pulling away to look down at her still-slim figure as I let my mind adjust to the prospect.

"A baby," she repeated, clasping my arms and looking behind her to Graham, tears lining her eyes.

Tommy came up behind me, and I stepped away so he could embrace Priscilla and then Graham. "Congratulations, little brother. I'm so happy for you both."

"You didn't know?" I asked as Sid and Lyle joined our little huddle.

Graham rested his arm across my shoulders. "Nope, I wanted to tell you all together."

Priscilla nodded, clasping her hands under her chin as she blinked through tears of joy. "I told my mom and sister over the phone a few weeks ago, but it was important to Graham for you all to hear it in person." She reached a hand out to Sid, who squeezed her fingers.

"A baby," I repeated again, wrapping my arms around Lyle and resting my cheek against his hair. They weren't moving. They were staying here. And there would be a <u>child</u>—a whole little person that was half Graham. Unbelievable. Tears sprang to my eyes again, the morning already so full of emotion, and the scene in front of me blurred.

"Aw, c'mere, Duck," Graham chuckled, pulling me off Lyle to tuck me between him and Priscilla.

She was crying, too, and I couldn't help but laugh as I hugged her again.

Who'd have ever thought I'd be losing it over becoming an aunt?

Olive practically guffawed when I shared the sentiment with her later that morning. "You're pulling my leg, surely. In case you haven't met: Mallory, meet Mallory, her family means the world to her. I'd be concerned if you <u>hadn't</u> cried at the news of a niece or nephew."

We were at Piney's shop, and I was helping her take inventory so she could have the rest of the day off. We had a lot of missed summer days to make up for now that Sid was back.

"Okay, okay, you might have a point," I acquiesced.

"Might?" She glanced at me over her shoulder, one eyebrow cocked.

"Might," I repeated, pulling a sheet of paper from her hand and checking the shelf of small wooden signs in front of me. You'd be surprised how many people go up into a mountain town and buy rustic decor for their homes. Even though the style down in Los Angeles, where most of our tourists come from, is much more glamorous, it's like they can't help but want a little piece of our quieter life to take home with them.

"All I've got left is the furniture, and then I'll be free to go."

"You read them off, and I'll count," I offered.

When we were finished, Olive dropped the paperwork at the back of the store where Piney was working in his shop, and I grabbed her hand and pulled her down the road and toward the lake.

The main beach is flooded with tourists this time of year, but locals know a more secluded spot just outside of town. You just have to wind your way through a little thicket of trees and brush to get to the shore.

I could hear my brothers' shouts and laughter as I made my way through the trees, Olive one step behind. The boys (minus Graham, who had work) had established a claim on the small beach inlet dubbed "Delight's Treasure," which is extremely cheesy, but I sure don't have anything more creative to call it.

"Well, look who it is," Tommy called from the water as he spotted us.

Sid, who crouched on the shore building a tower out of mud with Lyle, looked up and waved. "Olive! It's so good to see you." He stood to greet her with a short, tight hug.

"You look good, Sidney." Olive smiled. "So grown."

"I would say the same, but I don't think it counts as a compliment for a woman."

She laughed, shoving at his shoulder in a familiar way that made me grin. "I'm just saying you grew into yourself. That gangly dork of a kid from three years ago is now a grown man."

"Don't over-inflate his ego," I cautioned, but she wasn't

wrong. Sid was tall and lean, but more than just the muscle stretched over his torso, his face had changed. Gone was the round edge to his cheeks where his baby fat had lingered long into his teens, replaced by strong lines and eyes that still sparkled even if they held a deeper, more solemn awareness.

Christ. He's barely been back and already it was so easy for me to forget that he's been to war.

I shook off the urge to hug him close and instead moved over to the ice chest.

"What've we got?" I asked as I rifled through bags of fruit and chips to the tupperware container of paper-wrapped sandwiches at the bottom, resting on ice that had already begun to melt.

"Roast and Colby Jack," Lyle answered, running over to plop down on a towel next to us. "C'mon, Tommy, lunch time!"

I handed the sandwiches out, neat slices of roast topped with Colby Jack (except for Tommy's, which featured Kraft De Luxe Process Slices. He has a weird obsession with the stuff), lettuce, tomato, and horseradish sauce on Wonder Bread as we all sat to eat.

Sid's brows pulled together as he watched Olive take a bite, her fingers poised over her mouth as she chewed, laughing at something Lyle had said. When I looked back at Sid, he was looking at me intently, his bright copper eyebrows pulling further together.

I felt my own forehead wrinkle as I tipped my head to the side in question.

His eyes flicked to Olive and back to me. No, not to Olive, but to the food in her hands that she was happily devouring. I gave a small shrug. Was she not supposed to eat? He pressed his lips together and set his sandwich down to grab a cluster of grapes. I'd upset him, and a hot knot of frustration dropped into my stomach. I shouldn't have to question what his looks mean. I hated the thought that we could be out of step and decided he was being cryptic on purpose.

I ripped off a large bite, trying not to let it fester. Olive absently leaned into my side while talking, and I was more than happy to let that distract me from whatever Sid's problem was.

After lunch, Olive and I draped a couple of towels from tree branches to create a little alcove to change into our swimsuits and then joined the boys in the lake. Whatever weirdness that had taken place between me and Sid seemed to have dissipated, but I wasn't able to fully let go of my frustration until after I'd dunked his whole head underwater during a game of Marco Polo and then swam away before he could retaliate.

"There's not as many people here as I remember," Sid said later that afternoon as we sat on the shore, relaxing while Lyle walked along the waterline looking for skipping stones.

"Well, it is a Monday, so everyone who knows not to go to the tourist beach is probably working," I pointed out, taking a long drag from a cigarette. There was a group of teens further down, but other than that, we'd had the area to ourselves the whole day.

"Or most people are going to the popular beaches for safety," Olive said, digging her toes into the wet sand and resting her chin on her knees.

I flicked ash free, leaning back on one hand. "What's that supposed to mean?"

"Well, people would be avoiding secluded areas, wouldn't they?" she asked, plucking the cigarette from my fingers to take a puff. (She doesn't really smoke, but she'll share one with me every now and then. I won't derail the story by getting into how it makes my insides go all soupy when she does.)

I frowned, looking to Tommy for help, but he looked just as

confused as me. "What are you talking about?" he asked from her other side.

She sat straighter, dark eyes bright with morbid excitement as she looked at us. "Didn't you hear?" she asked, and I shook my head, silently urging her to spit it out already. She leaned back, checking to make sure Lyle was still out of earshot. "The Miller kids found a woman's body out in the woods south of town yesterday. It was mutilated beyond recognition."

I think we all froze, water lapping over our feet with a gentle slap.

"Where in the woods?" Tommy asked, lighting up a fresh cigarette, and Sid stiffened beside me, turning to look at him.

"On the other side of the old water plant, I think."

"Could it have been an animal attack?" I asked.

Olive shrugged. "I don't know. I only heard my dad talking about it with one of the deputies who stopped by to pick up an order this morning. But it sounds like they're pretty convinced it was homicide."

I shook my head, the thought absurd. Someone being killed <u>in Delight?</u> A body left at our doorstep? I could tell by the look on Tommy's face that he was experiencing the same feeling of disbelief as me.

"That's horrifying," Sid said softly. "That poor woman."

"I know." Olive shivered. "I can't even imagine."

I pressed into her side, letting my fingers drift through the silt at my feet. Tommy is friends with some of the local deputies, so I was sure he'd be at the bar later to try to pull some details out of them. Until then, the thought of someone bringing danger to Olive or my family was too big to wrap my head around.

As ridiculous as it might sound, the very notion of violence happening here is inconceivable. I know how to mark a potential threat. I like to think I would know if I'd locked eyes with someone who possessed a thirst for blood. I know how to read people at least that well.

The thing I keep circling back to is that this is our home. For as many years as we've been here, nothing has ever threatened our way of life or our peace. In a way, this town is protected because we're centered here. I don't know, but I do know how to ground myself.

Once we left the lake, I spent a good portion of my evening planning and preparing for the hunt. I might still have questions, but I at least feel more settled. Now, I believe that's the Beach Boys I'm hearing down the hall, so I'm going to wrap up here and see what trouble the boys are getting into.

# DEVOTED

Part Three

Having us all back together again must be making me nostalgic, because I woke up this morning thinking about the weeks following Daddy's death. How much better it seemed for me and the boys. How strangely miserable Momma was.

The depth of her grief confused me. I couldn't understand why she was so upset that he was gone. It had been weeks since anyone had been yelled at, since anyone had been smacked or spanked or slapped, since anything had been thrown to the floor or across the room in anger.

One morning, a couple weeks after, Sid had knocked over my glass of orange juice—it was my fault, I'd placed it too close to his elbow—and both of us had flinched as it splashed to the floor. My hands shot out to catch the glass as it rolled across the table, and Sid dropped to the floor with a napkin to start sopping it up.

Then Tommy had stood, offering Sid a handful of napkins and ruffling his hair before moving to the sink to wet a washcloth. I met Sid's gaze over the mess, and he gave me a little crooked smile, a mix of relief and disbelief on his freckled face. The complete and utter lack of response was so unexpected that my eyes filled with tears, and I cried. I cried with big, shuddering sobs that shook my small body as an overwhelming flood of confusion and hope—hope that this strange, tension-free scene could possibly be our new normal—consumed me.

"It's okay, Duck." Tommy set the washcloth on the table and scooped me into his arms, holding me on the floor next to the little puddle of orange juice. I wrapped my arms around his neck and buried my face against his shoulder, wanting to say sorry for putting my glass too close to the edge, wanting to say sorry for carrying on like a baby, but I couldn't stop crying long enough to say anything. "Just breathe," Tommy soothed, rubbing circles on my back. "It's all gonna be okay now."

And it was, even though the pantry grew bare and money grew tight and Tommy had to scrounge around for spare change to get groceries when the casseroles from the church stopped coming.

Speaking of church, Tommy still made us go every Sunday morning. Even though Momma rarely got out of bed at the time, not even to take care of Lyle, he made us wash up and put on our nice clothes and walked us down the road to the chapel.

It was maybe three or four weeks in when I finally threw a fit about it. "But Momma isn't making us go. Why do we have to?" I scowled, pushing away the washcloth Graham scrubbed across my face.

"Because we're good, church-going folk," Tommy said, helping Sid with his tie. "If we don't show up at church, then people will worry about us and start showing up around here."

The image of Tommy bashing Daddy over the head flashed across my vision, his bulk falling face-first into the pond. Goosebumps rippled across my arms at the thought of someone somehow discovering what had happened, and I tucked my small frame against Graham in search of comfort, the fight leaving my body. "Nobody's gonna take you away." I directed the words, half a plea, half a statement of reassurance, to Tommy.

Tommy gave Sid's tie a final tweak, ruffling his hair and turning to me with his classic lopsided grin. "I'd like to see them try."

But even back then, I saw that easy confidence fade into wary concern when he picked up Lyle from his bassinet and walked him into Momma's room.

"We're about to head out to church," his voice carried down the hall. "Do you feel up to watching the baby for a couple of hours while we're gone?"

I couldn't hear Momma's response, but when Tommy walked out, Lyle was missing from his arms.

"Is she better today?" Sid asked, a hopeful glimmer in his green eyes.

Tommy looked at Graham, something passing between them in the heartbeat before he turned to Sid. "Yeah, a bit."

"I miss her," Sid said.

Tommy gave him a sad smile. "Me, too, bud. She just needs a little more time."

I frowned, following my brothers out of the house. The fact that Momma couldn't see that things were so much better now confounded my little mind. Graham said it was a grown-up thing, that being alone in the world was scary, and that made even less sense to me. How could she feel alone when we were all together?

These thoughts stayed with me while I played tic-tac-toe on the back of the church bulletin with Sid during the service and after, when the preacher and his wife stopped us on the way out. Sid and Graham slipped by to run on the lawn with some of the other children, but I'd made the mistake of meeting Mrs. Forsythe's eyes and was pinned in place by the bald concern there. It was born of pity, but at the time I couldn't shake the feeling that it was my safety she was worried about, and I slipped my hand into Tommy's for fear she might think to take us away from him.

"How are things, Thomas? We've been praying for your family." Pastor Forsythe offered a kind smile, and I leaned into Tommy's leg, trying to hide.

"We're getting on alright, thank you, sir," Tommy replied, shaking his hand.

"We haven't seen your mother for a while."

"We could always stop by," Mrs. Forsythe added, her gaze finally leaving me. "It's our Christian duty to help, and I'd love to cook you a nice meal, help with laundry or whatever else."

I tipped my head up to look at Tommy, but if he was worried, I couldn't tell. "Thank you for the offer, Mrs. Forsythe, but we wouldn't want to impose. There's no need to go all the way out there."

"Nonsense, it's no trouble. We've got to take care of one another, you know. That's one of God's basic commandments."

Tommy lowered his eyes, smiling a sweet, shy smile. "You're too kind, ma'am. I'll let Momma know you offered to come by, and she can call you to schedule a time."

Mrs. Forythe nodded, placing a hand over her heart. "Of course, I'll be waiting for her call." She tried to catch my gaze again, but I just stared at the ground from behind Tommy's leg, unsure how to respond to the attention and not wanting to do or say the wrong thing.

Pastor Forsythe clapped Tommy on the shoulder, holding on for a moment longer than customary as he pondered whether or not to share what he was thinking. "God has proclaimed that the man is the head of the family, and if it's in the Good Book, then it's a claim I'll honor ... but maybe calling your daddy home early was His sovereign way of protecting you kids and your momma."

I don't remember what Tommy said to that, nor do I remember leaving church that day to head home. But I remember the disassociative, mind-numbing realization that sunk into my little head with his words, chilling me to the bone.

People <u>knew</u>. People knew about our dad's temper. Knew that he hit us. And they did nothing.

That discovery reshaped my entire understanding of the world.

Because God didn't save us. Tommy did. So if I sometimes idolize him … can I really be blamed? He is, after all, my very own personal savior.

Tommy was back to running calls this morning, but Graham took the day off to go to the carnival with us. He picked up me, Lyle, and Sid in the station wagon instead of walking from our house, and it was already hot enough that the air conditioning was running.

With their secret out, Priscilla was all bubbly joy in the passenger seat, talking the entire short drive to the fairgrounds, and she kept touching Graham—his arm, his hand, his leg. He smiled indulgently, letting her bask in her happiness and basking in it with her.

It was almost gross, it was so cute.

My own happiness (in the form of my carny boy) was also fast approaching, and I was so excited I could hardly sit still. My fingers tapped a rhythm against my knees as we pulled into the parking lot, and I was out of my seat and urging everyone along almost as soon as the car rolled to a stop.

"Jesus, Ducky, calm down before you bounce out of your skin," Sid joked, grabbing the hem of my shirt to physically slow me down to match the pace of the group.

Lyle grinned, wiggling his eyebrows in that way I think all younger siblings have of knowing how to elicit a reaction. "She wants to see a *boy*," he sang.

"Traitor," I mouthed to him with a (mostly) playful glare.

Sid let me go, catching my eye with a look that was part question, part knowing suspicion, and I shot him a grin that would rival the Cheshire cat's.

Priscilla let out an excited little squeal, moving to loop her arm through mine. "Okay, now *this* is an exciting development. A local boy? Surely not one of the carnival folk! They'll never settle down," she chattered, pulling me along.

Graham—Lord bless him—came to my rescue, extracting his wife from me. "There will be time for girl talk later, darling, not where Sid and Lyle are around to tease her out of her crush." He winked at me over her head.

I didn't head straight for my carny's ride, of course, but when we did meander near THE INVERSION, I made eye contact with him as I passed. But we didn't go on. A girl can't be too obvious, and the point was to let him think he was pursuing me.

"Let's go to the mirror maze," Lyle suggested a while later, pointing back across the carnival.

"You guys go ahead. I think I want to pop in and catch the end of the magic show," I said.

"All right, we'll catch you in a bit," Sid said, and I slipped into the stuffy shade of the circus tent by myself.

I found a seat at the back of the bleachers, watching as a man pulled a card from inside of a watermelon when it had presumably been in the deck his assistant held only moments before. I clapped along with the crowd, crossing my legs and leaning forward to rest my chin on my hand to watch the next trick.

"Fancy seein' you again." The flirtatious drawl curled up my spine in a way that was outright delicious.

I turned to look at my carny, dressed in much the same garb

as the last time I'd seen him. His shirt sleeves were cuffed this morning, stretched taut over defined arms, and I let him see me looking. "I'd ask if you were looking for me—"

"I was," he cut me off with an impish grin. "You never gave me your name, and I'd very much like to have it."

I gave him a suspicious look, then turned my eyes back to the show. "And why should I give it to you?"

"Because I'm guessing you're a townie, which means we could be seeing a lot of each other over the next few days, and I'd like to call you something you actually find agreeable."

"Oh, would you?"

"I am nothing if not a gentleman," he said with a wolfish smirk that suggested the opposite. And his Southern accent made it all sound even more solicitous.

I tilted my head to the side, watching the magician in the ring attempt to cut his lovely assistant in half. "So you say, but you haven't even given me your own name."

"I'll answer to anything you want me to, miss thing, but folks 'round here call me RJ."

The magician succeeded, and the crowd erupted in applause.

"Nice to meet you, RJ." I reached a hand out, and he shook it, his callouses rough and warm against my palm. I imagined shaving them off with a boning knife.

"Are you going to reciprocate?" His thumb brushed over the back of my hand before I pulled back.

With a dramatic instrumental accompaniment, the magician's assistant was whole again, and I waited for the cheers to die down before turning back to him. "I'm still considering." I smiled sweetly and hopped down from the bench, exiting the tent to find my brothers.

"Oh, come on, that's cold!" RJ protested, following me.

I spun around to face him as people started filing out. "Is it cold, or just practical? Why tell you my name when you'll be gone by the end of next week?"

He raised one shoulder with a slow, insolent grin, blue eyes sparkling in the sun. "That's a lot of time for a lot of adventure, by my count."

I held his gaze, trapping my lower lip between my teeth. "I guess we'll just have to see how good your math is."

"Hey, Duck!"

I looked over to where Graham stood on the other side of the crowd with Priscilla, waving. I lifted my arm and waved back to let him know I saw him. "I'll see you around, RJ," I said, before weaving my way through the chaos.

"How was the show?" Graham asked when I reached them, one eyebrow pointedly raised over the rim of his glasses.

"A wonderful time."

"Oh! Maybe we'll have to try to go this weekend. I'm sorry to have missed it," Priscilla said, wrapped around Graham's arm.

"Come on, Sid and Lyle are waiting in line for the haunted mansion. We can sneak in with them." He led us away, looking down at the top of her head with the mildest look of irritation before gesturing for me to move ahead of them.

I gave his elbow a sympathetic squeeze as I passed, knowing he just wanted to talk about what I had going on. But his wife was way too attuned to him to try to forge even a subtle conversation around it.

"RJ," I whispered to myself as I wove through the crowd. Naming him sent a thrilling surge of anticipation through me.

We didn't stay at the carnival late, heading home after a dinner of fair food, and it didn't take long for me to end up outside with Graham while Priscilla browsed our record collection, looking for something specific for her next Tupperware party.

"So what's the plan for the carny kid?" Graham asked, helping me spread fresh pine shavings in the chicken coop.

"I don't know yet." I brushed a stray lock of hair from my face, nudging one of the more belligerent hens out of the way with the toe of my sneaker. "He's a bit full of himself, but I think he enjoys the chase. I'm just going to play it cool for a while, give him only a bit at a time. I'll make sure he's into me enough that when I show up at their next stop, he'll follow me somewhere secluded without a fuss."

"That's most of a plan already," he pointed out, breaking up a compressed clump of shavings and letting them fall to the ground. "What'll that be, though, maybe two weekends from now?"

"Probably, yeah."

"Perfect. I'll make sure not to schedule anything so I can help you out when you're at the cabin."

Not that I'm not a perfectly capable woman, but one upside to having so many brothers is that I've never been forced to do all of the heavy lifting on my own. Hunting is fun, but butchering is work. Rewarding, but work. Especially when everyone I've ever taken has been bigger than me.

But while butchering is nothing more than a necessity for me, it's an art for Graham. He knows how to look at a muscle and see the best way to cut it, the best form to serve it in, whether that be cutlet, ground, sausage, steak, roast—he knows his way around meat. It's a gift. He even worked for the butcher in town for about a year when he was in high school, but the direct correlation made him nervous. And, in my opinion, I think having such a demanding job doing the thing he loved took a little of the joy out of it. So he shifted his deft fingers and desire to use his hands into mechanics and let his hobby stay a hobby.

"It's going to get tricky while Priscilla is pregnant," he sighed, finishing off the floor of the coop and rolling the top of the plastic sack. "With her family up north, she needs me more involved than she otherwise would."

"Nobody told you you had to knock her up," I said coyly, eyebrows raised.

Graham gave me a withering look. "It's not like I planned to, but, damn, Duck, can you blame a guy for not being able to resist when his lady is begging—"

"Okay, okay, enough," I interrupted, slamming my palms over my ears. "I understand how it happens, thank you."

"You're the one who asked," he laughed, following me out of the coop. "And it's not like you're a stranger to the baby-makin' dance."

"Graham, ew!" I shoved him.

"The ol' in-and-out."

I faked a gag.

"Havin' your corn ground."

"Stop," I laughed, picking up the pace to pull ahead of him. "You're so gross!"

"Poppin' batter in the oven," he continued, unperturbed.

"I might actually vomit," I declared, then turned and slapped my palm over his mouth as he prepared another euphemism. Even though he has at least seventy pounds and eight inches on me, he let me subdue him, only putting up the slightest fight to push me off before finally holding his hands up in surrender.

"I know this wasn't your decision, but there are some things I probably won't be able to help with or understand." Graham slid his free hand into his pocket, shuffling his hold on the bag of wood shavings. "Would you be willing to step in where I leave slack? Be there for her through the pregnancy and everything that comes after? It's been ages since I've been around a baby, but I remember how Mom was with the three of you, and ... well, Dad was obviously a less-than-stellar example for most things in life."

I hooked my arm through his, pulling closer to him as we neared the garage. "You don't even have to ask, stupid. Of course I'll help however I can. And don't you even once compare yourself to Dad." I looked up at him, waiting for his hazel eyes to find mine. "You're already five times the man—five times the father—he ever was."

He slung his arm around my shoulders and pulled me into his side, the coarse hairs of his beard scraping my temple as he pressed his cheek to the top of my head. "Thanks, Duck. That means more than you know."

We stashed the pine in the garage, where he stopped to dig around in the deep freezer. He loaded some of the marked packages of meat from the other day into a cooler, then gathered his wife and headed home.

As I watched them leave, I was struck with this sense of ... well, I don't even really know what I would call it. But I realized how true the words I spoke were. Graham will be a great father. His child will be loved unconditionally and taught all of the important lessons in life without fear of failure or lack of comfort. His child will grow up confident, knowing how to take care of itself, and it will carry on the Rathbone name, the Rathbone legacy that Graham and the rest of us have created for it.

Is it strange to call this future person it? What if I call it he but it ends up being a niece and she reads this back one day and thinks I'm a misogynist for assuming only a boy could carry on? But I digress. It's late now, and I need to let the dogs out for the night. Danny-dog's been staring at me for the past ten minutes and has started huffing impatiently. Silly old boy.

I fear this is going to be another long entry. I think I'm settled now, but hot creepers—this morning did not go as I expected, and that's saying nothing for this evening!

But morning first. Let me preemptively state: I missed Sid so much, but no one else has ever forced me to decipher my own emotions the way he does. I forgot what it was like having my conscience around.

My intention was to break the news about Jonah and Olive to Sid over breakfast. We hadn't talked about Jonah since his return, and I didn't want it to catch him by surprise. They'd already planned another date for tonight, and Olive would be coming over beforehand to get ready.

I made a sausage, egg, and potato scramble to help soften the blow. Lyle scarfed his portion down without breathing and was out the door to meet his friends almost before I'd even poured myself a glass of orange juice.

"How does he have so much energy?" Sid asked with a laugh, spearing a forkful of food. "I thought teens were supposed to be mopey."

"Olive is dating Jonah," I blurted with no tact.

Sid's fork stuttered on its way to his mouth as he looked at me, then he continued eating.

I shoved my own mouth full, wanting to say so much but also knowing that this was <u>his</u> thing and wanting to let him process it without me bowling over him.

"How're you dealing with that?"

I choked mid-swallow, coughing and reaching for my juice. When I'd finally settled, I patted my mouth daintily with a napkin, going for a composed air. "Pardon?"

"Are you okay?" He'd never taken his eyes from me through the whole scene.

"Me?" I asked, dropping my gaze to my bowl and stabbing through a clump of egg and potato with only slightly more force than necessary. "Why would I not be okay?"

"Ducky," he said evenly, and I peeked up to see one copper eyebrow arched pointedly. "You're telling me the prospect of Olive taking active steps toward marriage isn't at all upsetting?"

"Of course it is, but ..." I shrugged, taking a bite to give myself time to form an answer. "I've been preparing for it for years at this point. I came to terms with knowing she would never return my feelings ages ago, and I love her too much to bring her into ... all of this." I gestured vaguely with my fork, not even realizing until Sid snorted that it was topped with a segment of sausage. I popped it into my mouth. "I've also had time to sit with the news, and she's still in my life, regardless. But I didn't want you to be blindsided, and chances are high that you'll run into them ... run into <u>him</u>."

Sid sighed, pushing his food around for a moment. "I know that you blame Jonah for me leaving, but he's honestly nothing more than my past. Maybe he's a catalyst for better things, but there's no anger there for me anymore."

"But you loved him." I watched his face, confused by his complete lack of emotional reaction.

"I did," he agrees. "But it was a very naïve, very childish sort of love that I haven't held on to at all. I forgave Jonah before I even met Mak. I mean, yeah, he hurt me, but I know who I am now, and I've not only accepted it, I love myself. My family knows who I am, and they accept me and love me, too." He reached across the counter to squeeze my fingers. "Jonah doesn't have any of that. Honestly, I'm not sure he ever will. I pity him too much to still be hurt over the fact that he couldn't love me."

And that's Sid, too level-headed for pettiness and spite.

Not me, though.

I straightened, forking another large bite of hash into my mouth. "Well, I still hate him. And he's a spineless bastard to lead Olive along when he'll never love her the way she deserves."

Sid shrugged, taking a sip of coffee. "Have you told her any of this?"

"Of course not." My brows pulled together as I looked at him incredulously. "But if you've got any smart ideas in that head of yours about how to keep her from hitching her horse to that wagon without dragging you through the mud, then I'm open to suggestions."

Sid pushed around the food in his bowl again, focusing on the movement. "Have you stopped to consider that maybe he could actually love her?"

I snorted, sure he was joking.

"You've slept with men," he said, looking back up at me.

My eyes narrowed. "And?"

"You want to sleep with Olive."

My cheeks flushed. "Okay?"

Sid lifted his coffee cup. "All I'm saying is, it's possible for him to have been attracted to me and also be attracted to her. Maybe there's nothing to warn her of."

"No, but … that's not …" I spluttered, spinning to keep facing Sid as he walked his dishes to the sink. "She's not meant to be with him," I said with finality.

He lowered his bowl to the floor, letting Danny and Benny snarf up the remaining chunks of sausage, and then washed it and his mug, setting both on the drying rack. "If that's how you feel, maybe you should tell her."

I frowned. "You sure make it sound simple for someone who—" I snapped my jaw shut, cutting off a mean retort that I'd regret. But he was being hypocritical, and I couldn't quite douse that little flare of temper. "You _left_ when Jonah threatened to out you. Now you're back, and not even remotely concerned that he'll follow through? That he won't feel even more vindictive if it gets out that I also have homosexual urges and act on them with the woman he was courting? I'm glad you're happy, Sid, truly, but what world do you think we live in?" I keep my voice low and my eyes on my breakfast.

Sid was quiet for a while, and I picked at my food, forcing small bites even though I no longer had an appetite. "Jonah isn't a threat. I didn't see it back then, but he's too much of a coward to say anything. Regardless, life is full of risks. And I think you're choosing to take the wrong ones."

My frown deepened, but he left before I could reply. He'd given me too much to consider, and I was preoccupied as new guests checked in, almost missing when they let me know they wouldn't be in for dinner as they left for town. I still hadn't come to any conclusions about what I felt about the course that conversation had taken, much less what I was going to do about it, when Olive showed up after lunch.

She brought along a bag of cosmetics, hot rollers, and three different outfits. After depositing her things on my bed, she sat at my vanity while the rollers heated, and I carefully sectioned out her hair, brushing through the clumps of soft, dark curls.

Olive's hair reaches all the way past her waist when it's pulled straight, and as much as I adore her natural mix of spirals and waves, I love when she asks me to help heat style it. With as much hair as she has, it takes about an hour to set all the curlers, and playing with her hair is possibly the only activity I find more soothing than hunting. As I worked my way around her head, carefully rolling each section, I lost myself in the cadence of her voice. She was talking about some gossip she'd overheard in the women's Bible study earlier, but I kept drifting back to what Sid had said this morning.

I should tell her.

But telling her would be selfish. What would it do other than release a burden from my own chest? There is no future for us, not in her God-fearing circles and not with my family's proclivities. And then, even more distressing, was the chance of losing her. What if she was appalled by my desire for her?

But what if she returned those feelings? What if she thought about holding me, about kissing me, as much as I did about her?

I should tell her.

But …

And around and around in my head I went.

I had been just fine for years, and Sid had to go and mess it all up over sausage hash scramble, of all things.

I sighed heavily.

"Where'd you go?"

I met Olive's amused gaze in the mirror and blushed. "I'm sorry. I didn't mean to ignore you."

She tsked, rolling her eyes. "Do you ever?"

"I had a kind of intense talk with Sid this morning," I said, still not sure what exactly I would be divulging.

Olive frowned in concern. "How is he doing? My dad said sometimes when men come back from war, they're ... well, they're different. Because of what they've seen or done."

"Oh, no, nothing like that. He seems fine, I mean. We were just talking about ... life."

"Mmm," Olive hummed in understanding. "It feels like we have so many big decisions looming."

"And so many risks to calculate," I added, rolling up the last section of hair and pinning it in place. I took a deep breath, the words crawling up my throat, ready to spew free.

Olive smiled at our reflections, grabbing my hand over her shoulder. "I'm so glad we have each other to help figure everything out. I couldn't—I wouldn't want to do any of this without you, Mally." Her fingers threaded through mine, soft and warm, and she pressed a kiss to the back of my hand.

My stomach swooped, words lodged in my throat. But maybe I could find the courage to speak them.

And then she stood, twirling around toward the bed to scan the outfits she brought. The urge to uproot the baseline of our relationship left me when she released my hand. If there's one thing that's been drilled into me, it's that impulsivity leads to stupid mistakes. And I won't allow myself to make stupid mistakes where Olive is concerned.

"Which one do you think is best for a dinner in the city?"

"The city?" I repeated, looking over the options laid out in front of me.

"He's taking me to see *Cleopatra*," she said, and I thought that if any man were to take her to the movies, perhaps it was best that it was Jonah, who at least wouldn't try to do any more than hold her hand. (I refuse to allow any thought attributing validity to Sid's earlier sentiment that maybe Jonah could be interested in her that way. I'm already struggling enough, thank you.)

I helped Olive choose a pair of pants, a light blouse, and a cardigan to tie it all together. Once dressed, she did her makeup while we talked about our own trip planned for next month—*Lord of the Flies* is going to be screening, and she promised to see it with me because *Lord of the Flies* is one of my favorite books. Probably my favorite, actually, even though I think it's so entirely unrealistic that none of the boys resorted to cannibalism. And that's a completely unbiased observation. Not only would it have been a convenient source of food, cannibalism is also the highest form of dominance. I digress.

I carefully removed the curlers from her hair, pinning the front pieces back from her face.

"Ugh, you're a wizard, Mallory. I can never get my hair to comply like you." She fluffed the symmetrical, ordered curls in the mirror and then turned in her seat, wrapping her arms around my waist. "I'd ask you to teach me your magic, but I selfishly like being waited on," she admitted, tipping her face up to smile at me.

"I'm at your beck and call, Miss Piermont." I tapped the tip of her nose.

It was all going swell after that until Jonah came to the house to pick up Olive. She'd arranged it that way because she didn't want her parents putting him on the spot with an interrogation since this would be their first unchaperoned outing, and her mom had allowed it due to the excuse that I needed to help her with her hair.

If Olive had mentioned to Jonah that Sid was back home, I certainly couldn't tell. She opened the door when he knocked, and at first he was every part the gentleman, complimenting her outfit and saying how lucky he was to be taking her out. Then he froze in place when he spotted Sid on the couch playing a game of backgammon with Lyle.

Sid glanced up, registering the attention.

"You're back," Jonah said stupidly.

One side of Sid's mouth quirked up, and he dropped his gaze to the board to make a move. "Indeed, I am. Hope you've been well."

Jonah's eyes were glued to Sid, and I bristled, my lip twitching once in a desire to snarl. He had no right to look at my brother that way. Not after what he'd done, and doubly so not when he was dating Olive. "I have," Jonah said, recovering from his streak of dumbness. "It's ... Well, I hope the same for you."

"I can't complain," Sid replied, looking back up with a smooth smile and a diabolical little gleam in his green eyes. Despite what he may have said earlier, he was definitely enjoying his old paramour's discomfort. "I'm just glad to be home."

Jonah swallowed, returning a smile that was much less cocksure than before. "Well, welcome back."

"Enjoy your night," Sid said in dismissal, going back to his game.

Olive, presumably sensing none of the undertones in the house, grabbed Jonah's arm with a short squeal. "I'm so excited! It's been *ages* since I've been down to the city."

"There's a new drive-in chain that just opened up near the theater. We can stop for a burger and fries beforehand." He said this like it was the grandest gesture in the world, his chest puffing out a bit, and I struggled not to roll my eyes. Not that he wasn't being generous; dinner and a movie, plus the gas to get down there and back? It was a good evening, but he didn't have to be so hoity-toity about it, especially when Olive wasn't really a fan of—

"Oh, gosh, I *love* a good burger!" she chirped, cutting off my line of thought. My jaw actually dropped open a small amount.

Who was this squeaky, tittering girl?

"Thank you again for your help, Mally. I'll see you later." She reached over to squeeze my arm before following Jonah out the door.

Why was she acting so different around him? Had she been that way at the carnival?

"You look like Benny just stole your dinner," Lyle commented with a casual roll of dice.

Benny lifted his head from where he lay under the coffee table, then settled back down once he realized he wasn't being addressed.

"Was that not weird to you guys?"

"What, Jonah staring me down or Olive falling all over him?" Sid asked as Lyle slotted a point.

"Must be nice," Lyle sighed wistfully.

"She's too old for you, LJ," Sid joked, reaching over to ruffle Lyle's messy waves. "It's called flirting, Ducky." His eyes flicked back up to me, his gaze weighted. "A thing people do when they want someone to know they're interested ... or get a rise out of someone."

I clicked my tongue with a huff, trying to fight down the agitation rolling through my belly. "Gee, thanks for the explanation. I was entirely unaware." In equal measure, I wanted to dissect her behavior, be mad at her for it even though I had no right, let it eat up my insides, and also completely ignore everything about the situation.

I'll give you one guess which route I went with.

Knowing the perfect form of distraction, I stalked off into the mudroom, debating between sneakers or booties before finally deciding on the former, and plopped onto the couch to tie them.

"Where are you off to?" Sid asked.

I gave my laces a final tug and stood, planting my hands on my hips as the peace that came with action slowly washed over my agitation. "Hunting." I flashed him a bright smile.

Lyle wanted to come with me, but Sid wouldn't let him, and I was happy to let him be the enforcer. There were just some things I didn't want to do with any of my brothers around, and play the flirt was one of them.

Whether he'd meant to or not, Sid had a point about getting someone's attention or getting them to like you. And maybe it was simply a nice change of pace from my last mark of older-man-being-creepy, or maybe it was an intrinsic response to seeing Olive flirt with Jonah, but I wanted RJ to like me. Not that I didn't typically use my feminine wiles on most of my prey, but I wanted him to <u>actually</u> like me.

What can I say? Clearly, I'm frustrated as all get out, and having his trust and—dare I hope—his obsession before I slit his throat has a high chance of easing that.

I was confident my little ploy yesterday of refusing to give him my name was at least enough of a hook to have kept me on his mind, and now it was time to reel him in.

I headed straight for THE INVERSION, but instead of RJ's classic gray newsboy cap, I saw a much older man, tall, muscled, and sporting a thick, dark beard and bald head.

My brow furrowed in an exaggerated reaction to the part I played. I sucked my lower lip between my teeth, chewing gently as I turned in a slow circle, scanning the crowd. I spied the clown in the oversized pants that had been exchanging glances with RJ the day I'd singled him out, and walked over with a little wave.

"Good afternoon, pretty lady," he sang with an attempt at a bow. "Perhaps a flower?" He swept a long, skinny sheath of purple latex from his barrel pants and gave it a couple of perfunctory tugs.

"Oh, no thank you." I held up my hand to stop him, then tucked my hair behind my ear and gave him my best shy smile, looking up through my lashes. "I was wondering if you know the man who sometimes works the pendulum ride, RJ? And could you possibly let me know where to find him?"

The clown dropped his persona, his wide grin looking almost hungry with the red paint smeared over his mouth. "You're the one without a name, right?" he asked in a normal voice, tone full of humor.

I didn't have to work to conjure a blush, caught off guard to hear I'd been a point of discussion. "I was hoping to change that," I answered coyly, pulling myself together.

The clown waggled his brows, clearly pleased. "He's at the merry-go-round this evening," he said before inflating the long balloon in a single breath. "And here, this one's on the house." He skillfully twisted a daisy shape and handed it over with a wink. "Now you won't even have to tell him Jess sent ya."

"Thank you, Jess," I said, waving over my shoulder as I turned to weave through the people meandering about.

Sure enough, there he was, sitting next to the controls of the merry-go-round with his boots kicked up on the railing as he watched the white horses with brightly colored saddles move about. I walked up behind him, folding my arms over the rail and leaning forward. "How do you guys even move all this stuff?"

He startled, but recovered quickly, and when he turned his head to look at me, his eyes actually lit up. "Well, hello there, miss thing," he drawled, tipping his cap. Then a cheeky grin tugged up one corner of his mouth. "Or should I call you Duck?"

My head tilted to the side as I laughed, bringing a hand up over my lips. "You heard that, huh?"

"What kinda name is that, anyway?" he teased.

"You answer my question first, then I'll answer yours," I offered.

"What's your ques—oh, the rides?" *The rahhds.* "Well, I'll tell ya right now, it ain't easy or a good time. When we're movin' long distances, we use trains, but most of our stops we load it all up on big ol' flatbed trailers."

Impressive. "How long does it take you to set it all up?" I asked, genuinely curious.

He wagged a finger at me. "Nuh-uh, you said this would be a tit for tat kinda talk, and it's your turn to spill, missy." He dropped his feet, holding up his finger again. "Hold that thought."

RJ brought the ride to a stop, let the riders off, and ushered in a new group. Once the line was empty, he raised his voice to give a quick spiel about everyone staying seated and to let him know if they needed to puke, then he returned to the operator's station to start the ride.

Instead of reclining in his chair, he leaned forward, bracing his elbows on his knees so that we were eye to eye.

"Duck is what my brothers call me," I told him. "Because when we were little I would follow them around everywhere like a duckling."

"Well, ain't that endearing," he said, then tipped his head to the side. "So does that mean I'm still not gonna get your name?"

I grinned. "Maybe if you ask for it, but it's my turn."

"It takes all of us two days to take everything apart and another one to load it all up and hit the road. What's your name?"

I laughed, biting my lip and looking around like I was about to tell a secret. "Duck evolved from mallard, Mallory-mallard."

"A pleasure to make your acquaintance, Miss Mallory."

I fluttered my lashes sweetly. "I've yet to decide whether or not I feel the same."

I swear his pupils dilated, making his blue eyes appear darker despite the daylight. "Liar," he said, drawing it out, and my attention dropped to the way his mouth formed the word.

Damn my inability to cock a single eyebrow. They both climbed up my forehead. "Oh?"

He hummed an affirmative. "How many times have you been here since we opened? Not to mention that you sought me out on purpose. Even asked around to find me." He tapped a finger to the balloon flower in my hand without breaking eye contact.

"So you assume," I said, twirling the balloon. "Maybe I just really love carnivals."

He brushed a finger across the back of my hand, stilling my movement. "Maybe, but I doubt it."

He abruptly sat up, turning away to slow and halt the ride. I pressed my lips together against a grin. I had him locked, and he thought he had <u>me</u> locked, which was positively thrilling. I shook off the feel of his finger, flexing my hand against the lingering sensation. It wasn't so much the touch itself that bothered me, but the drag of it. Touch, pressure, I can handle, and even crave. But I loathe the feel of stuff moving across my skin. It grates against my nerves in the worst way.

But I was prepared to endure a small amount from RJ, who, yes, is an unapologetic womanizer—and don't worry, he'll absolutely pay for it—but ... and I'm only writing this because the whole point is to be honest here, right? And you aren't allowed to judge me anyway because you don't even exist outside of my imagination and this book. But holy moly, he sure is easy on the eyes, and I intend to take full advantage of that before he meets his demise. I watched him as he worked, admiring the way his trim waist narrowed down to a muscular backside that I wanted to sink my teeth into. (Figuratively and literally. I've got an excellent recipe for rump roast that I can't wait to use him for.)

There were still several hours left before closing, but RJ promised he would show me a good time if I stuck around, and I didn't have anything to do back home, so I shadowed him while he worked.

He taught me how to operate the merry-go-round, even going so far as to plant his newsie cap on my head. This didn't seem like it should be allowed, but I felt pretty confident that I wouldn't be able to injure or, God forbid, kill anyone on such a low-thrill ride, and a few of his coworkers came around and talked to us and didn't seem alarmed to find me at the controls, so I relaxed into it and enjoyed the day.

We worked until nine o'clock, but I use the term "worked" lightly. RJ obviously did anything that was more than pushing a few buttons and walking around to make sure everyone was seated, and we indulged in all the fair food we could eat. (Which, as a side note, we should be frying more things. I know we can't pass off tricep as fried chicken, but we could do some form of a cutlet or chicken-fried "steak.")

When the rides were finally shutting down, RJ offered me his arm with a mischievous grin. "Now the real fun begins."

I jokingly hesitated before slipping my arm through his. "Should I be scared?"

"Maybe just a little," he warned with a playful wink.

And I know what you're thinking. "Hey, Mallory, isn't it kind of stupid to be seen by so many of RJ's friends and coworkers if you're planning to kill him? Won't they be suspicious?" And to that I say: no, not really. See, if you recall a few days prior when I started watching him, he's a flirt. And the way his friend wasn't surprised or hesitant to point me his way earlier? I'd put my money (and future meals) on RJ finding a girl in every town they stop in. Once they hit the next town, they're not likely to assume that I followed him all the way there once he disappears. Any risk with him is calculated and likely to be worth it.

I'm a professional, remember?

We walked from the main carnival grounds to a circle of trailers and personal tents in the back, where a small group was gathered around a fire.

"RJ, you dog. Are you finally going to introduce us to your mystery woman?" called a half-dressed man running a damp cloth over his face. It took me a second to recognize him as the big-pantsed clown, but I was proud of my observational skills to place him on my own before RJ gave him a two-fingered salute that morphed into flipping the bird.

"I'll take that as a thank you for pointing her your way earlier," Jess replied with a cheeky grin.

RJ ushered me to a log by the fire, sitting down next to me and stretching his legs out in front of him. "So you've already met Jess, Rider, and Tara." He pointed out the people who'd stopped by to talk to us earlier, then introduced the rest of the circle I'd yet to meet. Mags, Di, Hock, Cookie, Fry, Gabby, and a couple others I can't remember.

"You drink, townie?" Tara asked, holding up a bottle of beer.

I nodded, barely catching the sound of the pressure release when she popped the top over the crackle of the fire. She handed one to me and one to RJ before settling down next to me. I didn't want to be rude, but I also couldn't contain my curiosity. "So, what's with the names?" I asked, taking a long swig. The yeasty flavor hit the back of my tongue, crisp and cold as I swallowed.

"Pretty judgemental for a girl called Duck," RJ teased, knocking his knee into mine.

"We get named when we join the crew," Gabby offered from across the fire. "Not all of us, of course, but most of us are here because there are places we don't want to be. The carnival lets us disappear for a while."

"Can't get drafted if you can't be found," Hock added, and several of the men raised their beers in agreement, RJ included.

"Tara comes from Tarot," Tara said. "Because I'm the mystic of the group. Jess is a jester, which he prefers over clown. Mags is a magician, Di is his distraction, so on and so forth. Some of our nicknames just come from our personalities. Like Hock, who would sell you your own soul if you let him work up a pitch, and Gabby, who only shuts up when she's sleeping."

"Guilty." The girl grinned, shoving her hand into a bag of kettle corn.

I took another swig of my beer, looking down at the place where RJ's knee still pressed against mine, then pulled my gaze up to his face. "And what about you?" I asked with a flutter of my lashes. "What's RJ stand for?"

"Bet you can't guess," he drawled, cocking an eyebrow.

"I bet I *cain*," I said, mocking the way he said *cain't*. "Is it 'Royal Jerk'?"

That earned me a nice round of laughter, and he slapped a hand to his chest in mock offense. "And here I've been trying to be such a gentleman."

I leaned my shoulder into him. "Okay, okay, a real guess … Ride … Jokester?"

"Close." He tapped my nose, and I wrinkled it up. "Ride Jockey."

"Rider was here first, so he got the cooler end of that deal," Gabby said.

The mountain of a man who I'd seen at some of the thrill rides gave me a broad smile. "I do more maintenance than operation, but basically all our heavy machinery are my babies." He downed the rest of his beer and tossed the bottle into the fire, where it shattered on a rock. "This RJ picked up on everything pretty quickly, though. It'll be a shame when you decide to move on," he directed the last statement to the man beside me.

The wording piqued my interest, and I looked over at him, watching the firelight dance in his eyes, turning the blue a liquid silver. "You're not the first RJ."

"And I won't be the last." He clinked the top of his bottle to mine. "They tried to call me Bumpkin at first."

"Country boy had a problem with that," Jess interjected. "And liked 'cunt' even less."

I'm no stranger to profanity, but was still surprised when even the other women around the fire were snickering at the comment.

RJ's arm snaked around me, his hand curling over my hip. "Had to throw a few punches to clear that one off, but I've never shied away from earning respect," he bragged, like casual violence is the epitome of manhood.

After the bonfire, RJ offered to walk me home, and I let him take me as far as the end of the drive.

We stood there under the light of the waning moon, and he looked at me like _he_ wanted to eat _me_, his blue eyes holding me captive in a way that made it hard to breathe. He leaned forward, and my stomach swooped, devoid of the usual repulsion that accompanied times like these, all eager anticipation.

I'm not actually interested in him. He's nothing but prey. This just happens to be an extraordinarily fun hunt. That's all.

I tipped my face up to him, closing my eyes, then felt his lips brush across the corner of my mouth. He placed the softest, feather-light kiss on my cheek before nipping at my jaw. My eyes flew open in surprise, and he pulled away with a devilish smirk.

"Good night, Mallory," he whispered, walking back down the road.

I stood there in the dark, fingers running over that small sting where his teeth had closed over my skin.

And now, as I sit on my bed, still reeling from everything, I give you the truth of the matter.

Physically, I'm <u>very</u> attracted to RJ, and I want him to want me even more strongly than I want him. Maybe it's just been a while, but I want to be touched. In a strictly salacious way. I want to feel him inside of me. And just when I'm at the height of my pleasure, I want to slit his throat and cover myself in the warmth of his blood.

It's messy and impractical and going to make clean-up a nightmare, but the thought is so erotic. ~~My womanhood~~ Nope, that's gross. I ache just imagining it.

And, you've got to think, how much better might a man taste if his last moments are spent in carnal pleasure? Will his meat be sweeter, unsullied by fear?

I can't wait to find out.

I can't tell if things are weird with Sid or not, and it's bugging me. I mean, I know that I feel like things are weird, but I don't know if he feels it too or if I'm just overthinking everything.

Sid was already in the kitchen by the time I crawled out of bed this morning. He'd put out juice, muffins, and eggs for the guests, and was set up at the stove, stirring something in a pot.

"What time did you finally make it home?" he asked.

"Not long after midnight. Thanks for taking care of breakfast." I leaned on the counter across from him, rubbing sleep from my eyes. "I had a couple of drinks with the carnies after closing."

I could tell from the tense set of his shoulders that he was frowning and let the silence linger until he was ready to speak.

"I wish you wouldn't ..." He paused, sighed in frustration, then turned off the burner and opened a cupboard. "Oatmeal?"

"Sure, thanks," I said, and he took two bowls down. "You don't have to worry about me," I assured him as he filled them. "I promise I'm being smart. I didn't drink anything I didn't see opened and didn't drink enough to lose control of my faculties or anything. You know I always have a syringe if I'm going to be eating out of the house, so it's not like I'm going to die by accidental nut ingestion. Not all of us are out of practice," I joked.

Sid's lips were pressed together as he handed me my breakfast. He dragged a hand down his face, and I handed him a spoon from the drawer behind me. "That's not ... I'm glad you're being safe, of course, and while I don't love the idea of you out late with strange men, I do know you can handle yourself. I meant ..."

I took a bite, cinnamon, nutmeg, and sugar warm on my tongue. Sid's oatmeal may as well be a dessert. I chewed slowly, taking another bite as I watched him struggle to find words. I used to be able to read him so easily, and I refuse to believe that only three years apart had caused us to be so far out of sync. Maybe he was worried about the other carnies noticing when RJ disappeared? But they have a high turnover rate, and, the icing on the cake, nobody even knows who he really is. You can't report someone missing if you don't know their name. Plus, they are clearly all cowards. Cowards don't stir up trouble by definition.

"They're hiding from the draft," I said, scooping a spoonful of steaming oats.

Sid ran a hand over his hair, the bright copper still so much shorter than I'm used to. "Yeah, I suppose that makes sense."

"Doesn't that make you mad?"

He shook his head with a sardonic chuckle, leaning back against the counter. "Is it really my place to judge them running from their fears when I did the same thing?"

"Your fear was Jonah outing you to the whole community for the sake of his own reputation. That feels a little different from being afraid to fight for your country," I defended.

"War isn't pretty, Ducky. It's real and dangerous and terrifying. And I was lucky enough to stay on a ship the entire time. So, no, I don't blame them for wanting to hide. It doesn't matter that I was more scared of rumors spreading through town and bringing disdain on you guys, and ... It doesn't matter now, anyway. I ran because of Jonah, but I think I also ran because of myself. I wasn't really okay with who I was, and it took me leaving to recognize things not just about myself, but about life." He looked at me, his chest rising with a deep breath, like he was preparing himself to say more.

Then Lyle came tromping into the kitchen, his hair flattened on one side and pillow lines across his cheek. "What's for breakfast?" he asked, walking over to the stove.

"Oatmeal. Want some?" Sid set his own bowl down to grab another from the cupboard.

Lyle's nose wrinkled up. "No sausage?"

"You're welcome to fix whatever you'd like," I said in a firm tone that meant to change his attitude.

His eyes rolled to me in a movement dense with sass, and he sighed, holding his hands out. "Oatmeal is fine." A pause as he watched it scooped into his bowl. "Thanks, Sid."

"You're welcome, bud." Sid ruffled his hair.

Lyle hopped up onto the counter next to him and kicked his feet while he ate. Sid gave me a look that I didn't know how to interpret. It was almost ... uneasy? unsure? Uncomfortable?

I really don't like that I can't read him anymore. At the same time, I don't want to admit to him that I can't. Because what if it's only one-sided? What if it's just me that feels this rift where we used to be so seamless? I thought he'd been about to broach my feelings for Olive again, but now I don't know. I made a mental note to bring it up with him again, but I haven't found the time yet this morning. And if it was about Olive, I don't want to argue.

After getting ready for the day, I found Sid and Lyle at the dining room table taking apart the Remington 721 rifle that stayed above the workbench in the mudroom.

The only time I can ever remember my mom being angry with my dad was when he brought that rifle home. It was an expense we probably couldn't afford, but he loved that gun. He taught Tommy and Graham how to shoot it and spent Sunday evenings after church cleaning it. The older boys barely touched it after he died.

But Sid had found an affinity for it, and he was good with it.

"We're gonna target shoot," Lyle informed me, watching intently as Sid pushed a small square of cloth through the barrel.

"But first we're going to take care of our firearm so that we know it's in good working condition and will fire properly," Sid added, pushing the cloth back through a second time. "Christ, has anyone even handled this since I left?"

"He's teaching me how to break it down to clean and put it back together, too." Lyle ignored the question. "Do you wanna shoot with us?"

"Maybe next time. I'm gonna run into town for a few things. Any requests?"

"We're out of aspic. And can you look for Spaghettios?"

"Not for the same meal, surely."

Lyle shrugged, pressing a thick spring between his fingers.

"Anything you need, Sid?" I asked.

He finally looked up at me, an easy smile erasing the furrow of concentration from his brow. "Nah, not that I can think of."

"Alright. Don't forget to tie Benny up while you're shooting. He's not used to guns."

"Yes, ma'am," they answered, and I left them to their work.

I'm home now (obviously) with groceries put away, and they're still out on the far side of the pond shooting cans. Benny is sitting at my feet, ears pricked and tense with nervous energy, but he's the only other one who seems at all bothered. I think I just need to get out of my head.

Olive called before dinner to fill me in on her date with Jonah, and somehow by the end of that conversation I'd invited her to join me at the carnival later.

Is it wrong that I wanted her there while I flirted with a guy, even if the flirting wasn't romantically motivated? I don't know. ~~I just wanted to be with her.~~ That's not true. I wanted her to be jealous, but knowing that was unlikely, I wanted to overshadow her night with Jonah, to do something <u>more</u> fun, and I hoped a post-carnival bonfire would fit the bill.

Regardless, she agreed.

I left the house around nine o'clock, Tommy giving me a knowing smirk and telling me to be safe and make wise choices. I only stuck my tongue out at him before skipping down the road. I met Olive at the end of our driveway, and she looped her arm through mine, buzzing with excitement.

It was only slightly awkward when I showed up with her, but between my well-practiced charms and RJ's smooth recovery from the initial surprise, I think it went well, and by the end of it all he seemed genuinely eager to have her tag along.

I think he supposed she might pose an interest for Jess or one of the other guys and potentially give them a distraction so he could have some alone time with me. Unfortunately for him, even if Olive was the kind of girl who would mess around behind someone's back, I certainly had no intention of being separated from her among this group of relative strangers.

While Gabby chatted Olive's ear off about the miserable life of dealing with curly hair, I went with RJ to the table set up a few yards away and watched as he filled three cups with beer. "Thank you for inviting us tonight. I mean, extending the invitation to Olive, too."

"Of course, miss thing." He handed me two of the cups, then touched his free hand to the small of my back to steer me toward the others. "Wouldn't want you to start questioning my intentions if I insisted on getting you alone every chance I had."

I bit the inside of my cheek against a smirk, leaning into his touch. "Are your intentions something I should be questioning?" I tilted my head to look at him, and the flash of firelight gave the blue of his eyes a particularly devilish glint.

"I can assure you my intentions are formed of the deepest respect," he whispered against my ear as his fingers drifted lower until his palm cupped my butt.

I jumped forward, shooting him a reproachful look and glancing around for good measure. "You're shameless," I reprimanded, trapping my lip between my teeth for a moment.

"Can't deny that." *Caint.* He winked.

I sat down next to Olive, handing her a beer, and joined in the general conversation around me. It wasn't long before someone produced a joint, the smell of hash joining the woodsmoke.

Olive's eyes tracked it around the circle, and she kept wiping her palms against her shorts. When it reached her, she pinched it between two fingers and looked at me, swallowing nervously. Firelight danced in her eyes, lighting the brown with honeyed gold. ~~If I had a crowbar, I would have cracked open my ribcage to~~

~~bathe my heart in that gilded light, holding the organ in cupped hands while my life's blood dripped through my fingers and Jesus Christ, Mallory, could you be any more of a simpering fool calm down.~~ I saw her indecision plainly.

"You don't have to," I whispered.

"What if I kind of really want to?" she asked, a nervous smile playing across her mouth.

I raised my cup to her in a salute and downed the rest of the beer, all casual.

She brought the joint to her lips, taking a shallow but lengthy drag. She coughed as she passed it, her eyes watering, and the circle laughed good-naturedly, applauding.

RJ plucked the rolled paper from my fingers, and I dropped my mouth open in protest as he took a deep drag, holding my gaze. Then he passed the joint off and cupped the back of my neck, pulling me closer.

My heart raced, and butterflies exploded through my stomach. As he touched his lips to mine and blew smoke into my lungs, I kept thinking how much I wanted it, how good it felt for him to think he had such a strong hold on me knowing I would ultimately be his demise. But with every frantic beat, my heart sang *Olive Olive Olive*. I didn't want her to see this.

Did I?

What if it made her jealous?

Then RJ pulled away with a lazy grin, and the smoke came billowing out of my lungs with a burning tickle. My eyes watered from the effort of suppressing the urge to cough, and then it passed, and my head buzzed with ... with everything, I think. What had I been thinking, dragging Olive into my hunt?

She slipped her hand into mine with a giggle and squeezed, our fingers naturally threading together.

I turned to her, and she buried her face in my shoulder. "No, don't look at me."

"Why?" I laughed, breathing in the smell of her shampoo.

She gave my hand another squeeze, pulling it into her lap so that all of my fingers were suddenly surrounded by her warmth. "I think I'm a little high."

"Well, hopefully. That's kind of the point," I teased, and she lifted her head as the joint made its way back around.

She took another hit, and I did, too, this time of my own volition. "Definitely high," she confirmed.

Jess strummed something lively on a guitar, and Mags stepped up to Olive, offering his hand. I resisted the urge to bare my teeth and growl, but she looked at me, her dark eyes glassy and sparkling and such an open happiness on her face, and then accepted, letting him pull her up into a dance. I watched, wary of him getting too handsy with her, but he did seem to truly be enjoying himself more so than overly interested in her. RJ stood and pulled me to join them.

I let him spin me around, laughing, but as I twirled and his hands drifted around my body, my mind slowed, everything seeming to happen in time with the thrum of my heart. RJ spun me, pulled my back to his front, and I tilted my head to the side when I felt his lips on my neck, an instinctual action, but my eyes found Olive, watching Mags lead her in a swing dance. What if he tried to touch her? Would she know whether she wanted it to happen or not right now?

Piney wasn't a big drinker, so, living in his house, Olive wasn't, either. I couldn't remember how many beers she'd had before smoking—just the one, right?—and the effort of trying to replay that short-term memory caused my feet to stutter to a stop.

"You okay?" RJ whispered against my neck, and I could feel

him, not hard but not quite flaccid, against my lower back. My mind spun, showing me my fantasy of killing him while we fucked, and want pulsed between my legs.

But Olive. I had brought Olive into this.

I needed to look out for her.

"I think I need something to drink," I said, suddenly aware of how dry my mouth was.

RJ led me back to the log we'd been sitting on. "Here, sit down for a bit. I'll get you something."

"Thanks." Being motionless for a moment helped me ground myself, and my mind was able to snap back into some semblance of focus. I let out a deep, slow breath, and whatever unease that had taken over me seemed to dissipate.

I watched Olive continue to dance, and as she spun around, she met my eyes and flashed me a thumbs up. I returned the gesture, and I'm not too proud to say I was awed by the uninhibited joy on her face. She wasn't worried about trying to be demure or poised, just being the authentic Olive I get when we're alone, and my chest constricted with the weight of my secret love.

RJ sat down next to me, placed a cup of wine in my hands, and slipped his arm around my waist. "How ya feeling?"

"Better now, thank you," I replied, leaning into him without taking my eyes from Olive. This hadn't been what I'd had in mind when I said I wanted a drink, but I took a sip with the hope that it would at least combat some of the cotton feel in my mouth. A bitter taste lingered on my tongue after I swallowed, sharp in contrast to the sweet view in front of me. Disinclined to experience the flavor again, I set the cup down at my feet as the party livened around us.

When another joint began its rounds, Olive skipped over to me, a little breathless, with a mischievous smile on her lips.

"Should I have more of the ... should I have more?"

I laughed as she rested her hands on my shoulders for stability. "Do you <u>want</u> more?"

"I feel like I shouldn't, but ..." Her eyes were wide as she dropped her voice to a whisper. "But I really want to."

I put my hands on either side of her face. "How do you feel right now?"

"Light." She grinned. "Floaty, a bit, but in a good way. Happy. And ..." I was probably just high—I know I was high—but it looked like her focus dropped to my mouth for a moment, and I think her cheeks went warmer beneath my palms. "And happy," she finished, eyes on mine.

"Alright, then, miss happy, take another hit." I tapped my finger to the sloped tip of her nose.

"You, too?" she asked, one hand sliding down my arm to grab mine.

I'd forgotten RJ existed until he spoke up from beside me. "Of course Mallory, too. Friends don't let friends party alone."

Something in me rebelled, wanting to refuse just on the principle that he'd insisted I had to. But I swallowed back the impulse, instead letting Olive tug me to my feet and accepting the wine RJ picked up from the ground to hand me again. I smiled, raising it to him before turning to follow Olive to the heady smell of burning bud.

I took only a small drag, just enough to coast on the high still lingering from earlier, and left Olive with Tara and Gabby while I went to hunt down something non-alcoholic. I found an unopened bottle of ginger ale and left the cup of wine in exchange.

"Goodness mercy, it's like you can read my mind." Olive swooned into me when I brought her the drink, and she downed nearly a third of it without stopping to breathe.

"It's because you're soulmates," Tara answered solemnly, twirling some sort of white crystal shard at her throat.

Olive giggled, looping her arm through mine as she gave the soda back to me, but I just stared at the other woman, trying to pick apart how she'd meant it as my heart fluttered in my chest like a damn chickadee.

The rest of the night was a blur of movement and laughter. A complete waste of time hunting, as my focus was on little other than Olive, but oh well. I did see RJ watching me every now and again with a strange look on his face that I didn't put effort into deciphering then and didn't focus on enough to recall exactly now, but he still seemed eager to see me again when we finally said goodnight.

Regardless, the walk back home with Olive was ...

Ach, okay, I had to shake out my hands real quick. Moving on.

Clouds were heavy in the sky, dampening the sound around us until everything felt muted—the crickets chirping, the soft rustling of leaves all fading into nothing. It felt perfect, and I didn't want to interrupt the moment with words.

We walked in companionable silence until we could see the distant light from my porch, and she squeezed her arm tighter around mine.

"Thank you for convincing me to come out," she said. "Tonight was ... fun. I had a lot of fun."

I tipped my head to rest on her shoulder, the smell of woodsmoke sharp in her hair. "Thank you for coming with me."

"Mallory?" Her voice was a whisper, and I lifted my head to face her. "How do you think you know when you've found your match?"

It felt like we were completely alone, the only two people in existence, and I didn't even think about it when I lifted my hand to her face, cupping her cheek as I pressed my forehead to hers. "When all the pieces just fit together, probably. Like me and you."

She laughed, her breath warm where it ghosted across my cheeks, contrasting with the cool night air. Her nose brushed against mine, and I contemplated tipping my chin, letting my lips graze hers. It would be so easy.

But I stayed still, ignoring the yearning ache in my chest until she stepped back with a sigh. "I wish being with Jonah was as easy as being with you."

I tucked her hair behind her ear, then let my hand fall to my side. "He's never been the easiest to decipher, has he?" I said, for lack of anything nicer.

"It's not even that." She shook her head. "He's sweet and attentive, but ..."

"But he never would've gone to a bonfire with the carnies," I supplied.

"Or smoked their drugs," she giggled, pulling me along toward the house. "And that's why you'll always be my favorite person." Her voice had grown softer, like she was offering a secret to the night.

I tried to ignore the way my heart wanted to crawl up my throat and throw itself at her feet. "Because I'll get high with you?"

She clicked her tongue against her teeth, dropping her hand to lace her fingers through mine. "No, dork. Because I'm always safe to be my full self with you."

"Always," I agreed.

We crept into the house quietly, getting ready for bed and then slipping into the sheets. We lay facing each other in the dark, but I couldn't keep my eyes open, and my mind was already drifting toward sleep.

Olive went home after breakfast this morning, and I recounted the last of yesterday's events before doing some chores around the yard. Once finished, I sat out by the pond with the dogs. Benny was soaked, playing fetch with a stick in the pond, and Danny sprawled next to me, contentedly snoozing after moseying around the property and making sure that all was in place.

Benny had just dropped his stick in my lap, staring at it with intent, tongue lolling out of his mouth as water streamed from his fur, when the rumble of an engine came from the road. The kind of growling engine reminiscent of a motorcycle.

It turned down the drive, spurring me to set the stick down and get to my feet. Danny raised his head, looking from me to the driveway for a moment, as though gauging my concern before he stood, throwing his head back to let out a few howling barks and trotting toward the front of the house.

Benny's ears perked, and I shrieked when he shook out his coat, sprinkling me with cool water. Then he darted off after Danny, his barks sharp and staccato compared to the hound's baying.

I followed at a slower pace. The engine cut off, and the dogs stopped barking shortly after. I could hear voices, but nothing distinct, and then I rounded the corner and saw the bike. It was sleek, all black and chrome, and gleaming in the sunlight. My jaw actually dropped, and I stepped closer to admire it.

"She's a '61 Triumph T100."

I stopped, looking over my shoulder to see an Asian man roughly my height, straight black hair grown out about an inch all over, brown skin just a shade lighter than Olive's, and bright, friendly eyes pushed narrower by his smile. And then the realization struck me. "Oh! Oh my God, hi!" I spun around and took a few steps closer.

Sid stood next to him, an arm around his waist and the brightest smile I think I've ever seen on his face. "Duck, this is Mak. Mak, this is my sister—"

"It's good to finally meet you, Mallory," Mak said, sticking his hand out.

I ignored it, rushing forward to throw my arms around him. "Oh my God," I repeated stupidly, soaking up every ounce of sheer happiness radiating from my brother and unable to process anything else. I stepped back, squeezing Sid's arm. And then it was like my brain finally clicked into gear, and everything came out in a rush. "I'm so glad you're here. I love your bike. You're staying here, right? How long are you in town? Have you eaten, I can—"

"Slow down," Sid interrupted with a laugh.

"Right." I wiped my hands on my shorts. "Right, sorry."

Mak shoved his hands into his pockets, his face flushed, and looked from his feet to Sid and then to me. "It's alright, really. I ... It means a lot to feel so welcomed." A playful grin broke across his face as he shot a sly glance at Sid before nodding to his bike. "I can teach you to ride, if you want."

If I didn't already like him on principle, that would have won me over. "Would you?!"

"I don't think that's a good idea," Sid cautioned at the same time.

I started to roll my eyes at him, but stopped in my tracks when Mak reached up and gave his cheek a placating pat. "Don't hurt yourself doing too much of that, Aka."

Sid shook his head, turning his face to the sky. "Hot creepers, having the two of you together is going to be the death of me, isn't it?"

Mak and I shared a conspiratorial smile, but otherwise ignored Sid's theatrics. "Lessons later," Mak promised. "How about a tour first?"

Sid and I formally introduced Danny and Benny, then showed Mak around the yard and the house. There were two free rooms upstairs that I gave him the pick of, then we ended back up in the kitchen, where Sid prepared a light lunch of grilled cheese and apples.

Lyle had, presumably, run off with his friends that morning, and when he hadn't returned by the time we'd finished lunch, Sid suggested they head into town to sight see. They invited me, but I could see how badly Sid wanted some time alone, so I declined.

With the house quiet, I did some management tasks for the bed and breakfast, all droll stuff, and now that I'm all caught up here, I'm contemplating a nap.

I want to see RJ again, to rebuild his confidence that he has me ensnared on account of how much I really didn't pay attention to him last night. ~~Plus, I could really use~~ ~~It's been a while since~~ Christ, could I be any more concerned about the wording of this? I miss sex. I want to come around something other than my own fingers. Judge me if you will (we've already established you can't).

But with it being Mak's first night in town, I don't want to be rude by skipping out yet again. So, for now, I'll probably just stay home and will definitely have that nap.

The rest of today was mostly uneventful. Sid called this afternoon to let me know that he and Mak would be grabbing dinner in town, and I told him to make sure they checked each other for ticks before coming home, which earned me an embarrassed exclamation on his end and a belly-deep laugh from Tommy, who was helping me prepare dinner.

The meal itself isn't worth mentioning other than the fact that I'd tried frying some cutlets. I used an altered schnitzel recipe, and while I think it could've used a touch more paprika and garlic, there were no leftovers, so it was a definite success.

Our guests were in the living room playing a game of Yahtzee when Sid and Mak made it home. I was personally annoyed by how formal it made the introduction with Tommy and Lyle, but the father had served in the Army during the second world war and seemed eager to exchange experiences.

Tommy excused himself, heading to bed, and Lyle drifted off soon after to read comics in their room, leaving me and the wife to try to extricate the boys from their conversation. Eventually, we were successful, and the three of us moved into the private part of the house.

Sid had looked frustrated when they came home, and I could tell he was still bothered. He hid it well, but there was a pull to his brow and he kept fidgeting with his fingers. I worried that someone had made a comment while they were out. Delight is pretty accepting as a general rule—or at least too well-mannered to be rude in public—but there are enough out-of-towners in the summer that it's possible they ran into an asshole or two who couldn't keep their racist comments to themselves.

Mak was in the shower (Siddy had kissed his temple before he left for the bathroom, and it was in fact the cutest damned thing I've ever witnessed) when Sid finally came into my room, leaning against the door after it closed with a soft *shnick* that made me look up.

I slipped a bookmark into *We Have Always Lived in the Castle* and patted the bedding beside me, pulling my knees up to my chest.

Sid sat on top of the covers, his back against the headboard and his arms resting over his knees.

"Mak is great," I said, setting the book on the nightstand and shifting to face him slightly.

That brought out his dimples, and he ran a hand over his hair almost bashfully. "He is. He likes you, too."

I smiled. I mean, of course it's obvious now, but I hadn't recognized how much I wanted to make a good impression until then. "He does?"

He gave my knees a little shove. "He'd better, if he wants to be a permanent part of my life," he joked, then continued more seriously. "It's the most surreal thing, Ducky. That he really chose me, that he wants to be with me out here in the real world." He tipped to the side, his head coming to rest on my shoulder, and I leaned my own against his.

"I love how happy he makes you. You deserve to be loved so wholly."

He was silent for a while, and then, so quiet I almost missed it, he said, "So do you."

My chest constricted, and I bit down hard on my cheek. I didn't want to have that conversation again. I know he said it because he believes it, because he loves me and wants me to have the world. But in that moment, I fought back a wave of irritation. Just because something worked for him didn't mean that it was what I needed or even wanted. So I said nothing, and eventually he sat up with a sigh, picking at the knee of his jeans with his mouth twisted in contemplation. I was so preoccupied with shoring up my defenses for whatever was coming next that I was entirely caught off guard when he actually spoke.

"Another body was found."

I blinked, the response pre-loaded on my tongue nowhere even close to appropriate.

Sid swallowed. Set his jaw. "I heard a couple of guys talking about it at the bar earlier. Another woman. Brutalized."

"Jesus," I whispered, wrapping my arms around my legs. "Do they know what happened?"

He shook his head. "Specific details haven't been made public yet, but they know she was abandoned in the woods after being tortured and probably raped. They know she was dumped there after being killed elsewhere. She hasn't been identified yet."

Unease crawled up my spine. Two bodies in the span of a week was not only bad for business, but how <u>dare</u> someone target <u>my</u> people? "This isn't good, Sid," I stated unnecessarily.

He scoffed. "No, no, it isn't."

I dug my fingers into my knees, trying to work out how to handle a murderer in Delight while my brain refused to grasp the concept, the idea not quite sinking in, slipping off the surface every time I tried to pull it under.

"Would you ..." Sid started, then paused, a hand running back and forth over his head. "Are you happy here?"

I cocked my head, confused by the abrupt change in subject. "Of course."

"Would you ever consider moving? Starting fresh where we didn't have ... I don't know, any of our history bogging us down?"

My brow furrowed. "I mean, if you guys wanted to relocate, of course I would be open to the idea, but ... I don't know. This is the only home I've ever known. I'm comfortable here. Where is this even coming from?"

"I don't know." Sid concentrated on the wall across from us for a moment. "It's nothing. Forget I said anything. I think it's just the mix of high emotions from Makoto being here and the talk at the bar, and I ... just forget it. I think I need some sleep." He gave an unconvincing chuckle. "I'll let you get to bed, too. Sorry if I worried you."

I frowned as he got up. "Well, I wasn't until now."

"I'm just ..." He waved his hands through the air a little helplessly. "I'm just a little rattled."

"Okay." Even though I had only grown more uneasy. His hand was on the knob before I spoke again. "Siddy?"

He paused, looking at me over his shoulder.

"You're not going to leave again, are you?"

"I won't ever leave you again. I promise."

That eased some of the tightness in my chest. And that's what I'm holding on to now, reflecting over all of this. We'll be okay. Because it's the five of us. Always.

# DEVASTATED

**Part Four**

Almost a whole year had come and gone before Momma recovered from Daddy's death. Tommy had gotten a job stocking at the grocery store, and Graham had picked up a paper route so that we could afford to feed ourselves. Sid tried to hunt with the rifle, but even after his eighth birthday, the gun was long and awkward in his hands, and ammo was expensive besides.

I remember the new school year had already started the first morning I woke up to Momma in the kitchen, making breakfast with Lyle propped on her hip.

I felt a strange mixture of scared and happy, and I hung in the doorway for a while, just watching her. Eventually, she saw me when she turned from the stove, and she jumped, throwing a hand to her heart with a little laugh.

"Mallory, honey, you scared me."

She smiled at me, and I ran over, throwing my arms around her legs.

"Well, good morning to you, too, sweet girl. Can you get your brothers up? I made breakfast."

I nodded, then ran back upstairs. Sid was still in our room, sleeping, and I crawled up next to him, shaking his shoulder.

"Siddy, wake up."

"Go 'way." He rolled over, burying his face in the blankets so that only a mop of red poked from the top.

"Momma made breakfast."

He slowly emerged, rubbing sleep from his eyes as he sat up. "She's better now?"

I shrugged, twisting my fingers into the fabric of my nightgown.

He got up, yawning as he grabbed my hand, and together we entered Tommy and Graham's room. They were both awake, talking quietly and sitting on the floor with a checkerboard between them, and looked up simultaneously when we walked in, their eyes wide and then relaxing when they saw us.

"Well look who's up early," Tommy greeted, smiling broadly and patting the ground next to them.

"Ducky says Momma made breakfast," Sid told them, staying put.

"She has Lyle," I added.

Tommy and Graham exchanged a look and then stood, Graham grabbing his glasses from the dresser as Tommy ushered us out the door.

That might have been the strangest breakfast of my life. Sid heaped spoonfuls of brown sugar into my bowl of oatmeal before adding some to his own, and Momma just watched us, not even a single admonishment about the amount of sugar we were using. She watched Tommy and Graham, too, and if she was trying to hide it, she was doing a terrible job. She smeared oatmeal over the side of Lyle's face twice because she was looking at the older boys.

Mostly just Tommy, though. It was like she couldn't take her eyes off of him, but not in the way that people watch something they love. It was different, and even if I didn't understand it, it made me uneasy.

There's no way Tommy didn't notice, but he sure acted like nothing was amiss. He ate with gusto, shared schoolyard gossip, and teased us like normal. When breakfast was over, he took his bowl to the sink, then came back over, reaching for Lyle. "I can get him cleaned up—"

"NO," Momma interrupted, lunging in front of him to grab the baby.

We all jumped at the outburst and stared at her.

She forced a chuckle, walking Lyle to the sink. "Sorry. I'm sorry. I just … I'm his mother, and I … I can take care of him." She stroked the back of his head, smoothing downy red curls.

I looked at Tommy just in time to see what would become his signature pacifying grin spread over his face, the apples of his cheeks round with boyish charm. "Of course. Sorry, Momma."

He left, heading upstairs to get ready for school, and first Graham, then Sid, followed. I stayed at the table, unsure of what had just happened, but sure that it felt wrong. Sure that I didn't like it.

Goosebumps broke out over my arms when Momma looked up from cleaning Lyle and saw me sitting there. She smiled a weird smile, sighing and nodding to herself. "You're a good girl, Mallory, aren't you?"

I bunched the fabric of my nightgown in my fists. "Yes, ma'am."

"Give me just a moment, and I'll help you braid your hair for school. Go on up and get dressed."

I hopped down from the table, but the words were already spilling from my mouth. "Tommy's been helping me with my hair."

Her face pinched together for a moment, then she smiled again. "Well, I can help you from now on, okay?"

"Okay, Momma."

She made me nervous, which was so confusing, because she was still my mother, and having her back from whatever fog she'd been in did make me happy. I relished the time she spent holding me and brushing my hair and reading me stories before bed.

She did these things with Sid, too, but only when he wasn't with Tommy and Graham. And when I did follow the older boys around like I used to, she would watch me with that pinched face, and it made me worry. So I hung back more, watching as she watched Tommy and growing more and more anxious by the day, sick with a mixture of happy to have her back and terrified to be drawn away from my brothers.

Those days when she tried so hard to be present feel like a fever dream. I was constantly on edge. I didn't quite feel safe with her, and finally getting held and coddled like I'd wanted from her after Daddy's death, I realized that I never had.

Momma had never hurt me, but she'd never kept me from being hurt, either. She would urge me to behave or do things a certain way with warnings of Daddy's temper, but she hadn't ever gone against him ... whereas, even at that young age, I'd already lost count of how many times Tommy had purposefully stepped into the line of fire, drawn Daddy's attention away from not just me, but Sid and Graham and even Momma.

And so, even while curled into her side, I would watch her, wondering how she could look at Tommy with so much ... hardness in her eyes. And I would watch Tommy pretend like he didn't notice, but shoot me a wink when she would pull me away from the boys, sneak in a reassuring touch to my hair, make sure I was included in their games during walks to school—all letting me know that no matter what might be happening, he was still there. He was aware, always looking out for us.

Who even cares about anything that happened this morning? An officer showed up today and I was alone. Sid and Mak are here now, but Tommy still isn't home, and there's a part of me that doesn't know how to feel about something this big until I know how <u>he</u> feels about it.

I was outside hanging sheets to dry when this man drove up. Even though the car wasn't marked and he was in a regular suit and tie, something about his presence instantly had me on edge. He hitched his belt up as he meandered over, looking from me to the dogs snuffling around his feet and back again. They weren't harming anything, and he was on their property, so I did nothing, just pinned another sheet in place and watched his approach with a blank smile.

He gave me a thorough once-over, snorting to himself when his eyes landed on my bare feet like he'd expect nothing less from a hippie than to let her dogs harass people. I gave him a once-over in return, clicking my tongue and returning to my laundry because a man too pompous to acknowledge friendly, well-behaved dogs wasn't worth my time.

"Excuse me, miss, I'm Detective Lachlan with the San Bernardino County Sheriff's Department. Is the homeowner around?"

I propped the now-empty basket on my hip and stuck out my hand. "He's not, but I manage the bed and breakfast and would be more than happy to help," I lied at the end there and hoped that he wasn't actually looking for Tommy specifically. But he hadn't mentioned him by name, so I shook off those initial jitters and relaxed into my well-practiced role when he clasped my hand in his.

"I suppose so, Miss ..."

"Rathbone."

"And you run the establishment?" he asked, pulling a small notebook from his chest pocket and flipping through it.

"Yes, sir. My brother does own it, but it's pretty much been in my hands for the past couple years," I babbled, friendly. Open. Just a young lady.

His stance relaxed, and he nodded, jotting a note in his little book. "I see. Well, Miss Rathbone, I have just a couple questions, if you don't mind. About a guest of yours earlier this month."

"Oh?" I cocked my head to the side. "Well, in that case, let's go on into the office so I can have my records in front of me." I led him to the house, Benny running ahead and Danny trotting faithfully at my heels, giving the officer a wary look. "Can I offer you a glass of water?" I asked once we'd stepped into the foyer.

"No, that's fine, thank you."

"If you don't mind waiting here just a moment. Usually I come in through the back when I'm doing chores, and ..." I trailed off, gesturing to my dirty feet.

"Oh, not at all," he said, tucking his hands in his pockets and failing at attempting not to look too eager about getting the chance to browse unobserved.

I hurried through the kitchen into the mudroom, grabbing a towel to dust off my feet and taking a moment to breathe and shake off any outward signs of unease his unexpected arrival may have left behind. I patted down my shirt and shorts, did one quick mental run-through to assure myself that the main house was all in order—we had guests, so of course everything was tidy—and moved back into the foyer.

He was in the living room, poking through the bookshelf full of books and games, and turned around when he heard me walk up. Nothing bashful or apologetic about him, just a man doing the things he's entitled to.

"This way, detective." I moved through the office door and propped it open before stepping behind the desk and taking a seat. It felt like a shift in the power balance, to be the one making these decisions first, and I waved my hand in offering toward a chair in front of me.

Instead of taking the opportunity to loom over me, he sat, perching on the edge of the chair. "What can you tell me about the Brewers?" he started without further preamble.

Aside from the fact that Donald's wife was much too pretty for him? But I frowned like I was struggling to recall who exactly he meant and flipped through my planner. "Ah, yes," I said when I'd found them, tapping the page. "Donald and Charlene. They were with us from the tenth through the twelfth, celebrating a wedding anniversary, if I remember correctly. Very sweet couple."

He nods, face serious. "And they checked out on the twelfth, you said?"

I looked down at the book again. "Saturday, that's right."

"Did they mention any other plans to you? Anywhere they might have wanted to visit before heading back home?"

I took a moment to think, then shook my head. "No, not that I recall."

He gave me a calculating look, slapping his notebook against his palm a couple times, before sitting back with a sigh. "Well, Miss Rathbone, neither seems to have been seen since they left here that morning. I'm sure you've heard by now that bodies were found out in the forest, and we've recently identified one of them as Charlene."

This shouldn't have come as a surprise, considering the detective in my house, and yet I sat there staring at him for a solid five seconds, trying to process what he'd just said. "Oh my God, did he kill her?"

He shifted, and I could see him trying to deliberate how much to share with me. "That was our initial suspicion, yes, but we found him dead in their car a day after we found Charlene."

"He killed himself?" I asked, a hand creeping up to rest at the base of my throat. Poor Charlene. If Donald had given any indication that he was abusive ... I could have saved her. But he'd truly seemed to worship the ground she walked on, and—

"We've ruled his death a homicide as well." The detective interrupted my spiraling thoughts.

Even as a sigh of relief wanted to heave from my chest, I struggled not to suck in another gasp. Our guests had been murdered.

"You said you're the operator of the bed and breakfast, correct? Can I get your first name and the names of anyone else living here?"

That's when my fingers started going numb. No one had seen them *since they were here*. Of course we were considered suspects. "Mallory," I answered, curling my hands into fists under the desk and then splaying them over my thighs, tapping each finger down the line and back to help regulate my breathing. My teeth felt a little buzzy. "My name is Mallory. Tommy—Thomas, I mean—is the homeowner, but he would never—"

"I'm just trying to gather facts right now, Miss Rathbone," he assured me. "Just doing my due diligence and tracing their final steps. Is it just the two of you here in permanent residence?"

"No, there's also Sidney and Lyle, but Lyle's only thirteen, and Sid just returned from service in the Navy on Sunday."

He jotted this down, nodding. "And was there anyone else here when they left that I could talk to?"

I looked back down at my planner. "The Masons. They checked out a day later. I have a name and address I could give you."

"That would be very helpful, thank you."

I flipped to the appropriate page and turned the book around, pointing to the proper line so he could copy it down. As he did so, the rumble of a motorcycle engine filtered into the house, followed by the joyful barking of the dogs as they herded it up the drive.

Lachlan raised an inquisitive brow. "Guests or a brother?"

"A brother and his guest," I answered, following him out of the office and to the front door. I slipped out ahead of him, watching as Mak parked the bike and shut off the engine. Anxiety flared in my gut as Sid dismounted, hefting a backpack over his shoulder and walking over to where I stood with Lachlan.

"Good afternoon." Lachlan stepped in front of me, introducing himself to Sid. "Detective Lachlan, San Bernardino County. I was just talking with your sister about some timelines."

"Is there a problem, sir?" Sid asked, shaking the offered hand.

Lachlan hitched his belt up and rested his hands on his hips. "Not yet. I'm just gathering some information right now. A couple of your guests were murdered at some point after they left your bed and breakfast. Now, which brother are you?"

"Sidney. I'm sorry, did you say it was <u>our guests</u> who were found out in the woods?"

"Yes, but, as I said, I'm just gathering information right now. I understand that you weren't in the area when the Brewers stayed here?"

Sid ran a hand over his hair with an apologetic smile. "To be honest with you, Detective, I couldn't tell you who the Brewers might be, and I'm honestly not too sure who our current guests are, either. The bed and breakfast is Mallory's business. Even so, I just got back home Sunday evening, and I've been busy catching up with family and everything I've missed over three years to really be mindful or help out at all."

"You were in the service, right?" Lachlan appraised him.

"Yes, sir. Petty Officer Third Class, assigned to the USS Coral Sea."

"Well, thank you for your service, Petty Officer. I believe I got everything I needed from your sister, but I'll be in touch if I need anything else."

Sid smiled in return, shaking his hand again. Only then did Lachlan's attention drift to where Mak was crouching to pet the dogs, and his eyes narrowed, his posture stiffening. Sid's posture also shifted, his shoulders going back and his own eyes hardening, even as his words remained cordial and respectful. "This is my shipmate, Petty Officer Nomura, who's been staying with us the past couple of days."

"That your bike, Nomura?" Lachlan asked.

Mak's arms hung at his sides, and he scratched Benny's ears when the dog nudged at his hand, though he kept his eyes on the man speaking to him. "Yes, sir."

"Mind if I get a peek at some papers stating such?"

My fingers wrapped around Sid's wrist as he stepped forward, keeping him from entering Lachlan's personal space. "Is that really necessary?" No cordiality in the question at all.

"Stay out of this, son. It doesn't concern you any."

I tightened my grip on Sid, straining to keep my arm at my side while he tried again to insert himself between the detective and Mak.

"Yes, sir, they're just right here in the saddlebag," Mak said, shooting a look at Sid. His eyes caught on where I held my brother, and he met my gaze with a barely perceptible nod as he unzipped one of the leather pouches strapped to the back of the bike.

"This is private property, Detective. You've no right to question him." The address sounded like a slur, the way Sid spat it.

Lachlan paused in taking the folded papers Mak handed him, looking over his shoulder with that one eyebrow raised. "It's my duty, Mr. Rathbone, to ensure the safety of this community. Especially in light of recent events." He turned back to Mak. "What day did you get into town ... Ma-ko-to?"

"Just yesterday, sir."

"You planning to stick around long?"

"I haven't really made any solid plans yet. Just enjoying the open spaces after being sequestered on a carrier for so long." Mak attempted a smile as he took the papers back.

"Right, well." Lachlan made the blandest effort to return it, then addressed the three of us. "Thank you for your cooperation. I'll be in touch if anything else comes up."

I released Sid as the detective walked back to his car, but I could feel him damn-near vibrating with pent up anger, he was holding himself so tense. I'd be lying if I said I didn't get a little thrill from it. My own heart thumped in my chest, blood racing through my muscles, poised and ready for action, to follow his lead.

"I should rip out his throat," Sid said so low it could have been a growl, and a ripple went through me in response. I could lunge from the porch, jump onto the hood of the car before Lachlan could turn around in the drive. He would stop, open the door with a look of appalled confusion, and then Sid would come up from behind him, tackling him to the ground and ripping a wet, meaty chunk from his throat with—

"Aka, look at me." Mak's calm voice derailed my train of thought, and I blinked, reality coming back into focus. Lachlan's car had disappeared down the drive, and Mak was standing in front of Sid, one hand pressed to his chest.

A shiver traveled down Sid's spine, then he breathed, tearing his eyes from the dust cloud on the road to meet Mak's imploring gaze.

"He doesn't matter. What he thinks doesn't matter."

Sid cupped Mak's face in his hands, and every line of him went soft. "I know."

Mak smiled and whispered in what I assume was Japanese, and I suddenly realized I was watching something personal and nearly tripped over my own feet trying to run back inside.

I'd barely made it to the kitchen when Sid followed me in. I grabbed a glass and filled it from the sink, just for something to do with my hands. I was rattled, and I hated the unfamiliar feel of it.

"Jesus Christ, Ducky." He dragged his hands down his face, but the nickname assured me he was just flustered, that we were a team in this unprecedented event. "Tell me they aren't ... tell me parts of them aren't in our freezer."

My heart actually sank into my stomach, I'm sure of it. "Are you really asking me that right now?" My voice pitched higher with hurt.

Sid shook his head. Swallowed. "I just need to hear you say it. Because I can't drag Mak into this." His eyes begged me to understand.

I'm still not sure that I do, but I relented, for him. "We didn't kill Charlene or Donald. Not the other lady they found, either. You know that's not how we do things." I felt sick under the weight of his gaze.

Sid searched my face, then sagged against the counter, pressing the heels of his hands over his eyes.

"He's got nothing on us, Siddy. He just wanted some information, that's all," I reiterated for both of our benefit. "I'll talk to Tommy tonight. We've got to figure out what's happening before more people get hurt." Before more attention could be drawn to town. There were way too many missing persons with links to Delight if you dug far enough back in their history. But Sid didn't need me to remind him of this.

He grabbed his own glass of water, drank it, then rubbed a nervous hand back and forth over his bright copper hair. "I won't have Mak involved in any of this. I won't sully what I have with him because of ... of our upbringing."

I placed a reassuring hand on his arm, waiting for him to look at me. "You know how much your happiness means to us—to <u>me</u>. I would never do anything to jeopardize that."

"I know," he sighed and looked like he wanted to say more, but instead looked out the window.

I followed his gaze to see Mak playing fetch with Benny. "What is it that he called you before?"

Sid's face flushed a delicate pink. "Red."

My eyebrows raised. "You must really love him if he gets away with that."

He shrugged, continuing to watch out the window. "It's different when he says it. But yeah, I do."

I leaned my head against Sid's shoulder and watched Benny spin in circles in anticipation of the next throw. "He fits in well."

"He does," Sid agreed, though something in his voice sounded almost reluctant. I'm trying not to dwell on that or let it get under my skin. I'm realizing now the guilt he must feel knowing there are so many things he can never tell Mak. Their situation is definitely not the same as Graham and Priscilla's. I would worry that Sid might leave if things get too complicated, but he just promised he wouldn't.

So I'm not worried about that. <u>I'm not.</u>

It was after eight by the time Tommy came home. I was just finishing up dishes from dinner when he entered through the back, offering a sheepish grin when he saw me. "Sorry I'm late; I was with Graham."

I sighed, pressing my fingers to my temple where a headache was forming. I just wanted to sleep.

I wanted to see RJ.

I wanted Olive to come by.

In truth, I just wanted someone to wrap me up and tell me everything was going to be okay.

"Did you eat?" I asked, and Tommy nodded, so I slipped past him, gesturing for him to follow as I walked outside and toward the pond. When we reached the dock, I sat, crossing my arms over my chest and trailing one foot through the water, letting the sensation ground me. Tommy bent down to hand me a cigarette, lighting it for me. I took a long drag before finally talking. "One of the women who was found earlier this week was Charlene Brewer."

I waited, watching his face as he tried to place the name. It only took a moment for his eyes to grow wide, and he lowered himself to sit beside me, flicking ash into the water. "What happened?"

"I don't know, but a detective came by today to retrace her last steps. Both her and her husband are dead. They never made it home after leaving here." I swallowed, digging my fingers into my arm.

"Fuck," Tommy breathed, his brows drawing together in concern. He took another puff, the tip of his cigarette glowing in the dark. "I'm sorry. I should have been here."

The apology settled me more than the nicotine, but I waved him off. "He was only asking questions."

"But it must have been unnerving, not knowing what he wanted, dealing with it all by yourself. Was Sid here?"

"They came back just as the detective was leaving. He ... he was rude to Mak."

Tommy's countenance darkened further. "The audacity of a man to come onto <u>my</u> property and harass my family."

"It was mostly okay," I assured him, trying to cool his temper before it boiled. "Honestly. The bigger problem is that someone is out there killing people in Delight. What do we do?"

"I'm not sure there's anything we can do, Duck. Just stay vigilant and continue to be careful the way we always have."

I blinked, taken aback by how unconcerned he seemed. "But they killed our <u>guests</u>. Plus a third person. Where did they come from? What do they want? And the reports about the women being beaten ... and raped," I choked out the last bit, the words wanting to stick in my throat. I looked up at Tommy with wide eyes that I knew showed all of the horror I felt.

"Hey now, nothing is going to happen to you, okay?" he soothed, draping an arm over my shoulders to pull me into his side. "I don't know who's out there or how long they plan to stick around, but you're going to be fine. <u>We're</u> going to be fine."

"How do you know that? How aren't you more concerned

about someone else encroaching on our territory and leaving desecrated bodies to rot in the woods?" Every fear I'd had over the last week came bubbling to the surface in the safety of the night, free to be spoken in the presence of my protector.

"You're smart enough not to let yourself become hunted. I know that much like I know the sun will rise. As far as who's doing all this, it could be any number of people. The carnies, a vagrant, some tourist who snapped, a jealous lover. If it makes you feel better, I'll talk to the local coppers tomorrow and see if they have any leads or will share anything that hasn't been made public yet, okay? At the very least, I'll tell them off for letting an out of towner come out here to harass you when you're by yourself. He could have come with one of the deputies you'd know if he wasn't trying to intimidate." He gave a single rueful shake of his head.

I sucked in another lungful of smoke, leaning into him. I knew he'd know how to handle it. "Thank you, Tommy."

"I'm sorry you were alone today." He dropped his arm, moved back so he could look me in the eyes. "Sometimes when I look at you, it's hard to believe you're the same person who used to be our little mallard. You don't need anyone to follow anymore; you're fully capable. I'm so proud of who you are."

My face grew warm, and I looked out across the water, shrugging because I didn't know how to deal with how much those words meant to me. But if I'm capable of forging my own path, it's because he and Graham and Sid showed me how.

I didn't want to undermine his sentiment by saying that I would always follow their lead where it mattered, so I'm leaving it here, because it's the truth.

We finished our cigarettes in silence, then he helped me up, and we headed back to the house. It was during that silence that I decided to go out. I didn't <u>need</u> to go to the carnival tonight, but

I needed the ritual of stalking prey to settle me after everything the day had entailed. Plus, I still had to make sure RJ thought he had me under his thumb, and tomorrow is the last day of the carnival before they start tearing down. So really, it only made sense that I get my time in.

Since it was already late, I went straight to the camp at the back of the grounds instead of going through the carnival, settling down on the steps of the trailer RJ shared with Jess, Hock, and Fry.

Jess showed up first, still slathered in face paint, and arched a brow. "Well, fancy seeing you here, townie."

"I come bearing gifts." I held up a tupperware container full of cookies. "A small thank you for everything you've all shared with me."

"You really know how to seduce a man," he said with an exaggerated flourish, waggling his eyebrows suggestively. "Let me slip into something more comfortable, and I'd love to accept your offering."

I laughed, familiar enough with his antics not to take him too seriously, and scooted over to allow him inside. He came out five minutes later in regular clothes, still wiping his face with a rag, and sat next to me on the narrow steps.

A small group had formed by the time RJ finally walked up, and I reveled in the way his eyes glittered when he saw me.

"I don't know how I feel about you looking so chummy with my woman, Jess."

Jess slung an arm over my shoulders and took a huge bite of cookie, grinning without shame.

My brows rose as I watched RJ's approach. "That's a pretty bold claim."

"You're on my doorstep, ain't ya?" He crouched down so he

was eye level with me, plucking a cookie from the tub.

"Technically, it's Hock's doorstep since his name's on the trailer," Jess spoke through a mouthful.

RJ looked at him evenly, pulling the tupperware from my lap without dropping his gaze and setting it on the ground beside him. Then, before I could even register what was happening, he sprang up from his crouch, scooping me up from the step (I'm embarrassed to admit I did shriek) and spinning around so that, by the time we stopped moving, he'd scooted Jess off the step and was sitting down with me on his lap.

I'm not a prudish woman. At this point, you know it, I know it, no one is trying to pretend otherwise. But I have never been handled that way, and I knew my face was red and flushed and could do nothing to hide it or stop it. RJ's fingers curled around my hip, and desire rolled through my belly in a wave that I had not at all been prepared for.

Jess's laughter broke the tension, and he pushed himself to his feet and dusted off. "Point taken, my brother." He picked up the cookies and led the small group to where the majority were gathered around the bonfire, and I was left alone with RJ.

I looked down at him, my heart rate spiking as his eyes met mine, watchful, calculating. I removed his newsboy cap and set it beside us, then slid my fingers into his hair. It was greasy from a day of sweat, but not intolerably so. And when his calloused hands slid under my shirt to caress my sides, I gasped. The drag across my skin had enough pressure not to make me want to crawl out of it, but I'm sure that more so had to do with the growing ache between my thighs.

"You're mine, not his." His voice was husky and quiet, and his face tipped toward mine.

I probably shouldn't have had the magnitude of response I

did, but, as mentioned before, I was stressed. It had been a while. And holy moly, I was turned on enough by his obvious desire for me that I had no chance of denying my body.

I kissed him, eager. I could taste his last cigarette on his breath mixed with the lingering sweetness of the single bite of cookie he'd eaten, and I wanted more of it. Gripping the back of his neck, I pulled myself closer.

His fingers dug into my hips, and he nipped my lower lip. "I want you so bad."

"Would you even know what to do with me?" I challenged breathily.

He rotated his grip on me so that the thumb of one hand dipped between my legs and pressed <u>right</u> where I craved friction the most, and I let out a little whimper. "I'm sure I could figure it out," he drawled. Then we were standing, and he led me into the camper. It was as cluttered as could be expected with four men living in it, but I wasn't really paying attention to the surroundings.

He sat down on a sheet-covered couch and pulled me to straddle his lap.

"Do you have a condom?" I asked, as his hands slipped under my shirt to grope my breasts.

"Yeah." He kissed down my neck. "Are you a virgin?"

I almost laughed, curling my fingers into the hem of his shirt to pull it over his head, and dragged my nails down his chest and abdomen to his belt. "Do you want me to be?"

His only answer was a groan as he pulled me into a deep, hungry kiss.

It didn't take long for the rest of our clothes to come off, and as soon as the rubber was on, I let him guide himself inside of me and lowered onto him.

I dropped my head back, eyes closed as I finally had that full feeling I'd been craving, and I sighed with pleasure.

He talked to me while he fucked me. Told me how good it felt and how I looked so pretty riding him. Made several comments about how tight and wet I was, and seemed very pleased about it.

While I was extremely turned on, there was no way for him to know that when I looked at him, I fantasized about how I would kill him. I pictured wrapping my hands around his throat and watching the blood vessels burst in his pretty blue eyes. I imagined strapping his hands over his head and carving along the sculpted lines of muscle that decorated his body. So, of course, I was wildly aroused. His life was in my hands and he didn't even know it yet. It's tantalizing, having that sort of power.

When I was close, I grabbed his hand, placing it between us for extra stimulation where I wanted it. Smart, filthy boy caught on quickly and worked to push me over the edge. I dropped my mouth to his neck, felt his flesh against my teeth, licked the salt of sweat from his skin. It would be so easy to snap my jaws closed around the pulse that beat against my tongue, to let his blood flow into my mouth and rip free a raw chunk of him. (I wasn't actually planning to, of course, though I had killed someone that way once before. Never again. Tendon got stuck between my teeth, and I became grossly ill from even just the couple mouthfuls of blood I'd swallowed. Alluring in theory, but not in practice. Anyway.) The warmth of him against my lips and the knowledge of his imminent death and consumption coalesced with the feel of him thrusting into me as his fingers circled against me, rolling tight until the pressure in me gave over to a blinding orgasm, and I turned my face to bite down on his shoulder as I cried out. My body convulsed around him, pleasure rippling through me in waves that left me panting.

He must have finished soon after me, because when I finally drifted back to myself, he'd gone still beneath me. I could feel his heart thudding against my palm, which was pressed to his chest, and he was stroking the length of my hair.

"God, that was amazing," he mumbled.

I hummed my agreement, trying not to shake him off. The movement on my back was starting to raise the wrong kind of goosebumps.

He chuckled, moving his hand to cup my cheek so he could tip my face up and kiss me. I let him take his time with it, and lightly trapped his bottom lip between my teeth when I finally pulled away and pushed off of him.

He watched me put on my bra and underwear with a lazy, appreciative gleam in his eye, but when I started stepping into my shorts, his hand shot out to grab my wrist. "Hey, what's the rush? Lie down with me for a bit. Share a drink with me." His lashes fluttered as he tried to coax me back to the couch.

I pulled free of his grasp, buttoning my shorts and grabbing my shirt from the floor. "Won't the others wonder where we are?" I asked pointedly, slipping it over my head and running my fingers through my hair.

"Oh, it's probably too late for that," he laughed, grabbing me again and pulling down. My hands gripped his shoulders, and I landed awkwardly on his lap, trying to avoid the condom that was still on his softening penis. "C'mon, Mal, stay a while. Let me pour us a drink. I promise they don't even miss us."

Do I need to explain how little desire I had to cuddle with this man on a sheet that was damp with our sex sweat, or can I just assume that you know? Great.

"I can't," I apologized, leaning forward to kiss his nose. "I promised my brothers I'd come home as soon as I delivered the cookies. I should go before they come looking for me."

As lies go, it was a good one. What guy wanted to face the brother of a girl he'd just casually defiled? And it worked, because I could tell by his face that he was done arguing. He looked a little crestfallen, so I leaned down to give him a last little peck and brushed my fingers over the indents of my teeth still in his shoulder. "This is a good look on you," I whispered.

By the time I got home, I really wished I'd at least visited the bathroom first. My underwear were uncomfortably wet with leftover arousal, which was also starting to dry. Luckily, the house was asleep, so I was free to move right to the shower without any awkward (for me) small talk first.

And now I'm enjoying a late-night snack, imagining how much better the shredded barbeque sandwich might taste if it were RJ, and feeling overall quite pleased with myself.

The day started strangely, but I was right to visit him. It was the exact pickup I needed. My head feels much clearer, and I can only imagine how good I'll sleep tonight. The hard work is done. It's all coasting from here.

If I don't laugh at the irony of how that last entry ends, I'll cry (again). I don't even know where to begin. This has already felt like the longest day of my life, and it's not even over yet. I just want to scream and tear something—more preferably some<u>one</u>—apart. But I can't do that right now, so I might as well see if getting it down will help, even if just to sort my thoughts.

Mak went back to LA this morning (that's where his family lives) with promises to be back soon. He even mentioned teaching me to ride the motorcycle when he returns. I can tell Sid wants to invite him to live with us, but is also hesitant to suggest it when there's hardly a chance for privacy with the bed and breakfast. We'll figure something out, though.

Graham and Priscilla were supposed to come over after church for a Father's Day lunch, but Priscilla was struggling with morning sickness, so they just went home instead. After we ate, Tommy left to bring them some food, and Sid and Lyle went down to the lake, leaving me alone to lounge and finally finish *We Have Always Lived in the Castle*. (The guests were out today, presumably at the lake or possibly the final day of the carnival. Thank God for small mercies.)

No sooner had I gotten comfy than the phone rang, and I stood up with a huff, crossing to the kitchen to answer it.

"Rathbone Bed and Breakfast."

"Duck, thank Christ. Is Tommy there?"

My stomach flipped at the breathless urgency in Graham's voice. "No, he just left to bring you lunch. What's wrong?"

He mumbled a string of curses. "Is everything—people might come by the house later. Is there—"

"What do you mean people might come by? Graham, you're scaring me." I clutched the cord to my chest.

"The police. Is everything in order at the house? There's no—there's nothing—"

"The police? What happened, why would they—"

"The other woman they found—I worked on her car. I was the last person to see her alive, Duck. They think I sabotaged her car so I could—and since that other couple stayed with you guys, they want to recheck for any other connections between them. They were just here, and I think they're going to the house next."

He was bordering on hysterical, and anxiety crawled up my throat. "But you didn't do anything, right? All they have is speculation; there's nothing they can pin you with."

"Of course I didn't do anything, but they have a warrant. They searched everything here. Priscilla is freaking out."

I pressed my shoulders to the wall, letting it take my weight. I was lightheaded and kept having to remind myself to breathe. Because none of this sounded so bad to me, but Graham was losing it, and that made me think that I was forgetting something vital.

"Graham, it's going to be okay. We didn't kill those people, and there's no reason for them to think we did."

A tight, high-pitched whine escaped him, a sound I hadn't heard from him since he was a kid and knew he'd done something that would incur our father's wrath, and my heart lodged in my throat. He cursed again. "I gotta go."

"Wait, Graham—" But the line was already dead.

I didn't read after that. I paced around the kitchen, smoking a cigarette and trying not to overthink anything, trying to calm down. I was just about to light a second when the phone rang again.

"Graham?" I clutched the plastic like it was a lifeline.

"No, it's Olive. Is everything okay?"

"No. Yes. I don't ..." I struggled with how much to tell her, still hadn't quite wrapped my brain around what was happening.

I should have known she could hear the distress in my voice, because the next thing I knew, she was saying matter-of-factly, "Sit tight, Mally. I'm coming over."

I had relocated to the couch, perched on the very edge with my legs crossed and my elbows braced on my knees when Olive came in.

The dogs got up to greet her as she moved to the living room window, throwing it open to let in some fresh air and giving me a reproachful look. I smiled, small, tight, sufficiently reprimanded, and tapped out my cigarette. "Now, tell me what happened," she said, sitting down next to me and taking my hand between hers.

I stared at where her thumb pressed against the back of my hand and chewed on the inside of my cheek. I could feel everywhere she touched me, from her palms around my fingers to her knee pressing against mine—and all of it was grounding. I wanted more, in quantity and in frequency and in quality.

She squeezed my hand, and I thought she might have been reading my mind until I looked up to find her watching me with amusement sparkling in her dark eyes. "Don't drift away on me. What's got you smoking like a chimney?"

Because she's Olive—and if there's any person on this Earth

I trust as much as I trust my brothers, it's her—I told her. In a convoluted jumble, I recounted the police visit yesterday, the Brewers' deaths, the second woman's connection to Graham, and his frantic phone call that had me more shaken up than all the rest.

To my surprise, Olive clicked her tongue in annoyance. "Well, if that isn't just the silliest nonsense I've ever heard, the police trying to rough up your poor brothers like that. I bet they're being pressured for answers and are just harassing people now because they have no real leads."

I melted internally, letting out a breath and leaning into her. "Thank you for listening. I feel better, having talked about it."

"It's just ridiculous! The thought of Tommy or Graham hurting anyone." She shook her head, removing one of her hands from mine to tuck my hair behind my ear, then cup my cheek. "It's all going to get sorted, I'm sure. Try not to worry too much."

I itched to grab another cigarette, needing something to occupy my hands and my mouth to distract from the intensity with which she looked at me, like she would raze the world for upsetting me. It felt like all of my fear and anxiety from before had been twisted into a tight little ball in my chest, ready to dissolve if I could only lean forward and taste the soft swell of her lips.

Then a knock sounded on the door, and the dogs both sat up, staring at it with pricked ears. I went to answer it, already knowing who it would be.

"Detective Lachlan, I can't say I expected to see you again," I said, not quite unfriendly.

He offered me a tight smile and gestured with his hand to the man beside him. "This is my partner, Detective Rosenfield. Do you mind if we come inside to talk with you?"

I steeled that cordial facade in place and opened the door

further, stepping aside. "Not at all, please."

They stepped inside. Benny trotted over to sniff at their feet and pants. Lachlan's nostrils flared slightly, but Rosenfield at least offered his hand for a sniff and scratched behind Benny's fluffy ears. Danny still sat by Olive, watching and leaning his weight against her legs.

Lachlan stopped when he saw her. "Oh, I was under the impression the bed and breakfast was solely operated by your family."

Olive blinked, then her eyes went wide, her cheeks flushing, and my control fractured. "It is." I bristled, brushing past the men into the sitting room. "I happen to be entertaining at the moment, and I must say, Detective, that your rash assumptions are not building my confidence in your ability to find whoever is out there killing people."

He had the gall to narrow his eyes at me, like I was the one out of line. That was the moment I decided he will be my next hunt, after RJ. Months down the road, he won't even see it coming, and I'll have come up with such a fun plan for him by then. "I'm glad you brought it up, Miss Rathbone, because I was hoping to ask a few more clarifying questions."

*Clarifying*, like there was any other point to asking a question in the first place. I stood there, waiting for him to begin.

"Can you confirm Thomas's whereabouts on Saturday the 12th and Sunday the 13th?"

"I was at the carnival on Saturday, but Tommy was here when I left and still here when I got home. I was with him all of Sunday morning until he and Graham went to the city to pick up Sid."

"Roughly how long would you say the two were gone Sunday?"

I frowned, trying to think back on it. "Probably around five or six hours."

Lachlan looked at Rosenfield, like I'd just confirmed something for them.

"I told you yesterday, the Brewers left Saturday morning. Tommy was here all day."

"How are you supposed to know that if you weren't around to confirm it?" Lachlan raised a condescending brow.

My nails dug into my palms with my effort to remain composed. "Tommy's always here on Saturdays. It's his morning to relax and his afternoon to do upkeep around the house."

Olive nodded, exchanging a concerned glance with me. "I've been around for a decade of Saturdays, sir. Tommy has always let her know if he plans to break that routine."

Lachlan looked at her like she'd called him a dimwit, but Rosenfield cut in. "I'm sure that's the case, but unfortunately, we can't take speculation as fact."

"Yet speculation is enough to hold my brothers under suspicion?" I challenged, folding my arms across my chest.

Lachlan cleared his throat. "Not entirely. There have been other developments," he said, not divulging anything further. "As it so happens, we've been granted a warrant to search the premises. Now, I'm not trying to dig into your personal life or uproot your home, so if you'd like to help me out, we can make this a painless process. Does Thomas have an office space? Can we see his room or anywhere he keeps personal effects?"

I swallowed, trying to shove my heart back down from where it had crawled into my throat. "Can I see it? The warrant?"

Lachlan pulled a folded paper from his breast pocket like he'd been waiting for me to ask, and I scanned the document. A warrant for the lawful search and seizure of the property and possessions of Thomas Milton Rathbone. My vision blurred when

I read his name, reminded that <u>all</u> of this is Tommy's. Because it can't be mine. For the first time, the fact made me bitter. This asshole somehow had every right to tear apart my home.

I handed the paper back and wet my lips, my mouth dry. "He uses the office for work stuff. It's that room there where we talked yesterday." I pointed.

Lachlan gestured to Rosenfield. "You go ahead and peruse in there while I take a look through his personal effects." Then he looked back to me expectantly, and I led him into the private portion of the house, into the bedroom Tommy and Lyle shared. The sick feeling in my stomach curdled into anger as I watched him sift through the closet, the dresser, look under the beds. He took his time snooping, and it felt so personal, even though he hadn't yet asked to go through my things as well.

A call came down the hall from Rosenfield, and I followed Lachlan to the office, where the other detective stood with a sheaf of documents in his hand, pulled from the very back of the desk drawer. Only years of practice kept me from stumbling or letting terror show on my face, even though it crawled just under my skin, enveloping me completely.

Lachlan took the file from Rosenfield and leafed through it, then looked at me. "Do you folks use the hunting cabin often?"

My eyebrows pulled into a frown. "Pardon?"

"The hunting cabin on the other side of the lake." He wiggled the papers in his hand. "Thomas purchased it in October of '56."

I shook my head. "I don't understand. We don't have a hunting cabin, and we certainly didn't have any money for one around that time."

The two detectives shared a look, then Rosenfield turned to me, pity clear in his kind eyes. I hated him, too, in that moment.

"I appreciate your cooperation, Miss Rathbone. We'll be out

of your hair now." And then they showed themselves out.

"What was that? What did they take?" Olive asked, moving to my side and slipping her arms around my waist.

I shook my head helplessly and leaned into her. "I don't know," I whispered, but I do know what you're probably thinking: "Mallory, weren't you just at a hunting cabin a few days ago? If we flip back—yes, right there. You butchered a man."

And you'd be perfectly right. But what you aren't privy to is what happened (Jesus, damn math, hold on) nine years ago, in the fall of 1956. So let me explain.

It had been the first truly cold morning of the season, and I was bundled into two pairs of socks as I sat at the table with my brothers eating pirate stew (which had been named by Lyle). I was eleven, and by that time, had not only grown used to the taste and texture of human meat, but preferred it.

Tommy cleared his throat, setting his spoon down to look at all of us. "The garage will no longer be a butcher room," he announced. "I've been saving up where I can and found someone to buy the few things of value Dad and Mom left behind, and I bought a place across the lake—a hunting cabin."

I looked at Sid, unsure what to do with the news, but he looked just as lost as I was. "You sold the gun?"

"No, that's yours, little brother."

"And you bought the cabin because ... we're <u>not</u> going to stop eating people?" he asked, a crease formed between his brows.

Tommy gave us his signature lopsided grin. "There's no sense giving up perfectly good food, but I don't like having them here. At our home. It's dangerous and stupid."

"That breaks rule five," I said.

Tommy nodded. "Nothing is going to be kept here anymore other than food. Graham and I will do all of the dressing from the cabin now, but I want you three to promise me something, and this is important." He met all of our eyes, holding Lyle's for the longest, making sure he understood the weight of the moment. "I'm telling you because you deserve to know, and I won't ever lie to you. It's the five of us, always. But if something ever happens, if anyone ever mentions it, you deny even the knowledge that the cabin is out there, understand? This way I can protect you, should the worst happen."

I pouted, not fully grasping what he meant. "Why do only you and Graham get to go to the secret place?"

Graham nudged my foot under the table. "Don't worry, Duck, it's not a clubhouse. Just a safety precaution. When you're old enough to hunt, you can go there, too."

I perked up at that. "When will I be old enough?"

Tommy tilted his head, watching me with amusement. "How about when you're fourteen, then you can start going with us."

I made them both promise, and then I started counting down the days. I also counted them for Sid, though the prospect that he would get that experience before me made me green with jealousy.

All that to say: even before the life of a hunter was bestowed upon me, I lived the life of a secret keeper. All for my brothers, who had never once done anything that would put the rest of us directly in the path of harm. I certainly didn't know then that that foreplanning, those constant reminders that we weren't to know anything about the cabin across the lake, would ever come into play.

But the detective had found the deed paperwork that showed Tommy as the legal owner of the property.

I wanted to vomit. I still do. But I reminded myself then and I keep reminding myself now: <u>nothing is out there</u>. Clothes get burned. Bones and organs buried with lye. And the basement itself is hidden. No one would know to look for it. And even if they did, it's empty. As for any stains, it's a hunting cabin. Of course, it would have a place to process whatever game was brought in.

Olive stayed with me until Sid and Lyle got home. When Lyle was busy flipping through the TV, I brought Sid into the kitchen to fill him in.

Afterwards, we were both quiet, and I could tell he didn't want to voice what was on his mind, but I didn't let that trouble me. Not when so much else was happening, and I needed the comfort that I'd been missing from him for so many years. I leaned my head against his shoulder. "I'm really glad you're here."

"Maybe this is …" he trailed off, started again, his voice quiet. "Maybe this is our sign to stop. Even if it wasn't them. Even if the cops won't be able to prove anything. Maybe this is our chance to quit while we're ahead."

I stiffened beside him, looking up to search his face. "You really think Graham and Tommy did this?"

He shrugged, refusing to meet my eyes. "I don't want to, but someone is killing people up here, and no one has reported any suspicious men milling about."

"Women can kill, too," I muttered.

That earned me a withering glance. "And brutally rape other women?"

I pressed my lips together. "There are so many people in town with the carnival, though. It's possible someone has been camped out somewhere, getting lost in the crowds. Maybe it's even the carnies themselves."

"And they've just been allowed to leave a trail of bodies in their wake across California? Seems counterintuitive to their attempt to hide from the draft, only to have police sniffing around at every turn."

I huffed. "No one told you you had to be so logical all the time."

He looked at me, green eyes open and raw in the way we always were with each other. "Believe me, I'm just as worried by all of this as you. I've been trying to piece it all together and ..." He looked down, his brow wrinkled. "I feel horrible for even thinking it, but at least if it <u>is</u> Tommy and Graham, I know you're safe."

And how am I supposed to be angry with him for thinking our brothers could have possibly done this when he's only worried about me?

None of it makes sense. The more I think about it the more confused I feel. And you know what the strangest part is? Even though in my soul I know Tommy and Graham would never hurt someone like that, even though never for a second have I considered that they might have killed those people, I never really thought to be scared.

Angry? Sure. Worried about detection, obviously. But scared for my own safety? Oh, God—for <u>Olive's</u>?

Now I am, or perhaps I always have been, but the emotion was disguised by anger, presenting as disgust for these murders. It's been so very long since I've felt threatened or had something tangible to fear. And if that's what this feeling is, I hate it.

I'm numb and I'm spiraling and I don't know where to start.

I watched through the living room window as the dogs ran up to greet Tommy when he finally came home. Benny dropped a dirt-crusted tennis ball at his feet, which he threw before crouching down to scratch Danny's ears.

I went out onto the porch, arms folded across my chest to keep from shaking apart. "That detective came back."

Tommy met my eyes briefly, the blue-green full of the same sadness as the smile he offered me. "I talked to Graham already." He threw the ball again for Benny. "Did they find out about the cabin?"

"Yeah."

"Fuck." He ran a hand through his hair, turning to rest his back against a post.

My chest grew tight, blood roaring in my ears as his composure cracked and resettled into something like acceptance. "Tommy?" I whispered, wanting to say something reassuring but needing to be reassured myself.

A car turned down the drive, and my heart plummeted when I saw the Sheriff's emblem painted on the door, the light mounted to the top.

Sid joined us on the porch to watch its approach.

"Benny, heel!" Tommy called when the border collie raced to guide the car up. Benny's ears perked, and he trotted over to us. Sid ushered him inside after Danny.

Sid and I exchanged a nervous glance while Tommy stepped down into the yard, toward where the car had parked. A second car pulled in behind them, one I recognized from Lachlan's visits.

"No," I breathed, moving forward on instinct.

Sid's hand shot out, grabbing my wrist.

My heart thudded against my chest, time seeming to slow so that I was forced to bear witness to every detail.

Two deputies stepped from the marked vehicle as Lachlan parked. Opened his door. He was wearing sunglasses, but I swear his eyes met mine. One corner of his mouth hitched up, ever so slightly. I wonder if he knew how much I wanted to tear that smug smirk from his face and shove it down his throat.

I trembled, every muscle in my body tense.

"Don't make this difficult, Tommy," one of the deputies said, his discomfort easy to read. He was local, had drank a beer with my brothers on more than one occasion.

Tommy lifted his chin, sunlight glinting off the golden-red strands of his hair. Wind curved through the yard, ruffling his curls, tugging at the hem of my dress and pulling my own hair across my face.

The deputy stepped closer, badge flashing on his chest, his hand pulling a pair of gleaming metal cuffs from his belt. "Place your hands on the back of your head."

Tommy complied, holding his head high.

"No," I whispered again, shaking my head. Sid's fingers tightened around my wrist.

The deputy moved around Tommy, pulling his hands down one after the other to secure behind his back.

Something shuddered behind my breastbone, the world narrowing to a singular point where my brother was being led toward the cruiser, and then widening back out to normal with a snap, and time sped back up.

I inhaled sharply, ripping free of Sid's grip to leap from the porch. "No! Let him go, he didn't do anything!" I ran for the man restraining Tommy and was caught around the waist by his partner. "Stop it, don't touch me! Let him go!" I screamed, scrabbling at the arms around my waist.

"You might want to take her inside, Sid. She doesn't need to see this."

I heard the man speak, and while it fed the indignation burning in my chest, I couldn't take my eyes from Tommy being walked to the back of their car, hands cuffed behind his back.

"Don't fight them." A second set of hands grabbed my arms, and I recognized Sid's voice.

Frantically, I turned to him, and the deputy released me. "Sid, Sid, don't let them take him. He hasn't done anything! They can't take him." My legs gave out, and I collapsed against his chest, tear-tracked cheeks soaking through the front of his shirt. I don't even remember starting to cry.

Sid caught me, keeping me on my feet. "Come inside, Ducky."

I let him lead me into the house and deposit me on the couch. I'd mostly pulled it together by then. Though tears still slid down my cheeks, the sobs had reduced to sporadic hitches in my breathing.

"I'm going to go talk to them and try to figure out what's happening," Sid spoke softly, smoothing my hair down. I only nodded in acknowledgment before he left.

I stood, moving to the kitchen to grab the phone, and dialed Graham's number with shaking hands. The line trilled in my ear as I leaned against the counter for support, but no one answered.

I was just replacing the receiver when Sid came back in, running his hand back and forth over his hair, his shoulders tight. He braced his hands on either side of the doorway, refusing to look at me as a flood of emotions crossed his face. Then he shook his head, turned, and slammed the heel of his hand against the wall, making me jump.

He pushed away from the wall and stalked into the living room, sinking down onto the couch and burying his face in his hands, his knee bouncing frantically.

Anger is not a novel emotion in our home, as you've probably guessed by now. I am well versed in how to handle a fit. But Sid's anger has always scared me. Its rarity makes it feel more volatile. And now I was caught between the animal instinct to stand back, away from possible danger, and the desire to go to my brother and offer comfort.

I hovered somewhere in the middle, not retreating, but not stepping closer, one hand reaching toward him.

"Bastards," he spat to the floor, and I flinched. "Self-absorbed, dim-witted, sick-headed <u>assholes</u>." He kicked the coffee table, shoving the wooden chest across the carpet so abruptly that Danny lurched to his feet and moved across the room, shooting a reproachful look over his shoulder.

Sid fell back into the couch, arms limp at his sides and legs still. I scratched Danny's head, then sat next to my brother, sideways, with my legs pulled up in front of me so that I could face him.

His eyes were on the ceiling and brimming with tears, and I watched the protrusion of his Adam's apple bob as he swallowed.

My own fear and anger had been dulled by Sid's reaction, but they flared to life again in the still and the quiet, and I was powerless to stop my own tears from falling.

"The police went to the cabin," Sid eventually said, sliding his gaze to me. His jaw clenched, overcome by anger again when he saw me crying. "I want to hate them." His fingers curled into the cushion between us, his nails scratching audibly over cloth. "Tommy and Graham. I want to hate them for letting our family be torn apart. I want to hate them for being cocky and selfish and v—" his jaw snapped shut, and he swallowed hard. "But I can't. I love them so much, even though I wish I didn't."

I watched him, tears streaming down my cheeks and my stomach twisted into knots. I didn't understand his anger with our brothers, and the confusion didn't do anything to calm my fears. But then he reached over, wrapping his arms around me, and held me as I cried. I felt his tears soak into my hair, and I knew that, whatever he may be struggling with, he needed me just as much as I needed him.

Priscilla called sometime after that in complete and utter shambles to tell us Graham had been arrested, too. They didn't give her any specifics from what I could gather, but they'd said something about the hunting cabin—which she truly had no clue about—and the recent murders.

I'm pretty certain my stomach is eating itself, trying to guess at what might have been found out there that could have led to an arrest in such a short amount of time. I keep going over the last time I was there with Tommy, but nothing was out of place. We cleaned up. We were smart.

At any rate, Sid and I had pulled ourselves together by the time Lyle came home (he'd left at some point to meet up with his friends before everything went south), and even if I had no appetite to speak of, there were still guests to worry about.

Sid talked to Lyle while I prepared dinner. Maybe it was

selfish of me to not want to hear it recounted or look my baby brother in the eyes and watch his face when he realized our den of safety had been breached, but I was only holding on to my own composure by a thread, so I was willing to let Sid carry that burden alone.

He came into the kitchen as I was stacking cobs of corn onto a platter. "He's upset, but still taking it about as good as can be expected."

"Did he have a lot of questions?"

Sid frowned down at the plate of Salisbury-style steaks I placed on a serving tray next to the corn. "None that I had the answers to."

"Grab that basket of rolls?" I asked, lifting the platter to take into the dining room. I set the food down and apologized for our absence from dinner. I didn't miss the suspicious look exchanged between the husband and wife when I mentioned a family emergency.

I filled the dogs' bowls, made a plate for Lyle, and grabbed a roll for myself, knowing I should try to eat something. Sid followed suit, and we moved into our private quarters. "Do you think they heard anything while in town today?" I asked quietly, setting the dog bowls down in the hall.

Sid shrugged, chewing on the edge of a nail. "It's not too hard to imagine so."

My stomach turned. All these years we've been carefully curating our social image. And now it's tarnished, if not completely shattered. And the only people I could ask about what my next steps should be are locked up in who knows what kind of conditions.

I swallowed down a fresh wave of tears, sitting in the boys' room with Sid and Lyle, trying our best to distract each other from the uncertainty and fear.

It was late by the time I cleaned up from dinner. I wanted to keep the dogs inside, but Benny was circling in the mudroom, ready to be let out for the night, so I gave them both extra kisses and scratches before opening the door for them.

I don't know that I'll sleep tonight, but I'm going to at least lay down. I can't help either of them right now, and being overtired isn't going to help anything, either. I just need to hold on to the hope that whatever Tommy and Graham are being charged with won't hold. They have no proof, and they can't just tear a family apart.

I had drifted off at some point when I heard the soft click of the door being opened, followed by Lyle's footsteps padding across the floor. He lifted the blankets, and I shifted over, giving him room to crawl in next to me like he hadn't done in so long. When he was younger, he'd sleep in my bed when he had nightmares or didn't feel good. But it had been years since he last came to me for comfort that way.

Emotion swelled in my chest as my little brother settled next to me on the mattress—the ache of Tommy and Graham's absence, fear for what might happen to them, but also a fierce protectiveness. I soaked in his warmth as we cuddled in the dark for a long while.

"We almost caught the forest on fire the other day."

I was so confused I thought he must be talking in his sleep. "What?"

Lyle sniffled. "Jake had a pack of M80s, and me and him and Tanner were setting them off up the mountain, throwing them at things, exploding empty cans. We didn't mean nothing by it. We were just messing around, you know? Well, one of them ... we lit it and meant to throw it into a clearing, but I threw it too high and the wind caught it. It exploded in some brush and a fire caught. Mr. Drear was out collecting firewood and heard us. He'd already been coming to investigate, but then he saw the fire building and ran over to stamp it out. He made Jake hand over the rest of the firecrackers and threatened to get the cops involved if he caught us doing something stupid like that again. We hadn't brought our whole stash, though. We still have some, just we don't set them off close to the Drear's now. So when Sid first told me that that detective had come by here … I thought 'Not the fireworks, please let it be anything but the fireworks.'" His voice cracked. "I wish I could take it back. I was so scared and stupid and this is so much worse. I wish I got in trouble and Tommy and Graham were still here."

"Oh, LJ." I held him close, silky strands of his hair tickling my nose.

He dragged his arm across his face, sniffling again. "What's going to happen to them?" he whispered.

"I don't know," I answered, shifting to rest my cheek against the crown of his head.

He was silent for so long I thought he fell asleep, but then he said, even quieter, "What's going to happen to us?"

"Nothing," I promised. "Nothing is going to happen to us." I held him tighter, and a fuse sparked in the center of my be-ing, burning through my veins until I was nothing but righteous anger.

That anger simmered in me, eating through my worry and anxiety and replacing them with the vibrating need for action. As Lyle's breathing evened out into sleep, I lay beside him, resolute in the knowledge that, no matter what it takes, I won't let any-thing happen to my family.

Maybe that didn't warrant recording, but I don't want to forget this feeling. For now, I'll slide back into bed next to my little brother, and tomorrow I'll do whatever has to be done to make sure that his life stays as easy as it's always been.

Despite how exhausted I was, how exhausted I still am, I was awake before six. I tried to go back to sleep, but my stomach was in knots and a headache throbbed in my temples, so I gave up, careful not to wake Lyle when I rolled out of bed.

Sid was already in the kitchen, standing at the sink with his gaze fixed out the window. He looked like he hadn't slept much more than I did.

"Morning," I said softly, stepping closer.

He wiped tears from his cheeks with the heel of his hand. "Oh, good morning."

"We had the same idea." I offered a wan smile as I pulled a glass down from a cupboard.

"No surprise there," he attempted to joke back, reaching to take the glass from me and filling it from the tap.

I rummaged through a drawer for medicine, shaking a couple of aspirin tablets into my palm. After tossing them down with a sip of water, I stood next to him, looking out the window and soaking up his warmth. "Anything exciting happening out there?"

"All quiet on the western front."

"Scholar," I ribbed him.

"One of us had to be," he whispered back.

I took a long drink of water in an attempt to combat the

sudden tightness in my throat, then tipped my head to the side to rest my temple against his shoulder. "Do you think they're okay?"

"Of course they are; they have each other."

I swallowed thickly, tears blurring my vision. "We have to get them out. We have to … to find whoever killed those people." My breathing hitched, and I squeezed my eyes shut.

Sid was quiet for a long while, then his arm draped around me, and I let him pull me to his chest. God, it is still so strange how tall he is, his chin resting at my crown. "They won't be able to explain the cabin, Ducky. A cabin they rarely took us to."

I shook my head, pushing away to meet his eyes. "We're all entitled to our privacy. We had secret places, too. Lyle probably has a getaway he hasn't shared with any of us. Does that make him a murderer?"

Sid's mouth set in a firm line, his chin jutting out slightly as he leveled me with a look. "That's not what makes them murderers any more than that's what makes us murderers."

I clenched my glass, the heat of anger rising in my cheeks. "That's different, and you know it."

His eyes never left my own, but instead of the anger I know he saw in mine, I only saw a deep, weary sadness in his. "Is it?" I opened my mouth to retort, but he cut me off, grabbing my shoulders. "We did what we had to to survive. We stayed together, and we stayed alive. I've made my peace with that, but—" his fingers dug into me as he bent to better meet my gaze. "Why is it still happening?"

The intensity with which he looked at me suffocated the flames of my anger. "We … because we need—"

"We don't." He interrupted firmly, his brow slashing into a fierce glare that I so rarely see from him. Sid let me go, shaking his head and dragging his hands down his face. "Do you know how crazy I feel every time I rationalize the fact that we ate our mother? I tell myself we were just kids, and we were starving and we had no money and couldn't ask anyone for help without the possibility of being taken away from one another. And even though I know it means I'm fucked in the head, I'm fine with it because we're alive and we're together. But it should've fucking stopped there. She should have been the only one."

His anger caught me off guard, and I took a step back from him. A creak from the floor upstairs interrupted my reply, both of our eyes flicking to the ceiling. Sid let out a frustrated breath, pressing the heels of his hands into his eyes, and continued more quietly, "No more meat. It's a stupid risk to take right now. We shouldn't even have any in the house."

I scoffed, scorn the most readily available defense mechanism. "I'm not going to throw out perfectly good food just because you left home and decided—"

"To grow a conscience?" he interrupted again, and I tucked my fists under my arms to avoid beating them against his chest. He opened his mouth, then snapped it shut, inhaling sharply through his nose. My own tension vibrated tight behind my chest even as the fight fled his body. "No meat. <u>Please</u>, Duck. I'm going to run down to the local sheriff's office. They should open soon, then I can try to find out what exactly our brothers are being charged with, where they're being held, and if we can see them, okay?" He gave my shoulder a squeeze before leaving me alone.

I was still reeling from that rollercoaster of a conversation as I made breakfast, bleary-eyed, sleep-deprived, and struck by a feeling of vertigo as I tried to sort through my feelings. A knock at the threshold to the kitchen made me jump, slinging a bit of scrambled eggs to the floor.

Benny rushed over, snuffling up the mess as I met the eyes of the woman staying with us.

"Sorry, I didn't mean to startle you, dear. But I wanted to let you know we'll be checking out early."

"Oh, is something wrong?"

She smoothed down the front of her shirt. Fussed with her hair. "Oh, no. Well, not exactly. You've been marvelous, the accommodations are great, and the girls love your dogs. But, um … well, my husband couldn't help but overhear about the … well, the incident yesterday, and we thought it best to get out of your hair while you work things out."

"It's not a bother, truly," I assured her, and I think I failed at keeping the desperation from my voice. I needed this bit of normalcy to help convince myself that everything was going to be okay. That this was just one small bump in the road and everything would be resolved and back to normal before long at all.

She tried to offer me a smile, but it wavered at the edges. "We just … well, I'm sure you can understand, dear, but we just don't feel … safe … staying here any longer."

"Oh." My heart plummeted, and I fought to keep the friendly smile on my face. "Right. Would you like a refund for your last night?"

"No, no, that's quite alright. I just wanted to let you know that we're headed out this morning."

I nodded, and she left.

Safe. She didn't feel <u>safe</u>.

My grip tightened around the spatula, and I longed to show her just how <u>safe</u> she was without my brothers around.

I pictured running after her, sliding my fingers into that nest of gleaming, perfectly styled curls and slamming her head into the wall. I would drag her into the kitchen, tie a gag around her mouth, and carve strips of bacon from her back while she was still breathing, then cook it up and serve it to her family while she slowly bled out on the floor.

By the time I shook my mind free of the fantasies, the eggs were burnt.

At some point after breakfast, a knock at the door interrupted my cleaning of the guest rooms. The sound wound a cold rope of fear around the base of my spine, and I went downstairs to find Priscilla, her eyes puffy and red.

She immediately fell into my arms, sobbing hysterically. "Oh, Mallory!"

I patted her on the back, guiding her to the couch. I let her cry for as long as she needed, not offering words of comfort that I didn't have. When she finally settled down, I grabbed a tissue from a side table and handed it to her.

She murmured a thank you before dabbing at her face and blowing her nose. "I'm sorry to have just broken down on you like this," she laughed sadly, sniffling. "Lord knows you're probably having just as hard of a time as I am, if not harder. I know how much you looked up to them. How much you loved them."

My heart sank into my stomach with her use of the past tense. I do look up to them. I do love them. "It's difficult, but I'm staying strong. We can figure this out."

Priscilla shook her head. "I'm going up north, to my parents and my sister. I wanted you to know where I was." Her hand stroked her stomach. "Come with me. Lyle and Sidney, too. We can all leave together."

I blinked. "What are you talking about? We have to stay here so we can help Graham and Tommy. We can't just leave them."

Priscilla's eyes filled with fresh tears, and she shook her head again, more vehemently. "I'm not raising my baby here. Not where people will only think of him or her as the child of a ... of a murderer."

"You can't leave! We'll find whoever really killed those women and clear their names. How will Graham feel when he gets released, only to find out you've taken his child away?" I clasped her hands, trying to make her see reason.

She met my eyes, her lips pressed together as fresh tears slipped down her cheeks. "They're not getting out, Mallory."

Cold took over my entire body as I recognized the emotion shining in her eyes for what it was.

Pity.

She pitied me. Because she truly believed that my brothers deserved to be behind bars. She believed that Graham—the man she'd married and shared a bed with—was capable of the sort of blind violence required to beat a person beyond recognition. And the women, the way they'd been violated ... I dropped her hands, my stomach lurching dangerously.

"It wasn't them," I breathed, and it sounded like a plea even to my own ears.

Priscilla didn't respond to my claim, only stood and smoothed her skirt down before resting a hand over her belly again. "I'm leaving today."

"But Graham—"

"No." The vehemence in her voice shocked me into silence. "No. I have no husband, and my baby has no father."

I stared up at her, unable to respond past the heat of anger spreading through my veins, chasing away the chill of dread.

"Goodbye, Mallory. Don't sacrifice your happiness for them. They don't deserve your blind loyalty."

And then she left. I stood up, pushing the coffee table onto its side with a scream. And I continued to scream, feeling my throat shred and my lungs ache for new air, but unable to stop because I was unable to articulate my rage at whoever was responsible for all of this. My rage at Priscilla for so quickly and easily giving up on Graham when she had claimed to love him so fully. My rage at my own inability to do anything to fix any of it.

Eventually, I fell to my knees next to the mess from the coffee table, fingers digging into the rug to keep from digging into my own skin as the pain of this new reality fully sank in.

Arms wrapped around me, and it wasn't until his cheek pressed against my shoulder that I remembered Lyle was home. I shifted, clutching him to me with my eyes squeezed shut. "I'm sorry. It's okay. I'm sorry." I'm not sure what exactly I was apologizing for, but I repeated it, holding onto him until the raging storm inside me eventually lulled.

I don't know how long we sat on the floor together before Sid finally came home, looking at the upended coffee table before lowering himself to the floor next to us. "What happened?" he asked softly.

I didn't want to tell him that I was falling apart. Didn't know how to explain that the very foundation of my life seemed to have been pulled from under my feet. So I said the only thing that made any sense. "Priscilla left." I lifted my gaze to meet his, scared of what I might see there and unsure why.

"She should be with her family right now," he said gently.

"We _are_ her family," I argued. Sid just gave me a look like he knew I didn't really believe that, and I scowled. "Graham is," I amended.

He sighed, started to speak, stopped and ran a hand over his hair. "I talked to the sheriff's department. They've been processed, and we can go see them."

Lyle sat up. "When? Today?"

Sid reached out to brush over-long auburn curls from his face. "Yeah, we'll go today."

"Did they tell you what they're being charged with?" I asked, Sid's gaze flicking to me before dropping, and the knots in my stomach tangled tighter. "Tell me."

His focus was glued to the mess of the tipped coffee table. "There were ... trophies. Saved from victims."

I stood, taking my time to wrap my head around the statement as I helped him set everything to rights. Lyle curled up on the couch, quiet, like he was afraid if he drew attention to himself we wouldn't talk in front of him. "No," I finally said. "No, that doesn't make sense."

Sid sighed, but I threw my hand up.

"Think of the rules." It came out almost begging. "They would never—" my voice hitched, and I took a second to breathe. "They would never do something so stupid. I refuse to believe it. Lachlan planted whatever it is they found. That's the only explanation."

Sid just looked at me, his eyes so sad that I wanted to slap the pity from his face and pummel his chest until he saw reason. "They're not infallible." He reached out to me, but I pulled back, folding my arms over my chest.

"How can you turn on them so easily? They're your <u>brothers</u>." Hurt and accusation laced my voice, and he flinched.

"I'm not turning on them," he said quietly, his shoulders dropping. "I'm just trying to do what I can to make sure that, no matter what happens next, you, Lyle, and I still have a life. Tommy knew it might eventually come to this, and he never wanted us to go down with him."

I glared at him, even though I knew he was right. But anger is easier to handle than despair, and I was loath to let it slip through my fingers.

"I'll make us some lunch," he said. "Then we can drive down to the city."

I ate in my room while writing. It's going to be a long drive in close quarters, and I needed this space to compose myself.

I'm so … drained. Like all of the fear and anger I've felt in the past twenty-four hours has sapped me of, well, everything, I guess. But we saw Tommy and Graham, and as much as that hurt, I know that they're okay and they're together, and that's good.

The drive down to San Bernardino was quiet, the energy in the truck charged with a hundred unspoken words. Lyle slipped his hand into mine once we made it into the city, and my surety from last night flared behind my chest: I would protect him at all costs. I would protect <u>us</u>. And unlike Sid, I wouldn't exclude Tommy and Graham from that sentiment.

Sid was all tense lines as he drove, jaw set and eyes forward, and I hated how much it affected me to see him that way. It was so hard to hold on to my anger with him. He was <u>mine</u> in a way the others weren't. We were supposed to be a unit. Why couldn't he see that supporting our older brothers was more important now than ever? I needed him to back them because backing them was, in turn, backing me.

We checked in at the jail, then sat at a table in a secure courtyard for several minutes, waiting.

I told myself I wasn't going to cry, but as soon as I saw a flash of strawberry blonde accompanied by dark copper, my vision blurred, and my throat tightened. I couldn't even see my brothers' faces as they rounded the corner, just man-shaped, blue-clad forms lumbering our way. I stood, blinking furiously to clear the tears, and Lyle raced forward, slamming into Tommy so hard that Graham had to steady him.

"No prolonged contact with the inmates," a guard called from the corner of the courtyard.

Tommy hugged Lyle, then passed him off to Graham as Sid and I stepped forward to greet them.

"Are you okay?" I asked after we'd all embraced and sat down at our assigned table.

Tommy gave me one of his half grins. "Food's not as good as home."

Graham removed his glasses, pressing the heels of his hands to his eyes. I thought maybe he was upset, but I caught the flicker of a grin beneath his beard before he smoothed his hands over his face to look at us. "Don't worry about us too much, okay?"

"What did they tell you about the trial so far?" Sid asked.

Tommy sighed, and with his grin gone, I could see how tired he really was. "Nothing yet. They're trying to link us to the murders from last week, but ..." he trailed off, looking at Graham with a sadness that I felt like a knife in my chest.

Graham folded his hands on the table, staring at them intently for several moments. He opened his mouth, closed it, and cast a pleading look at Tommy.

"What's going on?" I asked, gripping Sid's hand under the table. He'd caught Tommy's eye, and something passed between them, Sid giving the slightest shake of his head.

Tommy nodded at Graham, then dropped his gaze while Graham finally looked up, meeting all our eyes one by one. Tears shimmered in his, rimming the hazel with silver. "I fucked up. And you'll never know how much I regret what it's doing to the three of you." He gave us a watery smile, then looked down at his hands.

I didn't realize I was still squeezing Sid's hand until he squeezed back, and I loosened my ever-tightening grip a bit. "What do you mean?" I asked.

Graham ran his hands over his face again, then into his hair. "I kept things," he mumbled. "From the people we ate."

I tilted my head to the side, sure I'd misheard. I released Sid's hand, placing both my palms against the tabletop in an attempt to ground myself.

"I know it was selfish," Graham continued. "But I didn't think it would harm anything. I never took them from the cabin, and I kept them put away in the dresser. I didn't expect ..."

Sid inhaled, sharp enough that I glanced at him. His face was pinched into an expression somewhere between appalled and confused, and a muscle feathered in his temple when he clenched his teeth together. His gaze bored into both of them.

Graham swallowed, but Tommy spoke before he could defend himself. "Don't be mad at him. I knew they were there, and I let him keep them. This is on both of us, but if the blame should fall to a single person, it's me for not putting a stop to it."

Fresh tears filled my eyes. Because Tommy was always our protector. All of us, and the way Graham looked at him now, full of self shame but adoration for the man who'd been his other half since childhood, made my chest squeeze so tight I could hardly breathe.

"What did you keep?" Sid asked, and I got the oddest sense that he was holding something back.

Graham's mouth tightened, his lips shifting from side to side for a moment before he finally looked at Sid with a heavy sigh. "Teeth, mostly."

I looked at Tommy, who only shrugged. "You can see why that

asshole detective might have found that ... concerning."

"That's why the trial might take longer to be set," Graham added. "They're trying to pin us with the murders from last week, but now they're not sure what other charges to include."

"I don't ..." I shook my head. "<u>Teeth</u>, Graham? Why?" I needed there to be a rational reason for this, some meaning behind this detail that had allowed our family to be torn apart.

"I can't explain it," he answered apologetically. "It was compulsive. I liked the sound they made clicking against each other, and the smoothness of them. I don't know."

Sid looked horrified, like he was about to be sick, while on my other side, Lyle just looked lost.

"But if you didn't kill the Brewers and the other woman, they have to let you go, right? No one can prove you did anything bad to get the teeth," Lyle said.

Graham let loose a broken sort of chuckle. "You'd think so, wouldn't you, kid?"

"I wish it could be as simple as that," Tommy added. "But there's still nothing to prove we <u>didn't</u> kill anyone, so the whole situation is ... not great."

Lyle nodded, not looking any less confused, and I put my arm around his shoulders, squeezing him.

"Listen," Tommy started, shifting in his seat and looking at each of us in turn. "I'm so happy to see you all. I love you more than you could possibly know. But it's very important that you remember the rules, now more than ever. Maybe Graham and I broke them a bit, and we're dealing with the repercussions of that, but you three are clean of all of this. Promise me you'll stay out of trouble."

We did, and then silence overtook us. I wanted to distract them, to talk about something happier, but there was nothing I could think of.

"Have you guys heard from Priscilla?" Graham asked.

I winced.

Sid saved me from breaking the news. "She's going up north to stay with her family," he said gently.

Graham's brow knit together, and then his face fell. "She didn't even say goodbye?"

Tommy put a hand on his shoulder, squeezing. "We'll get through this. Just like everything else. The family that matters is here."

Graham nodded, and then, all too soon, our time was up, and a guard called over for us to leave.

I wasn't ready. Time was happening too fast. There was still so much I wanted to say and so much I couldn't.

I hugged Graham tight. "I'll watch out for the baby, I promise," I whispered, and he squeezed me.

No sooner had he let go than Tommy's arms circled my neck. "Don't fight for us, Duck. We'll be okay." I shook my head, but he tightened his hold on me, not letting me interrupt. "I am so proud of you, little mallard. Now it's time for you to fly the nest."

A sob escaped me as a guard called over that we had to separate, had held contact too long. Tommy passed me off to Sid as I tried to pull myself together.

"The mantle is yours now, little brother. Do better than I did."

I can't name what I felt hearing Tommy so resigned to his fate, but the strength of that emotion is what finally drained me. But maybe now that I'm empty, I'll be able to sleep. Maybe things will look better or be easier to figure out when I'm well-rested.

Ha—the me of last night was clearly delusional. There is no making this better. I want to scratch that out, but I won't. I don't think I should feel guilty for writing it. But that comes later.

Mak came back today. It feels important to note that there is still some good, even with everything else.

I was sitting on the couch with the dogs at my feet, a bowl of Cheerios in my lap, and "The Price is Right" on TV when I heard the rumble of his motorcycle. Both dogs raised their heads, ears perked at the sound. I set my bowl on the coffee table and rotated to watch through the curtains as Mak drove up.

Sid came out of the office, where he was looking through bank statements and tax documents—preparing for the responsibility of the house and businesses to fall to him should the worst happen. "Is that …?" he asked just as the engine cut off.

"It's Mak," I said, watching him dismount and unstrap a large duffel from the back. I turned to look at Sid, confusion and tentative hope washing over his face. He brushed his palms against his pants, ran a hand through his hair.

By the time he was done with his nervous fidgeting and stepping toward the door, Mak had already opened it. Danny and Benny scrambled up to greet him, crowding around his feet with tails wagging.

"I thought you'd look a little happier to see me, Aka." Mak let his duffel slide from his shoulder to the floor and leaned down to pet the dogs while maintaining eye contact with Sid.

My brother stood there looking rather helpless, his arms hanging at his sides. "I thought you weren't coming back. I thought we decided it was better if—"

"Nah," Mak cut him off with a soft smile. "<u>You</u> decided it was better for me not to get tangled up in whatever is happening with your family. <u>I</u> decided I'm not going to let you push me away."

Tears glistened in Sid's eyes, and his whole countenance changed, like he couldn't quite believe that someone was choosing him despite everything. He whispered, "Makoto." And then they were both moving across the room, their bodies meeting flush as they kissed. It was deep and passionate, and my heart fluttered in my chest before my cheeks heated with the realization that this was not meant for an audience. Sid's hand traveled down Mak's back to the swell of his bottom, tugging him even closer, and I tore my gaze away, gluing my eyes to the television and clearing my throat.

I saw them leap apart in my periphery. "Why don't you show Mak up to his room?" I suggested, my entire face hot, still not looking at them.

"Right, um." Sid moved to grab Mak's bag.

"Sorry, Mallory. I didn't see you there," Mak apologized, scratching the back of his neck.

I turned off the TV and grabbed my bowl from the coffee table. "It's fine, really." I finally met his eyes and smiled, blush high in my cheeks, I'm sure. "I'm going to take the dogs out for a bit, I think." My eyes darted to Sid, whose face was just as red as mine felt. The humor in the situation hit me then, and I grinned, shaking my head with a laugh.

Two brothers arrested for murder while one commits crimes of passion in a completely different sense only days after. We are a family of degenerates.

"We'll catch up later," I told Mak. Even though I still hadn't shaken that infernal blush, I winked at Sid, satisfied when his face went an even deeper shade of red. Then I scurried into the kitchen, depositing the bowl in the sink before calling the dogs outside with me.

I went down to the dock, trailing my feet in the water and throwing sticks for Benny while Danny stalked around the perimeter.

Sid having Mak around felt right. I understood why he'd wanted him to stay away initially, but I'm glad Mak didn't listen.

I replayed their kiss in my mind, biting my lip as I remembered how they moved together, hungry, but also almost reverent. Every time I can remember talking about physical pleasure with my brothers, it was either clinical or teasing. What I had witnessed, though? They downright cherished each other, and my heart ached for that kind of reciprocity.

I considered inviting Olive for dinner. It would be good to have a full table, and I missed her viscerally. She called yesterday to offer support and assure me that she was there for me no matter what happened, but the emotional strain of the last couple days made it feel like forever since I'd seen her. But, for once, we had an empty house. Sid and Mak wouldn't have to pretend at being friends, and I didn't want to take away an easy dinner from them. They deserved at least one night of being a normal couple. So I decided to call Olive later, update her on how I was doing, and suggest meeting up later in the week.

Sid and Mak eventually joined me outside, bringing with them a pitcher of lemonade and some peanut butter and jelly sandwiches. For a while, things felt perfectly normal. We talked about general life things and interests (outside of hunting, of course), and I relayed the most embarrassing stories I could remember about Sid as a kid while I fed my crust to the Canada geese brave enough to risk proximity to the dogs.

We were alerted to Lyle coming home by Benny, who sprinted off to herd the bicycle up the drive. He seemed a little upset as he walked up to us, but didn't want to talk about it outside of telling me that his friends were idiots, so I brought him inside to do some baking in an attempt to distract him.

We had a few dozen cloud cookies cooling on the counter and were in the living room playing rummy with Sid and Mak when a knock came at the door. My new aversion to the sound is so strong I almost vomited. Dread pooled in my stomach as I met Sid's eyes, swallowed the pre-sick spit pooling in my mouth, and went to the door.

Nothing could have prepared me to see Jonah on the other side.

"What are you doing here?" I sneered, too emotionally exhausted to bother keeping my emotions in check. (That's repetitive, but I'm still too exhausted to care what you think.)

"Mallory, excuse the intrusion." It wasn't until he spoke that I realized Mitch was standing behind Jonah, a covered casserole dish in one hand. "I understand you might not want visitors right now, but I wanted to drop off some food on behalf of myself and the Forsythes and let you know that we're praying for your family."

I softened at his sincerity, grateful he was still willing to be a friend in light of everything else. Maybe our standing in the community wasn't entirely wrecked after all. "Thank you, that's very thoughtful." I stepped forward to take the dish from him, the door swinging open wider.

Jonah cleared his throat. "Since Mitch was already coming over, I figured I would stop by as well to see if—" He paused, his gaze over my shoulder, and I knew he'd spotted Sid and Mak. Shock and hurt flashed across his face before he blinked it away and looked back at me. "Um, is Olive here? We had an argument yesterday, and she's not taking my calls."

Satisfaction spread from my core to the tips of my toes and fingers, and I allowed it to show in my face, tugging at the corners of my mouth. "No, I haven't seen her today, but I'll be sure to let her know you stopped by."

Mitch cleared his throat, resting a hand on Jonah's shoulder. "We'll get out of your hair, then. Please, don't hesitate to reach out if there's anything we can do for you all."

"Thank you, Mitch. We appreciate it."

"What did they bring us?" Lyle asked.

"Was that your old flame?" Mak asked Sid at the same time.

I peeked under the lid. "Looks like green bean casserole," I told Lyle, then added to Mak, "Jonah Forsythe, in the flesh."

"He looked at me like I smashed his birthday cake," Mak commented.

Sid shrugged. "Indulging in birthday cake might be a sin, so maybe you did him a favor."

"Sidney David, is that snark coming out of your mouth?" I propped a hand on my hip.

"I learned from the best." He fluttered his lashes at me.

And things felt normal for a while after that.

I wish I could stop there.

~~Maybe if I'd kept my mouth shut~~ No. What happened is <u>not on me</u>. Maybe I could have been ... not quite so quick to anger, but I'm not the one who ruined the peace of the night. I refuse to take responsibility for that.

I had moved the leftovers from the casserole into tupperware containers and washed the dish to return to Mrs. Forsythe on Sunday, then stepped out on the back porch for a smoke while I let the dogs out. The night felt quiet compared to the noise in the living room. Happy noise, exchanged for a happy quiet.

Music filtered out as Sid joined me on the porch, leaning against the pillar across from me and tipping forward slightly to stare up at the sky. "Mak is attempting to teach Lyle how to count cards," he chuckled.

"We've moved on to Blackjack, then?" I smiled, blowing smoke and watching it drift into the night.

"We're at least making an attempt." Sid took the cigarette from me, pulled in a lungful.

I felt so comfortable out there with him, just us and the crickets and the faint sound of music from inside. So, when I took the cigarette back, I spilled my heart. "We can have nights like this all the time when Tommy and Graham are released. We can shut down the bed and breakfast, so it won't matter if Mak moves in. Maybe Graham will move back, too."

Sid's mouth pressed into a thin line as he watched me flick ash to the ground. "They won't be let free after what was found at the cabin."

I rolled my eyes, stubborn in my hope. "What are a few teeth supposed to prove? Oddities shops throughout Los Angeles sell that and worse. It's not a crime to collect weird things."

"No, it's a crime to kill people," he said evenly.

I snubbed the cigarette out against the post I leaned beside, tossing the filter into a tin can at my feet. "Why do I bother wasting my breath if you're not even going to listen?" I snapped. "I'm not going to have this stupid fight with you again."

"Our brothers are <u>murderers</u>, Mallory." He threw his arms out in exasperation. "They're murderers, and they made us murderers as well! You're seriously going to stand there and act like they're innocent?" He gave me an incredulous look, begging me to explain my logic.

"They don't kill people, not like <u>that</u>, and you know it. They would never jeopardize us that way," I argued, my throat getting tight.

"They lied to you today. That's why Tommy told you not to fight for them. Because they <u>lied</u>, and they know they're going to be locked up forever."

Even in my irritation, my chest squeezed, my heart thumping erratically against my ribs as I searched Sid's face. "What are you talking about?"

"It wasn't a jar of goddam teeth that had Lachlan calling for their arrest, though it's true enough that Graham was collecting them. They were arrested because there was a <u>person</u> in the fucking basement."

That was almost enough to shock me out of my anger, but not quite. Paired with his tone of voice, like he was pointing out the obvious, it fanned the flames. "Don't try to sway me with bullshit propaganda, Sidney. They wouldn't hunt out of turn."

He snorted. "Well, they did. They had a man chained up down there and he was at least alive enough to say he'd seen the both of them."

"How would you even—"

"The deputies told me. When I went to the local office today to figure out where Graham and Tommy were being held and why, they told me what the arrest charges were. I didn't ... I didn't say anything earlier because I figured it might be easier for you to hear it from them."

I swallowed, hurt crashing through me in a fierce wave. My eyes stung as I tried to make sense of it. For the first time I can ever remember, anger struggled to rise to the surface, drowned by a betrayal that threatened to sweep me off my feet. I shook my head, gripping the post that held my weight. "Graham has been stressed with the baby. It's harder for him to spend time away from Priscilla now, and maybe—probably Tommy wanted him to have a release, and they didn't tell us because they didn't want me and Lyle to feel like ..." I had to stop, my voice breaking.

Sid let out a crazed bark of laughter, placing his hands on either side of his face. "Listen to yourself! You've been brainwashed. You're not a child anymore, for Christ's sake. Open your eyes and do some damned deductive reasoning."

"Fuck you," I seethed, cutting him off. Anger—finally—roiled through my gut, rising in my chest as tears at last flooded my eyes. "I'm smart enough to recognize whether or not someone has my best interest at heart. <u>Tommy saved my life</u>," I finished emphatically.

"Yeah, and he also made us <u>eat our mother</u>," Sid shot back, raising his voice.

"You told me just yesterday you were fine with that. We were <u>starving</u>. The state would have separated us if we asked anyone for help!"

Sid threw his hands up again. "The state would have separated us because <u>he killed our parents</u>!"

Tears slid freely down my cheeks, and a frustrated scream built in my chest. "He <u>didn't</u>," I choked out.

"Ducky." Sid's voice softened as he reached out to me, clasping my hands in his. "Our father was one thing. He was an abusive asshole who deserved to die before he ended up killing one of us. But you can't really think Mom's death was an accident," he pleaded with me to see reason.

"You think Tommy killed her," I said flatly, the realization smacking me in the chest.

"I know he killed her," he replied evenly. "He got a taste for blood early on and cultivated it in the rest of us before we were old enough to fully discern right from wrong. And Graham was no better for going along with it."

I swallowed past the lump in my throat, shaking my head as my heart cracked.

Sid squeezed my hands. "I know you love them. I do, too. They raised us. They were good to us. But regardless of whether or not they killed the Brewers and the other woman, the world is safer with them behind bars. We can have a chance at a normal life. We can leave all this behind."

My heart shattered, I think. Hundreds of broken shards raining down into the pit of my stomach, eviscerating the interior of me on the way. Every look, every stilted conversation since Sid had been home, suddenly made sense. The clues weren't subtle, but I'd refused to see them, to piece them together.

I'd lost him.

He'd been the other half of me for as long as I can remember, but no more.

I pulled my hands free and fled.

The keys were still in the truck, and I drove up a dirt road to the top of one of the mountains that overlooked the lake. I sat on the tailgate, wallowing in the pain and misery of having lost everything until I went numb, and then I sat longer, reveling in the peace that was nothing. I watched the moon track across the sky, and then I drove home.

The horizon is tinged with pink outside my window, and even now I can't tell if I'm actually tired or not. But I'm going to try to sleep. Tomorrow—today, I guess—I'll have to visit RJ one last time before I end up following him. Lord knows I need that pressure release now more than ever. But before that, I'll try to patch things up with Sid. As much as I don't want to admit it, he's another thing I need now more than ever. I just wish ... ~~I wish that he was more like us.~~ I wish he understood me still. The way he used to.

Or maybe he never did. Maybe he never really knew me at all.

# DEVOLVED

## Part Five

A few months had gone by since Momma had started trying to take care of us again, but things were somehow worse than ever. Even with Graham and Tommy both working, we were just scraping by to keep food on the table. Meat had become a Sunday-only luxury. Graham had grown out of his shoes and was wearing Tommy's hand-me-downs, leaving Tommy to wear Daddy's. He had to stuff socks in the toes because they were too big, but we couldn't afford new ones.

I vividly remember the day Momma came into my room as I was getting dressed for school. Some of the other girls had teased me about wearing boy's clothes the day before, and I was in the middle of an internal struggle between being ashamed of once again wearing a shirt that had previously been Sid's and thinking of Tommy's too-big boots when my saddle shoes had been bought new for my seventh birthday that summer. Momma tutted, pulling me from my thoughts as she placed the back of her hand to my forehead. "Get back into bed, honey, you've got a fever."

I frowned, touching my forehead. "I feel fine, Momma."

"Sometimes our bodies hold sickness before we're able to feel it," she told me. "You could be contagious. It's not safe for you to go to school today." My whole face wrinkled up, but before

I could say anything else, she scooped me up and laid me back down in bed. "Don't argue, Mallory. I said you have a fever, and you're staying home today."

I fisted my hands at my sides, a confusion-fueled anger churning in my chest. I didn't know how else to handle it other than to cry. Tears welled in my eyes and rolled down my cheeks. "I wanna go to sch-hool," I whined.

"Hush. Stay in bed." She smoothed my hair down and dropped a quick kiss to my temple, then left, shutting the door emphatically behind her.

Even almost a year after Daddy was gone, I was still scared to carry on, but I cried softly for a while, listening to my brothers leave for the day without me. When my tears had dried and my breathing had mostly evened out apart from some light sniffles and the occasional hiccup, I sat up, twisting the sheets in my hands as I contemplated the closed door.

Eventually, I worked up the courage to open it, padding hesitantly toward the stairs. "Momma?" I called, taking one step down.

"What is it?"

I hurried down the stairs to find her rooting around in the den. "Can I have breakfast?" I asked timidly.

She looked up, blinking at me for a moment before nodding. "Yes, of course. Fix yourself a bowl of cereal." Then she went back to what she was doing.

I passed Lyle sleeping in his playpen, a mostly empty bottle next to him. His hair had already begun darkening to Graham's reddish brown, and I remember so clearly my little child's mind feeling thankful for that, because I didn't want Sid to feel closer to him than to me because they were both true gingers. I stood on my tiptoes and stretched down as far as I could to try to pat

Lyle's back, but I still wasn't tall enough to reach him if he was lying down, so I let him be and fixed myself breakfast.

As I ate, I heard Momma running around the house, muttering to herself as she went. She hadn't moved so much since Daddy died, and a slow, creeping fear stole my appetite. I knew we couldn't waste food—cereal was expensive—but I couldn't make myself eat another bite as it turned to soggy mush in front of me.

Momma ran past the kitchen back into the den, hissing something that sounded a lot like a curse under her breath as she went. I got down from the table, moving to the living room.

"What are you doing?" I asked, my heart thumping against my chest as I watched my mother's erratic movements. "Momma?"

Lyle stirred in his playpen, fussing.

"Can you make sure your brother has his pacifier, sweetheart?" she tossed over her shoulder as she ran upstairs.

Lyle had sat up now, waking up more fully and working himself up into a true cry. I grabbed a pacifier from the coffee table, reaching to hand it to him. He grabbed it, bringing it sloppily to his mouth and sucking vigorously, alligator tears suspended in his big eyes, still more blue-green than hazel. I shrugged, just as clueless as him, and stretched to tousle the fine hairs on his head before following Momma upstairs.

She was in the nursery, pulling clothes from the dresser and shoving them into a bag.

"Momma?" Suddenly I did feel sick, and I twisted my hands into my shirt as I watched her.

She didn't even reprimand me for stretching out my clothes when she looked up, and I felt that uncomfortable tightness in my throat that meant tears weren't far off. "Pack a bag, sweetie. We're gonna go on a little trip."

I stood there, not fully understanding what was asked of me.

"I need you to be a big girl right now and listen to me." She kneeled in front of me, wiping a tear from my cheeks with her thumb. I still remember the soft, doughy feel as it dragged across my skin. "We need to go. It's not safe here. We'll come back, I promise, but first I have to make sure that you and Lyle are out of danger."

My lip trembled, and I shook my head. "But what about S-Sid a-and—"

Momma shushed me, her hands settling on my shoulders and holding me firm. "Your brothers … I don't know how much they know. I don't know if they'll try to side with him. But we'll come back, don't worry. Just pack your bag and let's go."

She stood, nodding to herself and wiping a tear from her own cheek with the heel of her hand. "We'll come back," she murmured to herself, turning, and I almost didn't hear it when she whispered, "Once he's gone, we'll come back for Graham and Sidney."

The world seemed to slow as my little brain processed what was happening, what it meant.

She was trying to take me away.

My heart slammed so hard in my chest I felt like I was going to vomit. "What about Tommy?" I asked, tears blurring my vision.

She stopped, shaking her head, then turned back to me. "I think … You're so young. You wouldn't understand, and—God—oh, sweetie, I wish you didn't have to. But he did something bad. I know you look up to him, but he's dangerous, and I've got to get you and the baby away before he can hurt you, too."

I shook my head. "No, he wouldn't ever," I defended him stubbornly. "He wouldn't ever hurt <u>nobody</u>, 'specially not us!"

Momma let out a shaky breath, crying now herself. "Trust me, sweetheart. It'll all be okay, but we need to leave. I can't … I can't do what I need to until I know you're safe."

"I <u>am</u> safe," I argued. Tommy and Graham had made sure of that.

She'd already stood back up, her back straight and resolute as she marched across the hall. "None of us are safe around that boy."

I don't think she was talking to me, but her words scared me enough to launch me into action. I ran after her, full of fear and an anger so bright and hot it pushed everything else out of my mind. "<u>No!</u>" I screamed, throwing my arms out as I rammed into her.

I know I hadn't truly known what I was doing. There was no forethought behind the action, no intent toward what might happen next. But it had happened, and Momma was so thin and frail from grief that I pushed her right off her feet as she passed the stairs.

She fell forward, her temple catching the banister. If it made a sound, I don't remember. All I could hear was my blood rushing in my ears. Her head bounced off the wood, and her body tipped sideways. Her feet flew over her head as she fell, and then I lost sight of her.

I stood still, my chest rising and falling quickly. It couldn't have been longer than a handful of seconds, but it felt like an eternity that I was lost in that torrent of terror-fueled anger. And then I snapped back to myself.

Immediately, I could hear Lyle shrieking. Not in pain, just in that baby way of being startled and upset.

I ran down the stairs, nearly slipping on a few drops of blood on the way. I clutched the banister while I regained my footing, then hopped over Momma's crumpled form and over to the playpen.

"Shhh, LJ, it's okay," I soothed, reaching in to pat his head.

"Duddy," he wailed (he was still months away from figuring out *k* sounds), reaching his arms up to be held.

"Momma?" I turned around, but she hadn't moved. I couldn't think with Lyle screaming, so I ran over to the couch and pulled a cushion free. After dragging it across the room, I positioned it to the side of the playpen, then grabbed the rail and pulled.

The contraption tipped over, toppling Lyle onto his side. The bounce against the cushion shocked him into momentary silence. His wide, watery eyes took up almost his whole face, and I giggled at how silly he looked, staring at me with his mouth open. My laugh made him laugh, and I dragged him upright, plopping onto the floor with him in my lap.

"See?" I told him. "You're alright, aren't you?"

He threw his weight into my chest, drool and probably snot touching my neck when he hugged me, babbling his baby nonsense.

"Ick." I pulled his blanket out of the playpen to wipe the wetness off and gently scooted him to the floor. "I'll be right over there, okay? I've gotta go check on Momma."

He said, "Mama-ma-ma," but seemed happy enough, so I stood up and turned back toward the stairs.

Her lack of movement started to sink in then, and I began to worry that I'd really, really messed up. "Momma?" I called softly, taking a few steps closer.

Her eyes were open, but her head was tilted at a really sharp angle, and there was a bulge in her neck that was starting to turn a little purple. It made me queasy to look at, so I scampered back over to Lyle and pulled him into my lap.

He made a happy cooing sound, throwing himself forward to

tug at the frilled hem of my socks.

I kicked my feet out of his reach. "Stop it, Lyle."

He looked up at me, laughing at my frustration, then saw Momma lying on the floor. "Mama-ma-ma-ma," he said, falling forward onto his hands and knees to crawl to her.

"Oh, no, no, no." I scooped him up under his arms and lugged him toward the kitchen.

Lyle screeched, slowly sliding from my grip as I tried to get him out of line of sight from Momma. "No!" he yelled at me when I set him down, and I pulled out a pot and some wooden spoons to try to distract him. He grabbed one of the spoons and threw it, screaming again.

"Lyle, stop it!" I went to get it and threw it back. It landed a few feet in front of him and slid across the floor.

He stopped screaming to watch it, then started giggling and threw it again.

I breathed a sigh of relief, glad he was done being so upset, at least for the moment, so I could try to think. I peeked around the corner, but Momma was still lying where I'd left her, and I was too scared to walk over there again.

Then I heard the back door open, and all my attention went to the mudroom. When Tommy stepped through, I ran to him, throwing my arms around his waist and burying my face in his shirt. I was relieved and scared, because I knew something was wrong with Momma, and I didn't want him to be mad at me, but I was so, so glad he was there.

"Whoa there, Duck, what's wrong?" He tried to pry me away, but I clung tighter, shaking my head. "Are you hurt? Where's Mom?"

"I'm sorry, I'm sorry, I didn't mean to!"

I let him push me back, looking over me and then over my

shoulder at Lyle on the kitchen floor. "Mallory, what happened?" He looked scared, and he used my real name, and I knew that I'd done something very, very bad. Tears flooded my eyes, and I shook my head, knowing that if I talked, I would cry.

Tommy moved into the kitchen, where he had a clear view of Momma lying at the foot of the stairs. He froze for a second before walking over with slow, deliberate steps. He knelt down, putting one hand on her neck, hovering it over her mouth and nose. I watched, clinging to the counter and sniffling despite my best efforts not to cry.

Tommy ran his hands through his hair, dragged them down his face, and crouched there next to Momma for what felt like a long time. When he finally stood and turned to face me, the color had drained from him, and his mouth was set in a firm line.

I swallowed, biting my lip to keep it from trembling, and determined to be brave as he approached.

"I'm going to need you to be a big girl for me. Can you do that?" He tried to look calm, but I could tell he was scared.

I nodded, sniffling as a single fat tear rolled down my cheek.

He swiped it away with his thumb before smoothing my hair down. I didn't recognize it then, but reflecting back, it's hard to miss that this is almost the exact interaction I'd had with my mother not too long before. But where one had unsettled me deeply, the other put me at ease. "I need you to watch LJ while I take care of Mom. It looks like you've been doing a good job of it already. Just stay in here until I come and get you, okay?"

"What are you gonna do, Tommy?"

He cocked his head to the side, studying me. "Did you push her down the stairs?"

I dropped my gaze to my feet, nodding slowly. "Is ... is she dead now, like Daddy?"

"Yes, she is."

"I didn't mean to," I whispered, blinking up at him. "She was gonna take me and Lyle away and I got scared and she said you were gonna hurt us and I got mad and ... I didn't mean to," I repeated the last part in a small voice.

Tommy took a long breath in, then released it in a rush and pulled me to him, leaning down so he could crush me to his chest. "I know, Duck." When he finally pulled away to meet my eyes, he continued. "Things are going to be a lot different going forward. Right now, I'm going to move her to the garage before Graham and Sid get home. Once we're all together, we'll talk about what's going to happen, okay? But while I'm ... while I'm moving her, I need you to stay in here with Lyle."

Everything was cleaned up by the time the other two came home from school. Tommy pulled Graham aside while Sid asked how I was feeling and filled me in on the playground gossip, and then Tommy rounded us all up, perching on the coffee table while we sat on the couch, Lyle in Graham's lap. Gently, and with all the steadfast authority he'd cultivated over us throughout our lives, he explained that Momma had an accident, that she'd tripped down the stairs. He told us how important it was that nobody found out what had happened, that we pretended she was still alive or else we'd be separated. He answered what questions he could, and I didn't look at Sid once the whole time, afraid he would see in my face that this new difficulty was my fault.

After, we all hugged each other, burying another secret beneath our sibling bond.

We had meat with dinner that night.

Sid and I didn't know what we were eating at first. It's entirely possible that the older boys never intended to tell us. But we discovered them moving her remains—the parts we couldn't eat—and by that time we'd had days of full bellies and no worries ... I don't expect you or anyone else to understand, because I can't even explain it myself. But we'd all been so content together, we had each other and life had felt settled. And we were young. Perhaps old enough to know better, but so impressionable and eager to emulate our brothers ... Maybe if we weren't so happy, if we hadn't felt so safe, we would have reacted differently, but by the time we learned the source of the meat filling our bellies, we mostly accepted it in stride.

I'm still not sure what emotions Tommy experienced that fateful afternoon or what transpired between him and Graham that resulted in the decision to cannibalize our mother. We never talked about it, and she'd been housebound for so long by that point that no one ever even questioned her absence as far as I'm aware. But I do know that the way Tommy handled everything that day anchored within me the knowledge that I could always count on him, always trust him. Tommy is safe. That has been the single unshakable cornerstone of my life.

I don't want to get ahead of myself, but I feel the need to warn you that Wednesday will be broken up between a few entries, depending on how much I get out at a time. I don't want to rush through it and forget something important, and I know there's no way I have the wherewithal to get it all out at once.

Here we go ...

*Wednesday, June 23rd, 1965*

I'm not sure what I expected the morning to be like. Sid—calm, gentle Sid—has never held on to arguments long. He doesn't hold grudges. I think I figured we could talk over a bowl of oatmeal as the morning sun streamed through the window and be done with whatever space had been driven between us last night.

I certainly didn't expect him to come downstairs (okay, that part about him sleeping in Mak's room I expected) and give me a long, hard stare before saying, "I'm going to start figuring out our finances today. Once I'm done sorting through the paperwork for the house and bed and breakfast, I'm going to the bank to see if they'll let me look at any of the account information."

My mouth dropped open. "You can't just take over our money—my business. And don't you dare say the bed and breakfast belongs to Tommy when you know damn well it's mine."

Sid looked somewhat abashed, but more than anything, he looked tired. "Yours in everything but legality, and I'm not trying to take it. I just want to make sure we have everything sorted so that we're prepared for what happens next. Whatever that may be."

I trembled with the reminder that I owned nothing in the eyes of the law. Bile crawled up my throat. My life is and has always been in the hands of whatever man had his name on the deed to this house, my money safely locked away in the same fashion. "I assume you have an idea of what will happen next, though." My eyes narrowed into a glare, my jaw set.

This time, Sid refused to be goaded into a fight. "I'm going by Graham's after the bank for the same reason. Whatever comes from the sale of his house and whatever he has in savings, we'll move into a new account for Priscilla and the baby. We'll need a lawyer to draft up paperwork giving me rights over everything before any real action can be taken, and when I meet with Tommy and Graham to have them sign it all, I'll make sure that they'll be taken care of, too, however long they may be locked up."

He talked about it all so ... so clinically, so detached. Nausea rolled in my stomach along with an emotion unfamiliar to me in context.

Hate.

But even as I identified the feeling as such, I knew that wasn't the full truth of it. I couldn't hate Sid any more than I could hate Danny or Benny. But I hated the words coming from his mouth. I hated what he was doing.

The shattered pieces of my heart speared into my ribs.

I took a shuddering breath, steeling myself. "Do Lyle and I get a say in the matter?"

Sid's shoulders drooped. "Christ, Ducky, of course you do. I'm not trying to play dictator with your lives. Like I've been saying for the past two days, I'm only trying to be prepared and make sure that you're taken care of. The same thing I've been doing my whole life. I'm not trying to fight with you." He looked at me with so much hurt on his face that I had to turn away.

How could I deal with *his* pain when I hadn't even processed my own? When his was partially rooted in the fact that he couldn't—or wouldn't—understand mine?

"Well, have fun with that, then. I think I'll take breakfast in my room." I grabbed my food and sequestered myself away until I heard the truck rumble off down the drive.

I was antsy, unable to sit still or focus long enough to read or write. With the house to myself—Mak left with Sid, and Lyle had gone out with his friends after one of them called this morning, whatever argument they'd gotten into solved with the boyhood ease of a little time—I did chores to keep myself busy and my mind occupied.

I let the dogs out while I swept and mopped, but Danny laid right by the door the whole time, his head on his paws. His eyes would turn up to me mournfully whenever I stepped out the door to empty the dustpan or dump a bucket of mop water.

I pulled them back inside through the heat of the day, and we lazed around only half watching whatever program was on. Lyle came home and flopped down next to me.

"Get up to anything fun today?"

He shrugged. "We went to the main shore and played some two-hand touch. But then the high schoolers got there and took over."

"Dumb high schoolers," I commiserated.

He grunted his affirmation.

Benny was the only one of us who seemed annoyed not to be zooming around, so I let him out to roam and chase the geese and stopped by the fridge on my way back to the couch. I didn't feel much like cooking, though, and offered up the idea of a scrounge-around dinner as I sat back down. Lyle agreed.

"Did you and Sid get in a fight last night?" he asked after a while.

I glanced over at him, but he wasn't looking at me, focused on digging dirt from under his fingernails. "Why do you ask?"

"You left, and he was really frustrated when he came back inside."

"Did he say anything?"

Lyle met my eyes and shook his head. "What happened?"

I chewed my lip, trying to decide what to tell him.

"I don't need to be protected. I know you all still see me as the baby, but I'm as old as Tommy was when he became man of the house," he said with a pout that undercut the sentiment.

I sighed, shifting so that I could lean my head against his shoulder. "Tommy grew up faster than the rest of us precisely so that we wouldn't have to."

"Did you fight about him?" he asked again, refusing to be steered from the subject.

"Yeah," I conceded. "Sid doesn't think they'll go free. He wants to start preparing for the worst, and ... that's hard for me to think about, is all." As much as I was still upset by last night's conversation and Sid's insistence that Tommy and Graham had lied to us, I couldn't bring myself to pit Lyle against any of his brothers or give reason to doubt them.

He was quiet for a while, and then he asked, "Will we have to leave Delight?"

"I don't know."

Danny raised his head, floppy ears perked forward. Then he lurched to his feet and ran, whining, to the front door as I heard the faint purr of the truck's engine coming up the drive. For better or worse, Sid was home.

I stood to open the door, and Danny ran out to the truck. He briefly greeted Sid and Mak, then circled the car, his head tilting to the side as he sniffed all around it, periodically letting out a high-pitched whine.

He was looking for Tommy.

My heart squeezed painfully, tears blurring my vision as I watched the bloodhound toss his head back and howl. The mournful sound tore through my soul.

I'm only a little ashamed to admit that I gathered all that emotion and bundled it into my anger with Sid. I didn't want to hear about how the bank trip went or what our options were for the house and the bed and breakfast. I wanted him to hurt like I hurt. Like Lyle hurt. Like Danny hurt. If a pure soul like Danny could love Tommy so fiercely, he couldn't be that bad at all, could he?

For the first time since Tommy was arrested, the need for action flooded my muscles, and my prey drive kicked on full force.

It was time to see RJ again.

I went inside to change, dressing in my favorite pair of denim shorts (They're cut-offs that I altered from an old pair of Sid's pants. They're worn and comfortable, but more importantly, they do <u>great</u> things for my butt.) and a red plaid button down tucked in, sleeves rolled and unbuttoned just enough to show a bit of cleavage. I brushed out my hair, teasing the roots to give it plenty of volume, and pinned it back from my face with a black head-band. Mascara, blush, and lipstick and my look was complete.

Not to be vain, but I would eat me.

I tied on my white sneakers and headed out.

All three boys glanced up when I walked past the living room, stopping by the kitchen to tuck a syringe into my pocket. The carnival was already packed away by now, but maybe there'd be cooking around a final bonfire. Better safe than sorry, at any rate.

"Where are you going?" Sid asked.

"The carnival grounds," I tossed the reply over my shoulder, "to visit a friend. I'll probably be out late."

I slipped out the door into the golden light of evening, but Sid followed, catching my arm before I could make it off the porch.

"What do you think you're doing?" he demanded quietly, even though the door was closed.

I jerked my arm out of his grasp. "I'm hunting, Sid." I met his eyes defiantly.

"And where are you planning to put him now that the cabin is a crime scene, hmm? Here at the house?"

"Of course not." I hadn't thought that far ahead, but there was still time to figure out those specifics. I tugged free of his hold, crossing my arms defiantly. "I'll cart him through the forest in a Radio Flyer if I have to. It's none of your concern. You take care of our family your way; I'll take care of it mine."

His expression went from shock to something heartbroken and desperate. "Don't do this. Don't be this stubborn, Ducky, please. I know you think you're proving something, but let go of this misguided loyalty before you get in trouble, too." His pleas came out as orders, and I bristled. "You don't have to be like them to be strong. Admitting you're in the wrong, changing—that's real strength. You don't have to be what Tommy made you."

It was the insinuation that I wasn't capable of thinking for myself that pushed me over the edge. I wanted to hurt him. So I threw in his face the only truth I have ever kept from him.

"Tommy didn't kill our mother," I said, tilting my chin up and meeting his gaze with a cold, even glare. "I did."

I watched the last light of love and hope sputter and die in my brother's eyes before I turned away, stalking off toward my prey.

In case you forgot, Sunday had been the last day of the carnival, with this week spent tearing everything down and preparing to move on to the next location. By the look of things, they were fully prepared to hit the road in the morning.

It's uncanny, the way the world had continued to move on while I was too caught up in my family falling apart to participate.

But I was finished wallowing and ready to reinsert myself into a prominent role in the making of things. I'd also worked out how to use my few days' disappearance to my benefit. If RJ knew that there was trouble at home, and I hinted that I might be thinking about leaving, he would have no suspicions when I showed up at their next stop. He might even suggest we go somewhere private so that we can talk and he can console me. All I had to do was plant that seed in his mind and make him believe that I would miss him.

The grounds looked completely different from when I last saw them, nothing but a dirt lot with sparse patches of grass and bits of machinery strapped to long trailers dotting the area. People milled about, but ignored me as I wove my way through bundles of canvas and cable and metalwork toward where the trailers and tents were still set up.

I rapped on the door of a familiar fifth wheel. Hock opened it, his surprise quickly fading into a warm amusement. "Got yourself a visitor, RJ," he spoke over his shoulder before stepping back to let me in. "Good to see you, townie."

"Hey, weren't we just about to go do a thing?" Jess ushered Hock out the door, giving me a salacious wink as he passed.

"Subtle," I said as the door latched behind me, leaving me alone with RJ.

"They're knuckleheads." He shot me an apologetic smile and held his hand out to guide me down next to him on the couch. The sheets and blankets were folded up and balancing behind us. "I'm glad to see you again. I thought I wouldn't have the chance."

I folded my hands in my lap, wringing them together a bit. "Sorry I've been absent. I didn't mean to be, after ..." I peeked up at him, blushing. "After last time. But it's been, well, quite a disruptive few days at home."

He tucked a finger under my chin, lifting my face so that I met his eyes. "I'm sorry to hear that. Did you wanna talk about it?"

I bit my lip, shrugging. "I don't want you to think less of me. I think ... well, people in town already do."

He cupped the back of my neck, pulling me in to place a kiss on my forehead. "Nothing could lessen my opinion of you, Mallory-mallard."

The audacity of this man using a name that didn't belong to him had my hackles raising. I pulled back, letting out a little shuddering breath as I calmed myself. He was not the enemy, and I was in control here. "Did you hear about those people who were killed last week? My brothers were arrested for the murders." I bit my lip, letting tears sting my eyes as I blinked woefully up at him.

His brows lifted, and he pushed a grease-stained hand through his blonde mop. "Oh, wow." Whatever he'd expected from me, it probably wasn't that. Based on the brief flash of relief I caught in his eyes, I almost thought maybe he'd expected me to say I was pregnant or something. "Well, screw whatever these fussy back-mountain inbreds think. Just because your brothers did something bad don't mean you had anything to do with it."

"My brothers _didn't_ kill them," I said, feeling my chest grow tight. It shouldn't matter what he thought about them—he'd be dead by July—but I couldn't stand the thought of a single other person thinking them capable of that kind of mindless brutality.

RJ gave me a sympathetic look, and the pity in his expression made my stomach curdle.

"It wasn't them," I repeated through gritted teeth.

His expression softened, an emotion I couldn't recognize in his eyes. He stood, moving to the kitchen. "This kind of crappy situation calls for a drink. Your brothers are lucky to have you, you know. Not many people are capable of that kind of loyalty." _That kahhnd of lohlltee_, I internally mimicked.

I huffed, the best show of humor I could muster in the moment. "I'm the one that's lucky to have them." I shook my head, sinking back into the cushions. "I just don't know what to do."

A soft _pop_ answered me as RJ uncorked a bottle of wine. "Is there anything I can do to help?" he asked, glancing at me as he poured two cups. "I can stay behind when the troupe leaves if you need me."

"No!" I said, too emphatically, and calmed my tone. "I mean, I don't think there's anything you can do. And I couldn't ask you to interrupt your life like that. I more meant ... Oh, I don't know. Maybe I have grown up too much for this town. Maybe I don't need to stick around." I offered a small smile and accepted the short glass tumbler he handed to me. "I really appreciate that you'd even offer, though."

RJ sat down next to me, draping an arm over the back of the couch behind me. I fought the urge to roll my eyes, but played my part of helpless girl and leaned into him. I hated that his warmth actually was a comfort. "Of course I would offer," he says, dropping his hand to my shoulder and making small circles over the bone with his thumb. "If anyone can understand the impulse to run away, it's current company."

The rhythmic slide of his skin over the fabric of my sleeve grated on me, and I fought the urge to shake him off.

"I know we agreed this was nothing serious, Mallory, but that don't mean I don't genuinely care about you."

I almost missed my reaction cue because I was too focused on the tight press of my teeth against each other, fighting the urge to sink them into his thumb for that maddening, incessant motion. I reached up to clasp his hand, squeezing his fingers and tipping my face up to look at him with wide eyes. "Thank you."

He kissed the tip of my nose, then clinked the rim of his glass to mine, leaned back, and took a long drink. I released him and brought my own cup to my mouth, taking a sip of the red wine.

It coated my tongue, the dry, fruity notes undercut with a familiar bitter aftertaste that brought me straight back to the night of the bonfire, watching Olive dance.

I bit the inside of my cheek, overcome with the thought that I'd made the wrong decision. Why hadn't I gone to see her instead? Why was I so hotheaded and quick to lean into anger? What I needed was comfort, but instead I'd chosen to exacerbate Sid's anger to prove some sort of point.

God, I was an idiot.

Taking another long drink of the bitter wine to drown my misery, I sank further into the couch, rolling my head to RJ. "Tell me more about what it's like living as a carny?" I requested, not really caring, but feeling like it was too soon after my arrival to leave. Now that I'd gotten into my own head, that's all I really wanted, and I was remiss to attempt any meaningful conversation.

RJ seemed more than happy to distract me in this way, though, regaling me with tales of his early days with the troupe while I drained the last of the wine from my glass. I rubbed my tongue against the roof of my mouth, trying not to pull a face at the lingering bitterness.

My thoughts had turned to how I'd handled things with Sid, and I felt sick with how cruel I'd been to him, throwing our mother's death in his face like that when he was so clearly struggling. I'd been selfish, so wrapped up in my own crap that I hadn't taken the time to notice any of the signs he'd been giving me since returning home. If I'd only thought to call Olive, she could have calmed me down, let me wallow in my own feelings without needing to wound someone else.

I chewed on the inside of my lip, the weight of my misery seeming to pull me deeper into the cushions. Blinking, I refocused my attention on RJ.

Or attempted to, at least. My vision kept wanting to slide away, and the quality of his voice was strange. I shook my head to clear it, pushing myself up on alarmingly noodle-like arms and immediately falling back into the couch. "RJ," I said, concentrating too hard for control of my tongue. "I feel ... strange."

"Don't worry, darlin'. It's probably just the stress. You're just fine, ain't ya?" he soothed.

My fingers let go of the empty glass, letting it rest between my thigh and the cushion, and the first cold touch of fear raised the hair on the back of my neck.

RJ stroked my hair, watching me with a pleased smile now.

"I'm sorry about your brothers. Bad luck for them, huh? But it'll make your disappearance less suspicious. I might even keep you for a while, being as you've already been considering splittin' town."

A breathy whimper passed my lips as I tried to push myself away from him, my hands feeling like they belonged to someone else. "What ...? What are you ... talking about?"

He grinned, running a knuckle along my cheek. "I want to tell you something before you slip under, in case I don't get another chance. 'Cause I got a feeling when you wake back up you won't be much inclined to listen, but it's important to me that you hear this, because it really is a compliment."

Too late, every alarm in my brain triggered, blaring as my heart thumped sluggishly against my ribs. Fear spread through me with an icy chill, amplifying the bitter taste lingering on my tongue.

That same bitter taste as the wine he had poured for me at the bonfire, unattended while I watched Olive. My mind unfolded now, bleary but slowly sharpening as adrenaline flooded my system. I remembered that night, my inebriated assumption that being with her had been better than any drug or drink, and ignoring it after that first initial sip of bitterness. RJ's soft insistence that I drink it anyway. His same insistence the night we copulated. The beat of my heart painfully stumbled up a notch, and I curled one arm up to press against my chest as my breathing hitched into quick, shallow pants.

I'd been drugged.

RJ clicked his tongue and slapped my cheek a couple of times. It stung, and I snapped my eyes to him, trying to pull back. "Hang on, Mallory, stay with me."

"I'm going ... to kill you," I seethed, fighting dizziness as I focused all of my energy on motor function.

"There she is." He grinned.

I dropped my hand to my lap, leaning back, away from him.

"You know no one's ever made me work so hard before? Sixteen months I've been doing this, and you were the first that ever presented a real challenge. I had so much fun luring you in, you know that? I'm really glad I was the one lucky enough to lay claim to you." He sighed wistfully, glancing away. "I wasn't sure you would come back. You're just so unpredictable. So I got a little greedy and let Jess talk me into settling for your little lover."

As soon as his eyes left me, I began the battle of worming my fingers into my pocket, but his words made me pause. I blinked, struggling to pull in a deep breath as a new form of terror stirred within me.

"I was a little worried, before you came back and damn near jumped my bones. I almost thought you were one of them homosexual perverts, the way the two of you eyed each other during the bonfire. But I guess that was just her."

Olive.

Fuck.

<u>He had Olive</u>.

Blood roared in my ears, my entire body going numb as rage attempted to boil through the drugs in my blood.

Looking smug as could be, RJ kissed my temple before rising to refill his wine.

I barely waited for his back to turn before leaning further into the cushions, shifting my hips to better get at my pocket. My fingers were still clumsy despite the fury and fear dousing me with adrenaline. Whatever he'd given me was doing its damndest to pull me under.

I finally managed to pull the syringe from my pocket, slinging my other arm over my lap to pull the cap from the needle. Sweat beaded my upper lip, every part of my body either buzzing or gone fully numb, and my vision kept swimming in and out as I tried to watch RJ's progress in the kitchen.

A sob caught in my throat as my fingers once again slipped from the plastic cap. I was running out of time. With a grunt of effort, I threw my hand up to my face, knocking into my cheek, but catching the end of the syringe between my teeth.

"Whoa, whatcha got there?" RJ asked.

I choked on a scream, jerking my head to the side to pull the cap free, then focusing on turning my wrist as my hand fell, plunging the needle into the meat of my thigh. I could barely feel the pinch when it broke skin, almost scared that I'd missed my leg altogether and sunk the needle into the couch. But RJ was making fast strides back to me, and it was all I could do to fumble my thumb over the plunger and press.

Want to know some fun medical trivia?

Anaphylaxis is a phenomenon created when the immune system mistakes a substance as harmful, resulting in an overreaction that can include hives, swelling, and difficulty breathing, among other things. The first response to severe anaphylaxis is to ensure that the individual suffering doesn't succumb to full shock—keep the airways open, keep the heart pumping—which is achieved through an intramuscular dose of epinephrine.

From a medication standpoint, epinephrine is a synthetically produced adrenaline, and the dosage to treat anaphylaxis is several times stronger than the amount of adrenaline typically produced by the body in a fight-or-flight response.

This may seem like a lot of random gee-whiz information, but remember my dandy little (extreme) nut allergy? This is the sort of thing you gain interest in after nearly being killed by banana bread. Anyway, back to the main event.

Pure adrenaline hit my bloodstream as RJ loomed over me, the groggy effect of the drug he'd given me washed away. My heart rate doubled; my chest expanded, giving my lungs room to inflate; and energy swept through my muscles.

All newly re-gained control of my body was given over to emotion.

In one motion, I grabbed my glass from beside me and swung it into RJ's head. The impact against his temple echoed up my arm, but the thick crystal didn't shatter. So I hit him again. And again, in quick succession, so that he was dazed enough to be pushed to the floor. I spit the cap from my mouth and pulled the syringe from my leg before sliding down to straddle him, bracing one wrist against the linoleum and slamming the bottom edge of the glass down on his hand. There was a series of satisfying pops as at least a few of his knuckles broke beneath my assault, and he cried out in agony.

I took the opportunity to shove the same glass edge into his mouth, forcing his jaw open as I took hold of his other wrist, pinning it to the ground with my weight while he cradled his broken hand to his chest. "If you struggle, I will make sure every last one of your teeth is broken, understand?" I pushed the glass further into his straining mouth to emphasize my point.

RJ let out a guttural noise, his teeth clicking and scraping against it, and I took that for agreement, easing up slightly.

"Where is she?" I demanded.

His chest heaved as he glared up at me, and I slowly pulled the glass from his mouth. "Go to hell, you filthy who—"

I slammed the glass into his face, and he screamed, bucking wildly underneath me as blood and shards of his front teeth fell to the back of his throat. He managed to roll, and I scrambled off of him as he braced himself on his knees and one good hand, the broken one placed shakily under his mouth as he coughed up blood and bone.

He wailed again, and I drove the glass into his temple. This time, the rim broke, slicing into his scalp as he fell to the floor. Blood dribbled from his mouth and leaked from the gash in his head as I stood over him. Then I dropped the glass and walked over to the kitchen, tearing through drawers. I found a paring knife that looked both sharp and sturdy and slid it through the two belt loops at my back, then spied a large toolbox just inside the bedroom and selected a long wrench with a lot of weight to it.

It would do.

I returned to RJ, whose chest still shuddered with breath, and knelt down, brushing blonde hair back from his bloody temple. "I had such plans for you." I sighed, taking that moment to mourn what would never be, and then I slammed the wrench down on the divot in his skull until there was a sizable dent.

Satisfied he wouldn't be coming after me, I slipped from the trailer.

I didn't need to go far to find Jess and Hock. They were leaning against a stack of crates only a few yards away, smoking while a transistor radio blared "Who Put the Bomp." Thankfully, they were alone.

I walked up to them, wrench hanging by my side. They both stood straight when they saw me, surprise plain on their faces because they never expected me to walk out of that trailer.

"Where is Olive?" I asked.

Hock shot Jess a glance, stepping closer to me. "I don't know what RJ told—"

I interrupted him by swinging the wrench into the side of his knee with a wet crack that was perfectly timed to the first *ram* in Barry's *ram-alama-ding-dong*. He dropped, but before a scream could fully claw its way from his chest, I had the wrench flying against the side of his face. The impact reverberated up my arms and completely cut off his cry as he slumped forward, blood spilling from his head.

Jess's shock morphed into terror as I stepped over Hock's body, adjusting my grip on the wrench as I went. "<u>Where is she?</u>" I demanded lowly.

Jess stammered silently before finding his voice. "There's a box trailer over by the bonfire circle. She's in there."

My head dropped to the side with a smile. "That wasn't so difficult, was it?"

"She's fine; we didn't touch her. RJ wanted her, but he'd been busy. So we were just holding her 'till ..." He swallowed thickly and changed tactics, his entire body trembling. "It wasn't personal, you understand. It's just our thing, our own little form of stress relief, y'know? RJ picked you, but then that got too complicated I guess, and—anyway, three of the others had already been discovered, see, so ..." He gave a shaky chuckle, shrugging with his arms out, as though apologetic.

And that's when I finally put two and two together.

The <u>carnies</u> had killed those people and gotten my brothers sent to jail.

This new information raged through me like a forest fire. They'd ruined my hunt. They'd torn apart my family. They'd taken Olive. Adrenaline still pumped through my blood, and I visibly trembled with the righteous desire for action.

Jess seemed to see what was boiling under my skin, because he took a step forward, hands still out in supplication. "Gabby's the one that flubbed the one guy, with the car. She's irresponsible. And it wasn't—it wasn't—please, don't kill me," he finished with a quiet, rather pathetic whimper.

I shifted my gaze from his face to over his shoulder, my brow knitting in confusion as I stepped forward with a sharp intake of breath.

Jess twisted to see what I was looking at, and I closed the distance between us, whipping the wrench between his legs as I did so. Air whistled between his teeth, and his hands cupped his balls. His whole face flushed purple in the moment before he dropped to his knees with a haggard, strangled cry. Spittle flew from between his lips as he tried to breathe through what I can imagine was great pain.

It was only right of me to put him out of his misery.

By the time the music faded out to the show host introducing one of Lesley Gore's greatest hits, the top of the wrench was clotted with blood, hair, and chips of bone, but I didn't waste time cleaning it as I stalked through the tents and trailers. I had to find Olive and get out of there before someone had the chance to find the bodies and raise an alarm.

The box trailer was where Jess had said it would be, and I set my wrench down on the bumper to unlatch it, flinching at the rattle of wood and metal when I pushed the door up.

But my fear of discovery was quickly overpowered by that flame of all-consuming rage when I saw Olive hunched against a stack of boxes, hands behind her back, ankles tied, and a gag around her mouth. Dried blood stuck to the side of her face, trickling from her hairline, and I could just distinguish the dark shadows of bruises across her arms and throat in the dim light.

"Olive," I breathed, vaulting up into the trailer. My knees hit the worn wooden floorboards, and I immediately went to work at the tight knot on her gag. Tears spilled down her cheeks, and she was trembling so hard I was surprised the whole trailer wasn't shaking. I gently shushed her, muttering some nonsense about everything being fine now when I was so full of the blinding desire for revenge that I struggled to keep my eyes focused.

Finally, I had the knot free and pulled it from her mouth before shifting to work on her hands. "You're here," she said raggedly, her breath hitching.

"Did they hurt you?" I asked, cursing as I chipped paint from a nail trying to dig at the knots.

"Just bumps and bruises, mostly, but my wrists really hurt. What are you doing here? Are you okay?"

"Hmm?" I was distracted, biting back a groan of frustration as my fingers slipped on the knots again. Then, in a burst of clarity, I remembered the knife I'd slipped into my belt loops and pulled it free. "Hold still." Her hands were free moments later, and she brought them in front of her, gingerly touching where her skin had been rubbed raw by the rough fibers while I moved back in front of her to cut through the bindings at her feet.

"Mallory, you ... Is that blood?"

I paused, registering for the first time the damp spray across my shirt, the drying speckles of gore over my legs. My heart lodged in my throat. She had never seen my violence, and I was suddenly scared of how she would react to knowing what I had done with the wrench.

I knew this was not the time for conversation, but I said it anyway as I finished cutting through the rope, then slid the knife back into my waistline so I could touch her. "They tried to drug me, and they told me they'd taken you. I ... I did what I had to." My fingers moved from her face down her arms, flitting over the exposed skin as I assured myself that she was okay.

Fresh tears glittered in the dark pools of her eyes, and she threw her arms around me. "I didn't think I would ever see you again." Her voice broke.

It felt like my ribs cracked open, and if she hadn't been pressed to my chest, I bet you could've seen my heart straining toward her like a Looney Tunes moment, if one could ever be so macabre.

I had almost lost her without even knowing she needed me, and that hurt more than anything else that had happened over the past few days. The thought was unbearable, tightening my chest to the point I couldn't breathe. Holding her there in the dark, the truth that had been holed away in my chest for five long years fought to burrow its way out of me. "I'm sorry it took me so long to find you," I choked out.

She just shook her head, then pulled back to scan my face like she was drinking me in, like she couldn't quite believe I was actually there.

I knew that it was only a matter of time before someone came looking for us, but I was so hopped up on adrenaline and the full weight of the relief at seeing her in one piece that I just … I don't remember deciding to move. One moment I was brushing her hair from her face, and the next I was leaning forward to kiss her.

Her lips were soft and warm, and the world completely unwound around me until her hands touched my shoulders. My heart plummeted to my stomach, and I braced myself for her to push me away, prepared myself to see the revulsion and horror in her eyes. But between one heartbeat and the next, her fingers curled into me, pulling me closer, and a small sigh escaped her.

Nothing I'd ever done could compare to the rush that filled me as her mouth moved against mine, as I swept my tongue over the swell of her bottom lip, threading my fingers into her hair and holding her there. She tasted sweeter than anything I had ever experienced, and it took all of my willpower to pull away from her.

Her eyes fluttered open, her mouth parted as she stared at me.

There was no time to decipher what was written on her face. "You are the most beautiful thing in this world, and I love you with all that I am," I whispered, needing her to know this, needing to acknowledge it for myself. I gripped her hands, looking away before she had a chance to reply. "We need to leave. Can you run?"

"Yeah," her voice sounded shaky, and her fingers laced

through mine. "I can manage."

My heart drilled a frantic rhythm in my chest as I helped her down from the trailer, grabbing the wrench along the way. I tried to lead her along through the shadows, toward the trees where we could make a run for it.

We'd almost made it when a cry broke out behind us. I swallowed against the urge to vomit, pulling Olive behind a stack of crates. "Go to the house and call the police."

"Mally, what? I'm not leaving you."

"I'll follow as soon as I can. I promise. I'm just going to create a distraction so they don't chase us down."

She shook her head, clinging to me. "No, I won't lea—"

"<u>Go</u>," I whispered the order with all the conviction within me, and she swallowed, tears cutting tracks through the dirt on her face as she finally nodded. "Into the woods, then south toward home."

Olive stared at me for one heartbeat that seemed to stretch on forever, and I was terrified to misinterpret what I thought I saw shining in her dark eyes. Then she kissed me, narrowing my entire awareness until she was the only thing that existed for a dangerous couple of seconds. "You'd better come back to me," she breathed against my mouth before turning to run for the treeline.

I only gave myself a short moment to watch her retreat before running back toward the center of camp, noise rising around me as I tightened my grip on the wrench and pulled the knife from my shorts.

I don't know how I killed so many of them. Maybe it was still an element of surprise, nobody expecting a girl to be deadly. Maybe it was just that most of the carnies weren't fighters. Maybe it was the meat that fueled my body, years of symbolic dominance manifesting physically in that streak of adrenaline and rage-fed violence.

Nobody even thought to check the woods, thanks to the trail of bodies I left following me deeper into camp.

The first was easiest to sneak up on. I think it was Di, the magician's assistant. I brought the wrench down at the junction of her neck and collarbone, the latter emitting a loud, wet *snap*. She screamed, high and shrill and full of agony, then I dragged the knife across her throat with a quick, sharp tug, not giving the blade a chance to catch on muscle and tendon.

I was moving before she hit the ground.

Wielding the wrench with one hand was more difficult than I expected, though. The next person I met tried to catch my swing, but misjudged it, and the weight of the tool broke his thumb. He howled with an anger that almost matched mine, grabbing my wrist with his opposite hand and pulling me closer. He didn't see the knife in my other hand, which I stabbed into his gut and pulled sideways and down, ripping open a gash in his abdomen.

He released me to hold in his intestines, and I ran, knowing he was as good as dead.

My wrist hurt where he'd ground my bones together, and I flexed it, trying to think. Distraction was my goal—keep as many of them preoccupied as possible so I could get away. And if a few of them barbecued in the process ...

I went back to RJ's trailer, knowing I'd be able to find stuff to start a fire and hoping they wouldn't expect me to return there.

I only ran into one person on the way, and he was armed with a pipe. It slammed into my arm, dull pain rippling down the bone in such a shocking wave that I dropped the knife. Tears sprung to my eyes, and I narrowly ducked a blow aimed at my head, dropping into a crouch and nearly falling backward.

With both hands around the handle of the wrench, I jammed it awkwardly toward his ankle, and he hopped to the side with a cry. Gritting my teeth against the pain in my own arm, I pushed forward, headbutting him right in the gut as the pipe glanced off my shoulder. I screamed, but kept my footing as he stumbled backward, then gathered all of the pain into anger and swung the wrench at his face.

Blood burst free from his nose or broken teeth or both, and I ran, sucking in breaths through the sharp, grinding agony in my shoulder. I was confused by the way it seemed to overtake my mind. No one had struck me since that day when I was six, and I was unused to that sort of pain.

I shook my head to clear it, hauling myself into RJ's trailer.

He was still lying on the floor, slowly rotting and useless. I spit on him for wasting my time, depriving me of my hunt, and most of all, for taking Olive. His stupid, pretty face wasn't so much to look at with his skull caved in and his teeth spilled down his throat.

I grabbed the sheet from the back of the couch, knotted one corner to the stove burner, and threw the rest out about the kitchen. I turned the burner on, watching as the fire caught the fabric, then turned to leave.

I stopped next to RJ, crouching beside him and pulling his jaw open wider so I could reach in a pinch a tooth between my fingers. I cleaned it on the hem of his shirt as the flames grew behind me, then slipped it into my pocket.

I left the trailer armed with my wrench, this time with the goal of leaving the campground and waiting for help to arrive. Sharp pain shot up my shoulder when I rotated it, bones grinding together in a way that churned my stomach, but I couldn't think of that now.

"You little bitch." Gabby materialized from the shadows ahead of me, a knife held in her outstretched hand. "You killed the boys."

Something popped in the trailer behind me, and then glass flew everywhere as the windows blew out, the entire thing going up in a ball of flame. Shards of debris stung my back and my legs as I tripped forward, away from the wall of heat.

Gabby flinched, and I took the opportunity to throw myself at her. We crashed into the dirt, and she yowled like a mad cougar as I scrambled on top of her, raising my arms. The pain from my shoulder sent a flare of light across my eyes. Before I could bring the wrench down, she stabbed me, her knife skating across my rib and ripping my side open with a fresh heat that tore a scream from my throat. She looked up at me with wide, terrified eyes, as though wondering why the blade hadn't sunk in, and then she looked at nothing, because I beat her face in with the wrench.

I scrambled off of her, pressing a hand to my side, trying to staunch the flow of blood as I hurried toward the edge of camp.

But I was exhausted, adrenaline flagging from my system as

I stumbled through the dark, firelight dancing behind me. And I'd taken too long with Gabby. People were coming to investigate the fire, and I was now leaving a trail of blood.

"Grab her!" someone called out, and my heart lurched into my throat. The thud of my pulse seemed to slow, blood roared in my ears, and I turned, dropping my side to hold the wrench in both hands as I faced the group of carnies behind me.

I would not lead them home, but neither would I go down without a fight. As I surveyed the group before me, I tried to calculate how long it had been since Olive had left. Sid would have called the sheriff, which meant help should arrive soon.

Soon. Such a relative word that really means nothing.

I grinned, blood splatters pulling with my stretched cheeks. The man approaching me went from angry to unnerved at my lack of perceptible fear, and I leapt at him, viciously swinging the wrench.

I caught his jaw, but fighting someone who's ready for you is an entirely different ball game. And so is fighting multiple opponents.

A few broken fingers, a few smashed teeth—I threw myself at them, screaming my rage, but they also landed a few blows of their own, and next thing I knew, I was on my knees in the dirt with a hand in my hair and a knife at my throat.

Drying blood pulled uncomfortably at the skin of my neck as my head was forced violently backwards, baring my throat. I laughed, licking blood from my lips and letting my eyelids drift closed. The tang of copper coated my tongue, thickening my saliva as I swallowed.

I was tired. My lungs ached, my legs stung from where they'd been peppered with shrapnel, and the muscles in my arms burned now that I'd finally stopped moving. My shoulder was a dull agony that fuzzied the edges of my focus, and my side continued to leak a wet warmth down my torso.

"Drop it," the man holding me ordered, and I felt the cold flat of a blade against my esophagus. I only laughed more—half for the fact that I hadn't even realized my fingers, sticky with my own congealing blood, were still wrapped around the wrench and half for the inefficient angle of the knife.

"Bite me," I invited.

His fist tightened in my hair. "I'm not joking around, girl. You've caused us a hell of a lot of problems tonight, and you're going to answer for it if I—" His rant was cut off as a gunshot split the night. Then he slumped to the side, releasing me.

There was a moment of stillness, as though no one could quite wrap their head around what had happened. Then another crack, another man—Mags, maybe?—spinning, a spray of blood flying out in an arc from the hole blown through his shoulder, and the camp erupted into chaos.

A blinding wave of relief washed over me as I pushed to my feet, lunging into a stumbling run toward the direction of the firing. I'm not into guns. I know almost nothing about them. But I know the sound of a Remington 721.

I saw the muzzle flash of the next shot. Sid was close, and I almost tripped over my feet in my rush to close the distance between us.

Between the gunshots and the trailer fire that was blazing strong in the night, threatening to spread as the wind picked up, I wasn't being pursued. Sid dropped the rifle, holding it to one side and reaching out a hand to me as I drew close.

As soon as my fingers grasped his, he turned with me and ran. "Just to the treeline, then we can stop," he promised, pulling me along.

I dug deep for a second wind, throwing my legs as far as I could, refusing to falter now when we were so close to making it out.

My lungs burned, my shoulder screamed with every movement, and I was quickly flagging. But then we were through the trees, and Sid pulled me to his chest before I could collapse to the forest floor.

I wrapped my arms around him, tears leaking from my eyes as I felt the steady beat of his heart against my cheek. All I could remember was the way he'd looked at me when I'd spoken to him earlier, thrown bitter truths in his face in a fit of anger that now felt so childish, and I clung to him tighter, not wanting to see what was in his eyes now that I was covered in blood, not just a hunter, but a killer by every definition.

Sid pushed gently at my shoulders. "You're bleeding, Ducky, let me look."

I kept my gaze downcast, stepping back as he peeled the soaked fabric of my shirt from my abdomen. "That's quite a knick there, sister." He bent down, removing one of his socks and pressing it to the wound. I hissed at the fresh pain, but didn't protest as he grabbed my hands, placing them over the makeshift bandage. "Keep some pressure there. We'll get it cleaned out when help arrives. Are you hurt anywhere else?" He scanned me from head to toe, brushing debris from my calves and thighs.

Carny blood covered my body; I could feel it drying on my skin, tight and itchy. "Just my shoulder, I think. It hurts to move."

He nodded, pulling me back to his chest, one hand cupped around the back of my head. The night was catching up to me, and my emotions were unraveling faster than I could string them back together. A lump formed in my throat, fresh tears cutting tracks through the blood on my cheeks.

The orange glow of the fire was joined by flashing red as emergency vehicles appeared around the bend in the road, and I prepared myself to pull it together, to tell this final part of the story so that my brothers' names might be cleared. But there was another reconciliation I needed to make first. Selfishly, the most important one.

"Siddy." I pulled back a little, looking up at him, surprised to find tears spilling down his freckled cheeks.

"I'm sorry."

It came from both of us, simultaneously.

Even though that was far from the end of the night, nothing that came after was bigger than that.

I haven't done much since Wednesday other than rest. The end of that night was a whirlwind. I gave my statement to the police while one of them cleaned and patched my side under Sid's watchful eye. They gave us a ride home so I could shower and change into clean clothes while they talked to Olive. We were given instructions to both see a doctor in the morning, then meet them at the sheriff's office for a more extensive debrief, but they left us alone to sleep for the night.

Olive's parents showed up while the police were still there, fawning over her and crying. She'd been gone for just over a day. They'd assumed she was just with me and had forgotten to call, and were overcome with guilt that she'd been taken and gratitude for me for having saved her. I think it was the first time Piney ever hugged me.

Much of yesterday is also a blur. I have eleven stitches in my left side and a hairline fracture across my right scapula. After the doctor, I retold what happened at the carnival grounds while Lachlan and Rosenfield listened intently, butting in to ask questions every now and again. Once satisfied, they told me that one of the carnies caved very quickly under interrogation, admitting to multiple murders across the West Coast and naming all who were involved in hopes of striking a plea bargain. Graham and

Tommy were still being held pending trial for kidnapping the man found at the cabin, but they were no longer being charged with manslaughter. There is also still the matter of the jar of teeth, which are being checked against dental records of missing persons, but only time will tell if anything comes of it.

Both Sid's actions and mine were filed under self defense.

The rest of yesterday I spent either asleep or writing down everything I remembered from Wednesday, then I finally caved and took some of the pain pills the doctor had given me.

I slept deeply, my body more exhausted than I'd realized. I didn't wake up today until well into the afternoon. Sid made me a sandwich while I called Olive. We didn't talk long, but it was good to hear her voice and learn that her injuries were much less severe than mine.

Sid watched me when I hung up, leading me over to the couch and handing me a grilled cheese. "How is she?"

I shrugged my good shoulder, a lump forming in my throat as I stared at the sandwich in my lap. Everything was suddenly so uncertain—<u>is</u> uncertain, and I still can't even begin to wrap my head around it. I wanted to fix whatever had broken between me and Sid, though. I couldn't begin to figure anything else out until I knew we were fully okay, and we hadn't talked yet. "Is Mak around?" I asked.

"He took Lyle for a grocery run a little before you woke up, and I wouldn't be surprised if they made a pit stop to peruse whatever comics hit the shelf last night."

I felt queasy and anxious, but forced myself to take a bite of food. Chew. Swallow. Another bite. I wanted to speak, but I didn't even know where to begin.

"I'm sorry for how heated things got the other day," Sid said softly.

I forced another bite, because if I tried to talk, I would cry.

He slumped into the couch at my side, scraping his thumbnail across the weave of his jeans. "I should have just talked to you when I got home, but I … I was scared, I guess. I'd spent so long away, and I didn't want to risk alienating myself from you guys. From you." He swallowed. "I don't want to be a part of this anymore, Ducky. I <u>can't</u>." He finally looked at me, his eyes full of the misery that laced his voice.

My chest tightened painfully, panic fluttering just beneath my skin as I met his gaze. I opened my mouth, but no words came out. I was frozen.

"But I also don't know how to exist if you hate me. I don't want to fight with you."

His words tapped something free, releasing the pressure building inside me. My vision blurred with tears. "<u>I</u> don't want to fight with <u>you</u>. I need you; I always have."

I think if we'd had this talk prior to the carnies almost killing me, it would have gone a lot differently. But that night shifted fundamental parts of both of us. We were both more willing to see things from the other's perspective. Sid was willing to give more ground than he otherwise would have, and I was much less quick to jump to the defensive.

We talked long into the evening, moving to the dock when Mak and Lyle returned. It wasn't an easy conversation, but it was necessary, and by the end of the night, we'd come to an understanding.

I can't explain the sheer panic that overwhelmed me at the thought of never hunting again. I need that control, that feeling of dominance. The men I've hunted, the people I've killed … society will never hinder their ilk from using the helplessness and weakness of others to make themselves feel powerful. But I can. And if they're dead anyway, what is the harm in eating them? Because I love that, too. It's part of what satiates me, and I just … I need it. It's too much a part of me. Maybe, eventually, I'll wean myself off, but thinking about doing so now makes it impossible to breathe.

I know Sid doesn't get it, and I understand why he doesn't want anything to do with it, but he agreed to let me keep hunting and to let me teach Lyle. That acquiescence was made under partial duress, because I think Sid knows that I would never exclude Lyle if he wanted to go, but the rules have been updated.

1. Only hunt people who have actively endangered the life of another.
2. No hunting within 100 miles or within county lines, whichever is further. (I won't tell Sid, but in a way, this added spatial challenge might make the hunt more fun.)
3. No feeding kills to other people.
4. No bringing anything home, restrictions to include but not limited to: clothing, accessories, body parts, and meat. Anything we want to consume has to be gone by the time we cross the threshold. (He tried to say only eat in the field, but I argued the ethics of wasting less if road trip snacks were allowed.)
5. One hunt per calendar year.
6. If any suspicion is brought up—if ever even once authorities question us again—it all stops.

This is the compromise we came to, sitting shoulder to shoulder in the moonlight. It looks so simple written down, when in reality we spent probably eight hours working everything out. When we finally stood to go inside, we met each other's eyes, and something deep within me settled. He offered his hand, and I took it, walking with him like we had as kids.

Despite our differences, I don't think we've ever been closer.

The weekend was blessedly uneventful. I helped Mak change the motorcycle's oil and top off fluids (Sid refused to let me get on it until my shoulder heals, but he's also setting aside funds while he goes through the household budget so that I can buy my own, so I'm not too upset about waiting a few more weeks) and we got a phone call from Graham and Tommy.

Though Olive and I have talked on the phone at least once every day, we hadn't seen each other in person, and we hadn't talked about anything that had happened the night I found her. I was terrified to see her and, inevitably, have a conversation that would change our relationship forever. Either that or blame the fact that I'd kissed her—that <u>she'd</u> kissed <u>me</u>—on heightened emotions or just ignore it altogether. So many fun options! I definitely haven't felt like vomiting any time I've thought about it.

That night at the carnival really is paramount, isn't it? The enormity of my past dilemma of whether it was possible to love hunting and also love Olive now seems blown out of proportion. If I were anyone else, would I have been able to save her? If I weren't already inclined to violence, she or I or both of us could be dead. And with the new rules in place, I feel confident that I can keep that portion of my life from ever bleeding over again.

Maybe some secrets are okay. Maybe I'm selfish and willing to accept that.

When Olive called this morning after breakfast, Sid caught my eye, one copper brow arched pointedly. I turned away from him, coiling the phone's cord around my index finger as my heart attempted to crawl up my throat. "Come over for dinner tonight?" I asked in a rush, interrupting her mid-sentence. She agreed, planning to head over after helping Piney at the store.

It was a torturously long day, and dear Sidney found the utmost amusement in my antsy disposition and teased me relentlessly.

"What's the big deal? It's not like she blames you for being kidnapped. You saved her." Lyle plopped onto the couch with a handful of licorice.

Sid and Mak exchanged a look, then Sid looked at me, brows high, asking if I was going to answer.

Lyle watched this, then looked at me in shock. "Wait, do you <u>like</u> her?" he asked, then his eyes went wide. "Have you liked her <u>this whole time</u>?"

"Shouldn't you be out roaming the woods with your friends or something?" I folded my arms over my chest.

"But I thought you liked boys," Lyle pressed.

Shrugging, I stole a piece of his candy. "I just like pretty people."

He tipped his head to the side and nodded, though his brows were knit thoughtfully.

Danny howled outside, excited, saving me from further conversation, but my stomach swooped as I realized there was a more important conversation I would no longer be able to put off. I stood as the front door opened, the dogs ushering Olive inside.

Sid stood as well, his hand pressing into the small of my back as he passed me. "Hey, Olive, we were just about to go fire up the grill—barbeque chicken tonight!"

"Nice to see you again, Olive," Mak greeted as he moved to follow Sid.

"You coming, LJ?" Sid waved for him to follow.

And just like that, we were alone. My hands were clammy. I struggled to remember how I used to ignore my feelings for her and act normal, because if she wanted to pretend that nothing had happened at the carnival grounds, I would let her. I needed to pull it together, but so far all I'd done was stare at her, realize I was staring, and look around the room like I hadn't seen the decor before.

Olive tucked a curl behind her ear, drawing my attention back to her. "I broke up with Jonah."

"What?" My heart skipped a beat, but her words had broken our stand-still. We moved to sit on the couch, angled to face one another.

"We got into a fight after your brothers were arrested. He actually believed they had done those horrible things, and, well, the short of it is that I told him he could go be nasty somewhere else, because I wasn't going to stand for it. He didn't appreciate that at all, but he appreciated it even less when I doubled down and told him we were through."

My heart fluttered as the words sank in. "You mean you guys were done even before ... because ..." I trailed off, shaking my head in disbelief as love swelled in my chest. Whatever awkward tension I'd been holding melted, and I threw my arms around her shoulders, crushing her to my chest. Hyacinth and bergamot enveloped me at the same moment as her arms. I felt like I could breathe for the first time in days.

Olive squeezed me, and a wave of pain spiraled out from my

shoulder blade. She jumped back when I yelped. "Oh, gosh, sorry! I forgot. Are you okay?"

I blinked away a sheen of tears that were more from emotion than pain and waved her off. "I'm fine, promise." I laughed lightly, smoothing a hand over her dark curls, coiling one around my finger, focusing on that because we were still sitting closer than before and the air between us was electric. "Thank you for sticking up for Tommy and Graham. It means everything to me." I glanced up, finally meeting her dark eyes and then unable to look anywhere else.

"Of course, Mally. I love your brothers like they're my own." She reached up, fingertips pressing against the line of my jaw, and everything inside me twisted into a pretzel of nerves and longing and hope. "But I just love you. I think I have for a really long time."

I leaned forward to brush my nose against hers because my words were stuck in my throat, my heart bursting in my chest and filling me with electric warmth. Her fingers curled into me, and I tipped my chin, allowing her to guide my lips to hers.

That kiss was somehow even better than the first time. Okay, so maybe it's not <u>somehow</u>, since this time she wasn't traumatized, and I wasn't covered in blood, but I mean it affected me just as deeply. She was warm and soft and sweet, and her fingers were in my hair, and my fingers were in her hair, and the entire world slipped away until all that existed was Olive and everywhere our bodies met.

My teeth closed gently over the swell of her lower lip, eliciting a breathy gasp from her, and she pulled at my hair, drawing herself closer. Heat pulsed through me in a wave of desire more heady than anything I've ever felt. I slid a hand down to Olive's hip, reveling in the soft curves of her, and we finally pulled apart a little. We were both breathless, and she laughed when our eyes met.

"Wow," I whispered, incapable of greater thought in the moment.

Olive smiled, almost shyly, and pressed a kiss to my cheek. "Agreed."

We eventually joined my brothers outside, but stole countless kisses throughout the evening whenever we had a moment alone. I didn't think it was possible to be any more in love with her, but now that I've held her and tasted her and touched her ... now that she's done all of that <u>to me</u>? Hot creepers. I'm done for. Thoroughly and happily done for.

It's been a few days. Whoops. I've almost felt too busy to worry about journaling—there's been so much going on, both good and bad, and being present with the people who need me has taken precedence.

Good first: Olive is in love with me (??!!) (I'm still squeaky over this). We're together almost always these days. My brothers all know, and Olive also now knows about Sid and Mak. We've even done a couple double dates, and it's all okay because everyone just assumes Olive is with Sid and I'm with Mak. I feel like I'm living in a dream. I'm so. Damned. Smitten.

Another thing: we're moving—Olive and Mak, too. As much as I love Delight, we've outgrown it. The reputation of the bed and breakfast is tainted, and Sid's right when he says that what we really need is a fresh start. So we're leaving California, off to brighter pastures or whatever. It's scary, but ... I'm excited. (Also, leaving California puts Lachlan well outside of the no-hunt boundary. He <u>will</u> get what's coming to him.)

Everything would be perfect if not for Tommy and Graham still being locked up. They approved of the move. Encouraged it, even. It would make it easier to keep in touch with Priscilla, for the sake of the baby, if she thought we'd cut all ties with them. They have a trial date set, finally. They're being charged with attempted manslaughter, which isn't great, but could be worse. So far, none of the teeth have turned up anything, so the boys' claim to have collected them from oddities shops hasn't been disproven. That in and of itself feels like a miracle, as does the fact that whoever is in charge of that type of thing is tired of wasting the man hours and budget to keep looking. We've heard the prosecutor is going to ask for a life sentence, but because there's no irrefutable proof anybody actually died, they would be eligible for parole in fifteen years. That's currently the worst-case scenario, and I remind myself of that daily.

Until today, we'd only had phone calls since that first visit. Going back again brought on so many different emotions. It was … difficult, to understate it.

Seeing our older brothers dressed in the same drab blue as the other inmates visiting in the courtyard made it impossible to forget that this was all their fault. If they hadn't hunted out of turn, breaking rules that <u>they</u> set that the <u>rest of us</u> managed to follow, our family would be whole right now. Avoidance has been easier than processing the betrayal, but being face-to-face with them forced me to confront everything I was feeling.

I knew they could see every bit of hurt and anger in my eyes. I didn't bother attempting to hide it from them.

Tommy didn't try to make an excuse. "I'm sorry. It was stupid and selfish." He looked at the three of us, mossy blue eyes full of remorse. His gaze trained on Sid. "I'm sorry for not owning up to it. You shouldn't have had to be the one to tell them. It was foolish of us to think it wouldn't come out."

"Cowardly, even," Graham added quietly.

He wasn't wrong.

"How many times?" I asked, voice tight.

Tommy and Graham exchanged a glance before Tommy

spoke. "Only a few. The first was after you finished high school. We had more free time and got greedy."

I know he was being honest, but the simplicity of the answer angered me. None of our lives would ever be the same because they'd been <u>bored</u>. "Well, I hope it was worth it," I snapped.

Graham flinched, which filled me with equal parts satisfaction and remorse, and one corner of Tommy's mouth pulled up in a sad smile. "We'll spend the rest of our lives regretting how much we've hurt you."

"We never should have broken your trust," Graham agreed solemnly, looking at each of us in turn.

Sid asked if there'd been any updates about their trial, and the conversation moved on to our own life updates after that. I was still struggling, still mad and hurt, but as I thought back to my talk with Sid, full of frustration and tears, I came to the same conclusion that the two of us had arrived at. If he could withhold judging me, I could withhold judging them. Especially now that there were no more secrets.

When the time came for us to say goodbye, I pulled a small lump from my pocket, clutching it as I squeezed Tommy, then Graham, in a tight hug. I caught Graham's hand before they stepped away. "I love you," I told them both, pressing RJ's tooth into Graham's palm.

The fact is, the bond we all grew as children is unbreakable, no matter how messed up we might be or how we learned to cope. It's the five of us, always and no matter what.

Acknowledgements

If this was your first time reading my work, thank you for taking a chance and spending your time in these pages! If you're a return reader, thank you for continuing to spend your time with my characters, in my worlds. For all of you, I hope you enjoyed this tale of family and rage and desire. I'm eternally grateful to each and every one of you who picked up this book.

As always, Josh, your love and support makes pursuing my dreams that much more attainable. Thank you for being the best partner and the most amazing event assistant.

To my brothers: I love you guys. You were my first friends—my first adventure buddies and partners in crime and confidants. And, yeah, you were the first people I fought with and screamed at and maybe we still know how to push each other's buttons, but you were the first people I ever shared my life with. You guys were right there with me for every defining experience of my formative years. For the first eighteen years of my life, I never had to do anything alone; I always had someone who'd have my back. There's so much I could say thank you for, but for brevity's sake, I'll keep it to this: you're some of my favorite people always and forever. I'm lucky to have you in my life. A book so centered on familial bonds would have been pretty damn difficult to write without you.

To the women who are the sisters I never had: this is still the best timeline, and I still don't know what I'd do without you. Murs, do we mention again all the time spent plotting and figuring out motivations and dynamics? I swear, the act of eating pizza while driving through Teller County now ignites some synapses in my brain to allow essential plot things to unfold where they were otherwise knotted beyond recognition. If it weren't for my hyperfixation on "Sunshine, Lollipops, and Rainbows" and you simultaneously vibing with 60s bops, this story never would have been born. Speaking of things this story never would have been born without—Taylor, I can't pinpoint exactly when we started the surprise cannibalism book club or how it became such a hyped sub-genre/plot occurrence between us, but I can say with certainty that this micro-obsession was paramount to the development of Mallory's story. Fangirling over horror books with you is one of my favorite things. (Access to Scout's kitten pants and beans is another.) Sarah, your enthusiasm for this story before it was drafted doubled my excitement to write it. I'll never forget standing in your kitchen telling you what I planned for this book and you immediately jumping on board for the vibes and dynamics. Please know I lived for every single "Carissa No" comment in the doc and took each reaction as a huge win.

There are a few other people who were fundamental to the writing of this book. Lea Ann, having your eyes on a manuscript is always a privilege, but I'm especially grateful this time around for your help with keeping everything in line with the time-period. Leanna and Morgan, thank you for going through an early draft of this story and helping point out where it needed beefing. Rachael and Kelsey, I'm so obsessed with your brains. I hope you know how highly I hold your opinions and how important your feedback was for polishing this manuscript. In that same vein,

Elle and Faith, thank you for also putting in time with this story to help make sure she was ready for the world! I appreciate you all so much.

Until next time,
Car

Though fiction has been her lifelong passion, Carissa spent seven years as an air traffic controller in the Air Force before pursuing her dream of writing. She grew up exploring the Sierra Nevadas of California, but now lives in Colorado with her husband and their pets. When not writing, Carissa can be found out seeking adventure, driving mountain roads, greeting wildlife, and consuming horror in any medium available.